THE MERCY KILLERS

Also by Lisa Reardon

Billy Dead

Blameless

THE MERCY KILLERS

~ a novel ~

Lisa Reardon

COUNTERPOINT
Berkeley, California

This book is a work of fiction. Names, characters, places, and incidents are the product of the author's imagination or are used fictitiously. Any resemblance to actual events is unintended and entirely coincidental.

Designed by Jeff Williams

Library of Congress Cataloging-in-Publication Data
Reardon, Lisa.
The mercy killers : a novel / by Lisa Reardon.
p. cm.
H.C.: ISBN 1-58243-318-6 (alk. paper)
P.B.: ISBN-10: 1-58243-337-2
ISBN-13: 978-1-58243-337-0
1. Ypsilanti (Mich.)—Fiction. I. Title.
PS3568.E26825M47 2004
813'.54—dc22 2004004999

COUNTERPOINT
2560 Ninth Street, Suite 318
Berkeley, CA 94710
www.counterpointpress.com

To Mick Weber,
with love

Acknowledgments

Heartfelt gratitude to Jennifer Rudolph Walsh, Dawn Seferian, and Jennifer Blakebrough-Raeburn for their help in bringing the book to fruition.

For their vital encouragement and feedback along the way, I thank Caryn Banker, George Galuschak, Pat Walter, and Mick Weber.

The following people assisted with research. I wish to thank them for offering their expertise and their stories: all the Vietnam veterans who shared their experiences through books, letters, films, Web sites, and e-mails; Derek and Caryn Banker; Andrew Fernandez; Dr. Dean Filandrinos; Butch's Custom Harley in St. Paul; Sarah Hauser; Margaret, Angela, Ramona, and Hunter Hicks; Heddy Honigman; Mary Hubbard; Jeffrey Lerer; Bill and Susan Long; Valerie Long; the National Vietnam Veterans Art Museum in Chicago; Jack Spack; Clarence (Jim) Whiteaker; and Vietnam Veterans of America, Jackson, Michigan.

ACKNOWLEDGMENTS

THE MERCY KILLERS

1

IT'S HARD TO THINK HOW DIFFERENT THEIR LIVES would have been if it weren't for the mess they got themselves into, if it weren't for that war, if they hadn't all been so young and stupid and scared.

On a rainy evening in the spring of 1967, Old Jerry hunkers on his bar stool like a liquor-soaked question mark. The topic of conversation is his long-awaited suicide.

The bartender brings him a shot of Stoli's. "From Olivia," he says. "A little early happy birthday for you." Old Jerry gives Olivia a nod and a wave across the bar. She waves back. Almost sets her chiffon hair scarf on fire with her cigarette. Old Jerry adds the shot to the other two he has got lined up.

"Everyone thinks it's a joke but I'm telling you, Gil, I want to die." Old Jerry tilts his shot glass at the bartender. "I'm seventy years old. I can't get my dick stiff, I can't take a solid dump, I smell bad."

"You don't smell bad when you take a bath." Gil McGurk, forty-one years old with arms like firewood, picks his teeth with a cocktail sword and works the daily word scramble in the newspaper.

"I can't take a bath."

"Why not?"

"Too skinny. Bones bruise my ass if I sit in the tub."

Gil's eyebrows go up, but he keeps at his puzzle.

"That's right. Bony old naked bastard sitting on a rubber stool with Mr. Limp Dick. I want to die."

"So kill yourself."

"Uh-huh. Uh-huh. A man who can't even piss straight, how's he gonna kill himself? I need some help."

"No."

Old Jerry scratches where his clothes hang loose. "I itch, too."

"Because you won't take a bath," replies Gil.

"We covered that, my friend. And if I weren't older than Jesus's final fart, I'd still want to kill myself after sitting in this place so long with a guy as boring as you." He swallows one of the shots. A watery trickle runs down his chin and leaves a few drops on the bar. He rubs at them with his bony wrist. The cuff of his ancient flannel shirt is as soft as a spaniel's ear. "Why don't you have a drink and quit being a prick?"

Gil puts the newspaper down. "Haven't had one in seven years, Jerry."

"Seven years of you being meaner than shit."

"Seven years of me not killing myself with booze."

"It doesn't work anyway, trust me. Tell me what's in the newspaper, will you? Read me how the country's going to hell."

Gil turns the paper over: "Rash of Auto Thefts in Willow Run."

"That's probably Gino's doing all by himself."

"Johnson Seeks the Hearts and Minds of the Vietnamese."

"There you go," Old Jerry says. "Read me that one."

Gil reads the first few paragraphs and then turns to page 6B to continue. Old Jerry mutters "cocksucker" once but Gil says to shut up or he won't finish. At the end of the article, Gil sets the paper down to take a delivery of Carlsberg. Old Jerry calls after him, "You see? Who wants to live when you got that going on in the world? What are we doing over there?"

Gil nods toward the TV. "Killing commies and getting rich."

Old Jerry watches Gil and the delivery guy carry the beer into the bar. "So what do I have to do to get a guy to kill me?"

"Just keep it up," Gil says. "Hey P.T., come and stock some of this."

P.T. is Old Jerry's grandson. In the back, near the pool tables, he sets aside his broom. He smiles at the old man, at Gil, at the clock on the wall, at the tap handle, and at the sink as he kneels behind the bar and puts the bottles in the cooler. He stays close to the edge so Gil won't trip over him. It happened the first day P.T. worked there. Gil said, "Okay, that's funny once." P.T. thought it would be funny every time. He has his grandpa's weedy-looking hair with five cowlicks that shoot strands in all directions. He is nineteen years old, and stands a foot taller than Old Jerry, Gil, or anyone else who walks into McGurk's.

When he's done with the beer, P.T. goes back to sweeping the floor behind the pool table. It's six o'clock on the button, so he plugs in the jukebox. Gil won't let anyone use the jukebox until six.

Old Jerry nurses his Stoli and watches P.T. pick the loose change out of the dustpan. He brushes a penny against his sleeve, puts it on his tongue, and closes his eyes. When Gil calls for him, he takes the penny from his tongue.

"I smelled a skunk." There were skunks when P.T. and his little brother were young. "I saw a skunk once, it was bigger than a garbage truck." No one listens. "So I threw a stick at it and it turned around and sprayed the whole house. Stank for two years."

"That so?" asks Gil.

"It happened when I was little, before Charlie was born." P.T.'s eyes looks like they were colored in with an old gray crayon. A dark red spot nestles in the outer corner of one eye.

"Seventy years." Old Jerry looks at Gil as if P.T. had proven his point. "I put in my time. I want out."

Gil gives P.T. a quarter and tells him to pick out some songs. The Ronettes fill the place. A man with an Afro walks in with his dog; the dog, an overgrown toad with fur, heads for a booth with customers in it, real customers who have never been in the place before, and shakes himself until it looks like it's raining as hard inside as it is outside. The customers leave. The man lounges onto a barstool and says, "C'mon cupcake. C'mon up here."

The dog jumps up on the stool next to his owner, spreading his wet dog stink across the bar. Gil washes his hands and dries them, working the towel over his knuckles.

"Black and Tan?" he asks.

"Yeah, and some peanuts," says the man. "Can I get a bowl of water for the lemon drop here?"

"Get it yourself." Gil tucks the hand towel into his belt. "And don't go putting it on the bar, Bobby. How many times I'm gonna tell you the dog don't drink at the bar?"

"Over here, sweet potato. C'mon." Bobby puts the bowl of water on the floor. "Nice to see Gil's having his usual good day."

~

Paris looks good in the rain, but Ypsilanti, Michigan, does not. Plastic fluorescent flags drip over used car lots. Dingy rivulets swirl along curbs and soak the socks of the careless. It's the wettest spring anyone can remember and the city bleeds dirt. Inside McGurk's, Old Jerry talks down the length of the bar. "Bobby, how come you don't go to a Negro bar where you belong?"

"Cause I like fucking with you crackers."

Gil sets Bobby's Black and Tan in front of him. "You got those tires for me yet?" he asks.

"No." Bobby shakes his head like he just doesn't understand it. "My brother-in-law Teddy, you know Teddy."

"Jesus," says Old Jerry, who's been hearing about Teddy for years.

"He knows a guy does Goodyear wholesale," Bobby continues. "Put them on for you, the whole shebang."

"So where are they?" Gil rubs at the spilled drink that Old Jerry missed.

"That's the thing," Bobby says. "He says the dude's in Georgia until the end of the week."

"I'm gonna have a blow out on these things I got."

"I know that. I know it. But what are you gonna do? The guy's in Georgia." Bobby nods, taking a sip of his beer. "Listen, tuna casserole." He drops a salted peanut on the floor for the dog. "Don't let me forget to call Teddy or Gil's gonna have both our butts in a sling."

"It's my birthday tomorrow," says Old Jerry.

"Get him a drink Gil, on me." Bobby nudges the dog with his toe. "Tell the man happy birthday."

When Old Jerry gets his drink he raises it and says, "You're all right, for a Negro," before gulping it down.

"Sho am 'bliged t'ya fo' sayin' so." He turns to Gil. "When's Katie coming in?"

"Night off," says Gil.

"Tell her I got something for her." Last week it was a new Electrolux. The week before that it was four pairs of shoes: same style, same size, four different colors.

"You got connections," Old Jerry says. "Can't you hire someone to take me out?"

"Sorry man."

"I'll pay for it."

"I don't fence death, old man."

"Pussy." Old Jerry finishes his last free shot and slowly unglues himself from the bar stool. "Come on, P.T. Let's go home and tape a plastic bag over my head."

P.T. pulls on the raincoat with the matching rain hat that his brother gave him last Christmas. When they step out to the parking lot, P.T. gazes up at the rain falling down in his face. "Mom's here," he says.

Old Jerry takes the boy's arm and walks. "That so?"

"She's right there." He smiles and waves up into the rain as he walks. "She tells you happy birthday."

After fifteen years of this nonsense, Old Jerry is starting to believe that his daughter really does visit P.T. from the grave. He shrugs. "Thanks."

2

LATER THE SAME NIGHT OLD JERRY'S OTHER GRANDSON is making his way down the dark corridor of a stranger's house. The owners shouldn't be home for another hour. He starts with the master bedroom, dumping a whole jewelry box into his duffel bag. He'll sort it out later, let Sheila and Katherine have the cheap stuff. He grabs a leather coat from the closet; looks like it might fit his brother. Cufflinks, watch. *Why do these jokers always have two watches?* He checks inside all the dresser drawers, then the night stand. Finds the March issue of *Playboy* under a stack of *Outdoor Life* and throws it on the bed so the wife'll see it first off when she walks in.

Something rustles in the hall. He pulls out his Colt and holds it with both hands so he won't shake. He waits behind the bedroom door and listens. Quiet, then a quick rustling like someone trying not to be heard. *What are the odds of two guys robbing the same house at the same time?* He closes one eye and peers through a crack between the door hinges. No one in the hall. The sound comes again, from one of the kids' rooms. He puts the gun behind him, not wanting to give the kid a heart attack. But the place is all dark; no one leaves their kid home alone in the dark. More rustling. His legs are frozen with fear. Ten minutes go by. The other guy's standing there frozen, too, because for a long time all is quiet. He figures to hell with it, probably someone he knows anyway, and walks into the hall. Now there's a rustling, a squeak, and metal rattling. He shoves the Colt out in front of him, steps into the room and yells, "Hold it."

It's a guinea pig, squealing and circling its cage. Charlie almost shoots it just to get some feeling back in his legs. The animal stops running and watches Charlie out of one eye as he opens the cage door and makes a grab for it. After four tries and a bite on the thumb, he holds the guinea pig good and firm. He sticks it in the pocket of his windbreaker and zips it almost closed.

A horn honks down the street. Two long blasts. *Shit.* Charlie runs for his duffel bag as headlights from the driveway sweep across the wall. He runs down the stairs trying to put the gun away, keep hold of the duffel bag, and not crush the guinea pig. He swipes a box of animal crackers off the kitchen counter on his way out. In thirty seconds the patio door is closed, curtains drawn, everything like they left it. The couple enter the house, arguing about who left the upstairs light on until she sees the skin mag on the bed.

By then, Charlie's inside Gino's '66 lemon-yellow Marlin and speeding away. He lights an Old Gold to top off the buzz of scaring himself to death over a rat. "Pull over," he tells Gino. "Let me throw this stuff in the trunk." Charlie stashes his take and returns to the front seat. The Marlin moves easily into traffic.

"Where to?" asks Gino.

"Swing over to Sheila's," says Charlie. He pulls the guinea pig from his pocket. "Look."

"Where'd you get it?"

"Stole it from the kid's room."

"What you gotta do that for?"

"It's for Bro." Charlie drops it back in his pocket and zips up.

His friend lets it drop; no use arguing about it. "Reach in the glove box, will you?"

Charlie pulls out a bag and rolls a joint. "You're low."

"Yeah."

They drive back to Ypsilanti in peace, sharing the joint and watching the wipers slide across the windshield. They've been friends since third grade, when they discovered in one another the same propensity for silence. The only sound is an occasional quick inhalation of smoke, and the tapping of the roach clip against the ashtray. They pull into the parking lot behind Sheila and Katherine's apartment. Charlie leans across the seat and lays on the horn. Three short beeps. They sit watching the wipers some more. Charlie tries again, three short beeps, twice. A window opens and a young woman's face appears. Charlie rolls down his window in time to hear her shout, "Shut up."

"Tell Sheila to get out here."

"She's not here. Stop the honking." Katie leans out and peers inside the Marlin for a glimpse of Gino's bottle-blue eyes and falling black hair. "Hi, Gino."

Gino says hi into the steering wheel. "Gino says hi back," yells Charlie. "Where is she?"

"I don't know. You guys want to come up?"

Gino shakes his head. Charlie yells, "No, Gino's gotta get home."

"Well, be quiet. I was sleeping." She reaches up to close the window. "Bye, Gino."

Charlie waves as they pull away. "I got a couple of dime bags at home," he says, rolling another joint. "You want one?"

~

Carrying the evening's haul, Charlie and Gino climb the urine-laced steps to the apartment. CKLW blares Motown hits from the radio in the kitchen. Old Jerry had moved into town soon after his daughter died. When the boys' dad finally went back down south, they went to stay with their grandpa in his tiny apartment in town. Between P.T.'s job at McGurk's, Charlie's stealing, and Old Jerry's Social Security checks, they made enough to keep the boys fed and the old man drunk.

Charlie bangs his knee on the hide-a-bed that he and his brother sleep on in the living room. "Bro?" He reaches in the end table drawer, tosses a dime bag to Gino, and looks around. "Bro?"

"In here," comes P.T.'s quiet voice from the bedroom. Charlie walks in and sees his grandfather lying on the bed, blue. His brother sits on the bed with a pillow on his lap, holding the old man's hand. "Now, do not be mad." P.T. stands up and sits down several times, as if forcing himself to stay in the room. "Do not be mad," he says again.

Charlie feels for a pulse all around the old man's wrist, his neck, but gives up. "Shit."

"Do not yell."

"I'm not yelling."

Gino appears behind Charlie. "He's really dead?"

"What happened?" asks Charlie.

"We had a contest to see who could hold their breath the longest, and I won." P.T. continues to stand up and sit down.

"That's not what happened," says Charlie with the eerie patience of panic. "Tell me what happened."

P.T. thinks for a moment. "A huge fat man came to the door and wanted us to buy some magazines but he did not have *Sports Illustrated* and grandpa said for him to go to hell and the man said we better buy some magazines or he would sit on us and grandpa said go ahead and try it blubber butt and the man came inside and sat on grandpa until he was dead and I had to call the police and they said—"

"That's not what happened either," says Charlie. "Tell me the truth and stop jumping up and down."

"He asked me to please smother him and I did. With a pillow." He holds up the pillow as proof. "Do not go making it into a bad thing, either."

"Don't talk, okay?" Charlie pulls the covers up under Old Jerry's chin and sits on the chair beside the bed, plucking at one eyebrow. "Shit. Shit."

Charlie stares at his shoe laces, at one frayed end where the plastic tip has come off. He rubs his sleeve across his nose a few times. Old Jerry used to drive them around in his convertible, getting up to eighty on the highway with the boys standing up in the back. He took them to ride the ponies out on Carpenter Road. He'd tell them to punch him in the stomach and, when they did, he'd fart. Old Jerry may have been a mangy drunk but he was the best grandpa any kid could ask for.

"Can we still have the birthday party tomorrow?" P.T. asks.

"Put the pillow down."

"Yeah, but what are we going to do?"

"Don't nobody talk, all right?"

"Do not yell." P.T. sits on the bed with his legs crossed Indian-style so as not to spring to his feet again. "I hate it, you yelling."

Looking at the two of them, Gino is surprised at how much they look alike. Charlie is shorter and darker, and somehow manages to look more deranged than his older brother, but there is a funny resemblance there all the same. "You want to call an ambulance?" he asks.

P.T. gazes down at Old Jerry's face. "He looks a lot better than Mom did."

"I asked you to shut up, didn't I?" Charlie stands up. "Why would I want to hear that? What's that got to do with anything?"

"I asked you not to yell!"

"Well, Jesus Christ, Bro. You make it sound like . . ." Charlie deflates at P.T.'s look. "Sorry. Hey, it's okay." He glances at Gino still standing in the doorway behind him. Gino's look says, "Don't ask me."

"Listen. This is what we're gonna do," Charlie goes on. "Far as we know, nothing happened. We don't know where he is. We'll act like everything's cool, we'll have the birthday party tomorrow, and we'll be as surprised as everybody when he doesn't show up."

P.T. gives his brother a skeptical frown. "What if Gil or someone asks where he is?"

"Say you don't know."

"What if someone asks me when was the last time I saw him?"

"Say you don't know."

"How can I not know the last time I saw him?" P.T. plucks at the torn hem of the pillowcase. "That would be retarded."

"You're right. That's a good point." Charlie smiles. "Just make something up. You're good at that."

"Why?"

"Because we gotta make this look like an accident."

"Why?"

"Because if they find out you did this, you'll go to jail."

"Who is they?"

"Police."

"All right."

"Okay. Ready?" When P.T. nods, Charlie asks, "Hey, P.T., where's Old Jerry?"

"I do not know."

"Well when's the last time you saw him?"

"The last time I saw my grandpa, he was on his way over to the Big Top Party Store this morning to get some corn flakes and cigarettes because I ate all of them last night and he said he would be back in a minute but he did not come back."

"That's right."

"That's perfect," adds Gino.

P.T. turns around. "Hi, Gino."

"Hi."

"Okay, you go to bed." Charlie tries not to dwell on how much P.T. looks like their dad. "We'll take care of it."

"How? How are you going to take care of it?"

"That's a secret."

"Secrets are no good." P.T. had started out of the room, but now he turns back toward the bed. "Do not keep secrets on me."

"Sorry." Charlie flops Old Jerry's hand up and down on the covers, distracted. "We're going to hide him."

"Where?"

"Why you gotta know where?"

"Because it is interesting and I want to know."

Charlie gets up. In eighteen years he's never won an argument with his brother. "I don't know yet," he says. "I honestly don't know."

"I guess what I want to know is, are you going to hide him behind the couch?"

"No. Not behind the couch."

"Okay then." P.T. turns to leave, but this time Charlie stops him.

"Why?"

"I already have some stuff hid there." P.T. leaves the room without saying good night. Gino lets him pass without taking his eyes off the dead body. Charlie sits staring at his grandpa, waiting for a good idea. "This is bad."

Gino nods. "I'm not touching him."

"We have to."

"This is not cool." He shakes his head. "I don't groove with stiffs."

"We'll wrap him in sheets and carry him out the back way."

"Where everybody can see us?"

"It's raining. Ain't nobody gonna be watching."

"There's always somebody watching." He gives it some thought. "You know how I feel about dead things." Charlie nods, but Gino can see his whole head shaking.

Twenty minutes later they have four empty dresser drawers stacked in the back seat of the Marlin. The hollowed out dresser rests in the trunk, Old Jerry wrapped in sheets inside it. Even though the corpse didn't weigh much, they got stuck twice on the stair landings. Gino ties a rubber hose around the back bumper to keep the trunk lid down. Charlie ties a red rag to the dresser so the police won't pull them over.

"Where to?" asks Gino.

"Ford Lake."

Back in the Marlin, Gino pulls the dime bag from his coat pocket. "Here."

Charlie rolls a joint with shaking hands as they drive back through town toward the lake. On the third try, he gets it lit.

"He'd have burned the apartment down sooner or later," Charlie says.

Old Jerry fell asleep with lit cigarettes. Once P.T. drew a treasure map and Old Jerry tried to make it look old by burning the edges of the paper with his lighter. Burned the kitchen curtains, too. Charlie laughs softly.

Gino glances over. "What?"

"I don't know. Old Jerry always talking about the different ways to off himself." He turns to look at the trunk. "Bet he never pictured this."

~

It's miserable work, getting Old Jerry out of the trunk. They unwind the rain-soaked sheets and throw him into the water. The splash brings Charlie's stomach to his mouth. He swallows several times and shouts at the rippling water. "Happy now?"

Gino gives a small laugh. "Happy birthday, old man." He imitates Old Jerry's voice: "Best goddamned birthday present I ever had."

"What do we do with the dresser?"

"Take it to my place," says Gino. "Keep it in the garage."

"Never to be seen again," says Charlie. "You gonna sell it by the drawer?" Gino runs Washtenaw County's best chop shop out of his garage. In the car Charlie rolls another joint. "I just remembered a joke."

"No."

"This is a good one. This is perfect. 'A good friend helps you move. A *really* good friend helps you move the body.'"

Gino chokes on his hit of weed. "Once maybe," he says. "That's the last corpse this boy's gonna lay a hand on."

"Fuck."

"What?"

Charlie feels around in the pocket of his windbreaker. He holds out his hand. The guinea pig sits up in his palm, blinking.

~

April 14, 1967. At 2:12 in the morning, as Old Jerry slowly floats to the surface of Ford Lake, Charlie returns home to find P.T. waiting up at the kitchen table.

"Mom said it would be okay."

"Yeah." Charlie sits across from him. "Listen, Bro . . . "

At 2:14, Gil locks up the cash drawer and turns off the lights. The neon sign outside fizzes into darkness.

At the same time, Katie and Sheila share a beer in their bathroom. Katie pulls thin strands of Sheila's hair through a plastic cap, applies the peroxide for frosted highlights. It's going to be a surprise tomorrow for Charlie.

At 2:36, Gino pulls into his driveway and unloads the dresser from his trunk. He lives outside of town where the roads are black and the sky reels with stars. He stands against the bright yellow hood and smells the combination of new grass and gasoline. He thinks about his parents, who died years ago; how his father used to stand in the yard on nights like this while his mother called quietly to him through the screen door. That's all he remembers of either of them.

3

THE NEXT DAY, CHARLIE TELLS P.T. NOT TO GO TO McGurk's until it's time for the party. He and Sheila set off for the bakery to order a chocolate cake with chocolate frosting. Sheila goes off about how Old Jerry is allergic to chocolate. "Gil won't even let him eat a little piece," she says.

"To hell with Gil, okay? Gil can kiss my ass."

"Chocolate cake, chocolate frosting," the bakery guy repeats. He's a big guy, the kind of guy you want to see working in a bakery. "Want it to say anything?"

"Happy Birth—"

Charlie cuts her off. "'Seventy Years,'" he says. "None of that 'happy birthday' crap."

"You want that spelled out or in numbers?"

"Numbers. And an exclamation point. In blue."

She stays quiet until they're back in the car. "Dickhead *ojo de culo*. Can you pull the porcupine out of your ass now?"

"You and Katie get the decorations?"

She reaches in the back seat, rifles through a paper bag, and puts on a shiny blue party hat. It has silver fringe along the brim that looks like a big caterpillar. A bunch of blue feathers bob from the top of the cone.

"What about the noisemakers? He likes noisemakers."

She digs around in the bag and brings out a noisemaker, the paper kind that unrolls when you blow in it. It's blue, with blue feathers shooting out. "Got two dozen."

"Good girl." Charlie laughs and honks the horn for the hell of it. For a moment, Old Jerry's alive and sitting on his usual barstool at McGurk's, waiting for his party. "He'll piss himself when he sees that."

"He pisses himself already." She leans over to kiss him, then props her feet on the dashboard. Sheila is five feet tall. Her long black hair hangs straight down her back like a horse's tail. The smile she gives Charlie now is wicked. "Let's stop at my place and fuck."

When Charlie and Sheila arrive at McGurk's that evening, P.T. is already there. Sheila tosses the bags on a table and carries the cake to the back room.

"Hey, Daddy-O," she says on her way behind the bar.

"How's daughter number two?" says Gil.

"Dry."

Gil pours her a beer. Sheila's been friends with his daughter Katherine for so long, Gil considers her his. No one else claims her.

Charlie, carrying a shoe box under one arm, heads for P.T. and fakes a lame punch at his face. P.T. doesn't blink, just touches his knuckles against Charlie's.

"I thought you were going to wait for us to pick you up."

"I walked over."

"I brought you a hamster." Charlie reaches in the box, pulls out the guinea pig, and drops it on the bar.

"That's a guinea pig," Bobby says, one hand on his dog.

"Thank you." P.T. picks the thing up. It drops little shits onto the bar.

"Get it out of here." Gil tosses a cocktail napkin at Charlie. "Clean that up."

Charlie pulls a handful of crumbled crackers out of his pocket. "He likes these."

"Don't feed him too much," says Bobby. "He'll burst."

"He ain't gonna burst," Charlie says. P.T. and the guinea pig squeak back and forth to one another.

"Yeah, he will," says Bobby, both hands on the dog now. "They're too dumb to know when to stop eating and then they split open. Saw it happen once."

"Maybe that was a gerbil," says P.T.

"Maybe you can get him off my bar," says Gil. "This ain't the goddamn Detroit Zoo."

P.T. takes the hamster to the back room and comes out with an old Budweiser box. In the corner he carefully places a clean ashtray for a water dish. He shreds paper napkins and scatters them inside the box. He shows it to Sheila.

"That's beautiful."

"Thank you," says P.T. "Her name is Marigold."

Sheila pulls balloons and decorations from a bag. "You and Marigold want to help me?"

"Because Mary is too plain, and she has gold fur, and besides that she lays gold eggs."

"Guinea pigs don't lay eggs." She hands him several balloons. "Blow these up for me, will you?"

"Yes she does. She did it in the back room where no one could see, and I put the eggs in my pocket to show you guys, but I sat on them and they turned into feathers and blew away."

Sheila nods. "Marigold's a good name, then. Where is he?"

"Who?" asks P.T.

"Who. Give me a break. The birthday boy."

"I do not know."

"I expected him here by noon," says Gil, "sucking up the free drinks."

"I figured he was here," says Charlie. "You ain't seen him?" He glances all around the bar as if they might have missed him in the gloom. "He better not pass out somewhere and miss his own party." He turns to P.T. "Hey, Bro, when's the last time you seen him?"

"The last time I saw grandpa, he was on his way to the Big Top Party Store to get corn flakes and bread and milk and cigarettes and peanut butter because I ate it all."

Bobby pulls party hats out of a bag while he and the dog watch Mutual of Omaha's *Wild Kingdom* on the TV above the bar. "Water buffalo gotta be about the nastiest thing the Big Man ever set on earth. Look, cream puff. You see that? That one there looks just like Ladybird, doesn't it?" The dog looks up at the TV. "That's the kind of thing you run into if you let them draft you."

"Come on, Bobby," Gil says. "Take the dog home before the place fills up."

"I'm waiting for Gino. He's bringing a guy, got a deal I might like," Bobby says. "Whatever the stuff is, dude swears it'll be easier to move than toads off a lit stove."

"Buying off someone you don't know?"

"He sounded like a brother. You can't tell anymore, everyone trying to sound like James Brown," Bobby says. "Gino's bringing him, so we should be cool."

The front door opens, a black guy walks in, and Bobby laughs. "Look who busted out." Bobby gives the guy some kind of black power handshake. Bobby's no more a Black Panther than Hubert Humphrey.

"Mr. Robert Royce himself," says the guy. "I heard they shipped your ass off to Vietnam."

"It'll never happen." Bobby motions for Gil to get the guy a drink. "Heard you had two more years."

"Good behavior. Staying out, too."

"Call me when you get tired of working the car wash." Bobby looks around. "Where's Old Jerry?"

"Drunk somewhere," says Sheila from the top of a ladder where she is taping streamers to the wall. Charlie and P.T. sit across from each other blowing up balloons, the guinea pig box between them. Each has a hunk of bangs hanging over his forehead. For not looking alike, they look a lot alike. The door opens again and a blonde walks in. Nobody's ever seen her before. Gil leans close to Bobby. "Get the goddamn dog off the bar stool. Now."

The blonde's so tiny she has to hitch her butt up high to get herself seated. P.T.'s the only one not staring a hole through her. She's with some punk with staring eyes, looking like he's on something.

"What can I get for you, young lady?"

"Rum-and-Coke," she says, chewing on a little wad of gum. "Separate."

Gil nods, slaps one hand on the counter, and leans down to grab a glass from under the bar. "Coming up," he says with an impersonal tone that isn't fooling the punk boyfriend. The blonde lets out a streak of gum snapping that even gets P.T.'s attention. It sounds like a pea-shooter going off in her mouth. When the cartridge is empty, she goes back to chewing, nice and quiet. The boyfriend asks twice for a Pabst. Gil ignores him.

"Hey," says Bobby, moving in. "What's that accent you got?"

"Miss'ippi."

"Hear that, turnip?" Bobby tells the dog. "She's all the way from Mississippi."

"What kind of name is Turnip?" she asks.

"That's not his name."

"What's his name?"

"Here you go." Gil gives her his Dean Martin smile as he sets out a hefty shot of Bacardi, a glass of ice, and bottle of Coke. "That's three-fifty," he tells the boyfriend, smile gone.

"What's a matter with you, Todd?" she says without looking at him. "Pay the man."

"Hey, Gil," says Charlie. When he gets no answer, he shouts. "Gil!"

Gil walks over to his table, pulling the dish towel out of his belt and wiping his hands hard enough to skin a knuckle. "What are you, blind?" he says.

"Can I get another Miller?"

"I'm handing the lady her drink, I'm working up a good line. All of a sudden, everyone in the place is screaming my name."

"Sorry." Charlie takes a better look at the Mississippi Blonde. "Sorry," he says again.

"Yeah." Gil turns away, but Charlie grabs his arm. Gil hasn't been laid in five months. He shoves Charlie in the chest, hard enough to plant his butt forever into his chair. "In a minute."

This catches the Mississippi Blonde's eye. She watches as Gil walks behind the bar and takes her boyfriend's money. She sits up all straight and high-titted, sips on her rum-and-Coke, and smiles. Doesn't look much older than sixteen. She pops her gum like an automatic rifle and winks at Gil. Sheila leans over the counter. "Careful, Daddy-O."

Front door opens. This time a Mexican comes in and looks around. He sees the dog and looks at Bobby. Gino comes in behind, nods to Bobby, and leads the Mexican to a table in the back.

"Give me three Buds," says Bobby.

"Don't you have any Negro friends you can drink with?"

"You don't think I'd bring them in here, do you?" Bobby carries the beer to the Mexican's table, the dog on his heels. Gil keeps one eye on the blonde while he watches the Mexican hold his hand out to Bobby.

"Joey Ortiz."

"Robert Royce. How you doing?" Bobby gives him a prison handshake. "All right, my man," Bobby says, "tell me what you got."

Gil talks to the Mississippi Blonde while her boyfriend steams. At the table in back, Gino hunkers down while Bobby and Ortiz talk. He gives P.T. a peace sign across the room. P.T. gives one back, losing his grip on a balloon. It circles over his head until it's empty, then drops on the table. P.T. does it a few more times before Charlie tells him to stop.

In comes Katherine, carrying a huge bouquet of flowers. "Am I late? Where's Old Jerry?"

"You were supposed to take over the bar an hour ago."

"Took me forever to find white tulips."

Gil hands her the glass swordfish vase from behind the bar. "Why'd it have to be white tulips?"

"It just did." She pulls off her coat and throws it at the overloaded coat rack. "Where is he?"

"Not here yet. You said you'd be here an hour ago."

"I know. I know."

"You get it from your mother, so help me." He turns to the blonde. "Her mother was late for her own funeral. Had to dig the casket back up and throw her in."

That's what he tells everyone. Katherine's mother is alive, playing house with some over-sexed Mr. Clean in Ann Arbor: "Father Knows Best" when her mom was around, and all hands when he had Katherine alone. Last thing her mother said to her was, "You are not going to ruin this for me with your lies, do you hear?" Katherine quit school and came to live with her dad.

She grabs the vase and fills it with water, then arranges the flowers while looking all over the room for Gino. The Mississippi Blonde gazes up at Katherine, who stands five feet eleven in her bare feet. With heels and a bouffant she scares most men. When Katherine winks at her, the Mississippi Blonde snaps her gum and says, "Gee."

"Gosh." Katherine replies. "Isn't it past your bedtime?"

Todd Dolph, the boyfriend, leans over the blonde like she's a pet cat. "Shut up," he tells Katherine.

"Take it easy, lover boy."

Gil puts a beer down in front of his daughter, tells her to go up to her room if she's going to start a fight. *Nineteen years old,* she thinks, *sending me to my room.* Not a word to the crater-faced boyfriend who started it. She pours herself a beer and drinks half of it before putting the cold mug against her forehead.

"Is it humid in here or what?"

As Katherine comes out from behind the bar, Todd the boyfriend looks at her all cold-eyed like he's going to backhand her. She's two inches taller than he is, and probably outweighs him by thirty pounds. She ruffles his oily yellow hair. "Peace, pencil-dick."

In the bathroom, Katherine teases the bouffant back into shape, freshens her frosted pink lipstick, checks for food in her teeth, and returns to the bar looking as sweet as she can manage. She comes up behind Gino and glances at the stranger sitting with him. She never saw this one before, wonders where he gets them. Bobby's little rabies-trap barks at her from under their table.

"One little spin on a bar stool," she says to the dog. "Get over it."

Bobby leans back in his chair. "Katie girl, you look beautiful."

She puts her hands on Gino's shoulders. "Hi."

"Hi, Katydid."

She looks at the Mexican seated next to him. "Who's this?"

"Just doing business, sweetheart. Relax."

Bobby and the Mexican lean into one another and talk. Katherine rubs Gino's shoulders. She feels the muscles through his knit shirt. Her stomach drops between her legs.

"Took the kids to see *Dr. Strangelove* yesterday." Gino's favorite subject, his niece and nephew. His brother's a Republican, so the niece and nephew are Gino's personal reclamation project. "I'll never have any of my own," he said once. "So I gotta save these two." Last weekend he had them over to his house to make tie-dyed T-shirts. He claims it's political, but the truth is he loves those kids. Katherine's hands move from his shoulders to his neck underneath all that black hair. He reaches up and squeezes her hand, gives it a little kiss, and lets go. "I'm working, sweetheart."

Bobby asks, "When you gonna give him up, girl?"

"When I die. He's it for me." She says it loud enough for both the Mexican and the blonde at the bar to hear. But the blonde's got no eyes for anyone but Gil.

"Come on, Miss'ippi Mud Pie," she says to Bobby's dog. "Tell us ya name, honey." She holds a cracker with a slice of salami in front of the dog's nose. "Tell me ya real name, sugar, and I'll give ya six of these."

Gino lets Katie put a party hat on him. For the ten thousandth time she asks him, "When are you gonna come over to my side and give it a try?"

"You're my friend, Katydid." Gino smiles and kisses her forehead, then walks away.

"I never saw anyone so pathetic over a homo," Sheila tells her.

Katie fell in love with Gino when he first pulled into the parking lot of McGurk's four years ago in a red Mustang convertible, one of the first ever made. The top was down and the sunlight made his hair shine like black mink. Katie sat on the fire escape, smoking a joint with Bobby. Gino got out of the car, looked up and smiled. She dropped the joint.

"Hey Gino," Bobby said, standing up to knock the joint out of his lap. "Where'd you get your hands on that?"

"Robert Royce," Gino replied. "Figured I'd find you here."

Katie nudged Bobby's leg. "Introduce me."

Gino's blue eyes landed on her like an atomic bomb; they looked trapped and glittery behind those thick black lashes. He was twenty years old at the time, and Katie was only seventeen, but he drove away that day with her heart dragging off the tailpipe. Bobby told her later that Gino had been away, doing time for car theft. She told Bobby that she'd have Gino or the sun would never shine again. Bobby laughed and let her figure it out for herself.

Gil's busy pouring free drinks for the Mississippi Blonde, who snaps her gum at him and reaches all the way over the bar for an ashtray, giving him a clean view down to her navel. He lights her Camel for her and she grins at him, still chewing her gum. She inhales hard enough to suck the ash down half an inch. She's a pro. Her boyfriend's gone. He couldn't pick her up and drag her out, so he left her there. Gil's having a good time. Bobby offers to tell Katherine the dog's real name if she'll sleep with him.

"No," she says, "no, no, and by the way, no." She holds an Oreo just out of the dog's reach.

"You're a mean girl, Katie."

"Mean?" She yanks the Oreo away from the hair ball as he leans in for a bite. "Me?"

"Gil tell you I got something for you?"

"What is it?"

"Case of nail polish remover." He traces his finger along the peace sign on the back of her right hand. "My brother-in-law knows a guy owns a tattoo joint in Depot Town."

"Yeah. I know." She watches as Gino dances with Olivia; he holds her up so she doesn't fall and break a hip.

"I can get you anything you want."

"I want you to shut your pie hole."

"Spider? Rose? The guy's an artist. Did a gorgeous snake crawling down a girl's thigh, right out of her snake nest."

"Her what?"

"You know. Her snatch."

"No thanks."

"I got a cousin, his wife works at a nail salon. You want a set of those claws for free?"

"What's wrong with you?" she asks.

"Never mind."

"What are you, trying to buy me?"

"It's not the money," he says. "The money's not the point."

She looks over her shoulder for Gil, then whispers, "Then what *is* the point?"

Bobby shakes his head in disgust. "If you don't get it, I can't explain it to you."

Someone in the crowd says, "See, they found his head in the desert." Katherine wishes she was part of that conversation. Gil brings her gin without the tonic.

"Shouldn't somebody go check on Jerry?" Katherine asks.

"It's early." Gil leans forward on the bar with his Orange Crush, watching everybody dance to *Woolly Bully.* "Bunch of lunatics, but it's nice when everyone's here."

Sheila returns from the pay phone in back. "I called the apartment, he's not there."

The little blonde smiles at Gil. He pulls out his Polaroid and says to her, "Smile like you love me." She does. He snaps the picture and counts to sixty before peeling back the paper. "Damn, sweetheart. Look at you." He yells across the bar, "Come on, boys. Get up here for a picture."

P.T. comes first, dragging Charlie with him. Bobby has to hold Gino up at the bar, he's so drunk. That leaves P.T. to hold the dog. Charlie scowls, his eyes staring and his hair falling in his face. Bobby says for Gil to hurry up and shoot the picture before

Gino falls down, but it's too late. They lurch off to the side just as the bulb goes off.

When Gil peels back the cover, P.T.'s got the dog in front of his face, Charlie stares into the camera like Charles Manson, and Bobby's reaching off to the side where Gino is a blur, cut in half at the edge of the picture. Gil sticks the photo on the mirror over the cash register.

"There's a classic," he says. "Three and a half Stooges."

The boys scatter. P.T. lifts a tray of dirty glasses to take to the back. The blonde leans forward and taps him lightly on the shoulder. "Hi, you."

"Hi, you," he says back.

"How old are you?" she asks.

"Nineteen."

"My goodness." She peers at the red mark that mars the white of his left eye. "What happened to your eye?"

"I forgot."

She tilts her head to the side, looks up at him, tries not to blow smoke in his face. "What's your name?"

"You are a pretty girl," he tells her. She smiles and gives a little laugh. He asks her, "Why are you a prostitute?"

She holds her cigarette in front of her mouth for a second before smashing it into an ashtray. "Did I ask for that?" Her little eyebrows go down in a straight line. "Did I ask you how come you're some kind of a retard or whatever the heck you are?" He holds the rack of dirty glasses and blinks. Katherine moves in to knock her ass on the floor, but Bobby holds her arm. Charlie stands back and watches. "Lord God, I thought you were cute, you know. You're a cute kid. Was I asking for wisecracks from some guy who can't even count to ten?"

"I can count to ten."

"Congratulations."

"I was curious," P.T. tells her. "It is interesting, and I was curious."

"If you're curious, give me thirty bucks and I'll tell you all about it," says the Mississippi Blonde. She crosses one leg over the other.

"If you get thirty bucks, I'm Tiny Tim," says Katherine.

"No, thank you," says P.T., carrying the rack of glasses to the storeroom and returning with a clean dishrag. He wipes the bar, lifting first the blonde's ashtray, then her drink, to make a clean swipe like he's seen Gil do a million times. Gino comes up for a refill. "What will you have?" asks P.T. Gil lets him do that from time to time, act like he's the bartender.

Gino puts his arm around Katherine's shoulder. "How's it going, Katydid?"

"I love you."

"You having a good time?"

"Have some pity."

"You don't want a pity fuck," he says.

"Yes I do."

He laughs and carries the two drinks to the back. Gil has one elbow on the cash register, swizzle stick in his mouth; he listens to the little blonde. She's already written off P.T. "Aw, Gil honey, you oughta seen it. We'd go in the old tar pits after midnight. Use the flashlights to scare the bullfrogs so they'd freeze, okay?" Gil nods like she's telling him the Eighth Deadly Sin. "Some of the little guys are near a foot long, too," she says. "So you pick 'em up by the back of the neck and throw 'em in a wet sack. Next morning, you just reach in there, grab 'em by the feet, and bash their heads against a tree until their eyes bug and their little tongues stick out the sides." Gil nods again. Bobby listens, open-mouthed. "When you know they's good and stunned, then you can cut their heads off without it hurting 'em, so it's humane. Then you bread 'em, fry 'em up, and serve 'em with coleslaw, French fries, and ketchup."

Charlie plays Percy Sledge on the jukebox. He and Sheila dance together slow and sweet. Gil dances with the little blonde while P.T. covers the bar.

"Come on, Katie girl." Bobby weaves in front of Katherine, his party hat perched high on top of his Afro. "Let's dance." As the bar swings around in slow motion, Katherine looks over the top of Bobby's Afro at all the party decorations. "Too bad Old Jerry's missing his party."

4

OFFICER JORGE TAVERA TRANSFERRED TO THE YPSILANTI police force three months ago. Officer Townsend, the old rhino he's got for a partner, treats him like a cherry. "Transferred from Ann Arbor, huh?" he said every day for the first week. It didn't matter that Tavera had already put in eight years on the force; Townsend said Ann Arbor was about as dangerous as desk duty.

Tonight they're looking for someone who might know Jerry Moody, a body that came in a few hours ago, probable drowning. The landlady at the last known address says to check at the bar up on Michigan Avenue.

"Which bar?" asks Tavera.

"On the corner." She looks at him like he's simple. "You know. The bar."

Townsend stares at Tavera with bloodshot eyes. "You want to let me handle this?"

Blinking neon stutters out "McGurk's Ta Room," where the "p" is missing. Small grimy windows squint at them as they pull up. Inside, duct tape keeps the bar stools from coughing out their stuffing. The colors had been scrubbed from the tin ashtrays. The smell of wet dog yawns from the corners. Townsend yells above the music, asking the bartender if anyone here knows a guy named Jerry Moody.

"Who?"

"Jerry Moody. Supposed to be a customer here?"

Gil motions for Katherine to turn off the juke box. She pulls out the plug and the place goes silent just as P.T. says, "Jerry Moody is my grandpa."

"What's your name?"

Before P.T. can answer, Charlie gets in Townsend's face. "Why you asking?"

"Who are you?"

"Charlie Simpkins."

"He's my little brother," offers P.T., balancing Marigold on his shoulder. Charlie puts his foot on P.T.'s foot and presses down hard. P.T. sits down. "Who are you?" he asks.

"We're looking for next of kin," Tavera says. "Jerry Moody was found in Ford Lake this afternoon."

The bar stays silent. Olivia stares at the red tip of her cigarette. Bobby picks up the dog and holds it on his lap. Gil takes the swizzle stick out of his mouth and reaches for one of Charlie's Old Golds. Officer Tavera tries not to stare at P.T., whose colorless hair sticks out in all directions.

Charlie lays a hand on P.T.'s shoulder, startling the guinea pig, who bites him. "Fucker," mutters Charlie as he sucks on his finger.

P.T. says, "How did you find him so fast?"

"We need someone to ID the body," Tavera says.

"I gotta get my jacket." Charlie goes behind the bar to the back room. Then he comes out, looks around, says, "It ain't back there." Tavera stands by the door, waiting. Townsend keeps an eye on Charlie as he goes to the coat hooks in back near the pool table. He whispers to Gino, "Take him home."

P.T. calls, "Charlie?"

"Uh-huh?"

"You didn't wear a jacket."

Charlie returns to the front. "I'm gonna go with these guys for a minute," he says, "then I'll be back. You okay?"

P.T. nods. Katherine puts her arm around P.T. as Charlie follows the officers out of the bar. The silence is steadfast until the door closes behind them.

~

At the city morgue, Tavera leads Charlie down a tin can of a corridor. "You and the seven-foot wonder are brothers?"

Charlie looks at Tavera like he might take him down, right there with all the other bodies. "He had an accident when he was a kid. You wanna make another crack about it, lard ass?"

"What kind of accident?"

"You a fucking social worker?"

"We're going to want to talk to him."

"Why?"

"We'd like both of you to come in the morning and give a statement."

"About what?"

"We'll ask you some questions, that's all. Regulation stuff."

When the sheet is pulled off his grandfather's face, Charlie steps backwards and nearly stumbles into Tavera. It doesn't look like Old Jerry anymore. It looks like something that lived in the basement when he was a kid, something that hid under the bed or crouched behind the sofa when he and his brother were left alone at night. His legs freeze with a double-edged fear; the imagined monster was bad enough, but his father when he finally came home was worse. Charlie closes his eyes and hears again the tires in the driveway, the terrible slam of the car door. He hears his brother whisper for him to run upstairs to bed quick, then the sounds coming up through the floor, his brother's head hitting the wall as Charlie hid deep under the covers. He pushes past Tavera and vomits onto the floor. Someone brings him a cup of water; he uses it to splash his face. A voice speaks quietly to Townsend in the background. Charlie follows the officers into the hallway where it's easier to breathe.

"Mr. Simpkins," says Tavera. "Can you think of anyone who might have wanted to see Jerry Moody dead?"

"Besides himself? No." Charlie smiles, but he rubs his hands together to get rid of the rubbery feeling. They both seem to expect him to say something more. "Why?"

"Mr. Moody was deceased when he went into the lake." Charlie nods five or six times, lifts his eyebrows, and nods some more while he listens. "We're going to want to ask you some more questions. We'll send someone to pick up your brother."

"Why?"

"I told you we would have to question him."

"Tonight?"

"Mr. Simpkins, are you at all interested in finding out what happened to your grandfather?"

Tavera watches Charlie with a growing sense that something's wrong. "When was the last time you saw him?" The question comes out softly, hardly an accusation at all.

Charlie can't get the thumping out of his head. Thump, his brother hitting the wall, the floor, over and over. Charlie takes a deep breath and speaks to drown out the noise in his head. "I guess the last time I saw him would be when I dumped him in the lake."

So the confession goes: Charlie waited until Old Jerry passed out, smothered him with a pillow, and threw the body in the lake. Tavera drives Charlie to the station and gets a detailed account before placing him under arrest.

~

The opinion around McGurk's is that Charlie did the right thing by giving Old Jerry what he wanted for his birthday.

Sheila visits Charlie while he's waiting for his trial.

"When we bought the cake?" she says. "You'd already killed him when we bought the cake?" Charlie nods. He's never lied to Sheila before, and he does a terrible job now. In five minutes she's wrangled the truth out of him. "It's not going to work," she tells him. "And even if it could work, you can't do it."

"I'm not fighting with you about this."

"That's right. Because I'll tell them myself."

He grabs her wrist and squeezes hard. "Keep your voice down."

"Let go."

"You open your mouth, I swear to God—"

"What? What'll you do?" When Charlie lets go of her, she leans in closer to him. "I'm pregnant."

He looks at her from a huge distance, as if he were already in prison, as if all this were her fault. "Get rid of it."

Two minutes later, Officer Jorge Tavera enters the visitors' room to break up the fight. Sheila has thrown a chair across the table, even managed to throw two punches in Charlie's face. Tavera gets her up against the wall and handcuffed as another officer leads Charlie away. Sheila keeps her eyes on Charlie. "You're crazy," she yells. "You're crazier than your brother."

"Don't be like that." Charlie tries to quiet her down before she says more in front of Tavera.

"If you do this, you can forget about me."

"That's your call."

"I mean it. That's it." Charlie disappears through the door. She rubs at one eye with her knuckle until she sees starbursts, trying to take in what just happened. She yells at the closed door. *"Coma la mierda, hijo de una puta."*

"Llámame Jorge," replies Tavera behind her.

"Nobody's talking to you, asshole." Tavera reads Sheila her rights. She interrupts to ask for a cigarette. Tavera reaches in her shirt pocket, pulls out a Viceroy and sticks it in her mouth. He lights it as he continues the Miranda. She takes a deep drag. "You done?"

"Assaulting a prisoner," he says, "no buena."

"How about assaulting an officer?"

"How old are you?" When she doesn't answer he tries again. "Got any ID?"

She holds the cigarette butt in her teeth and flicks the ashes on the table with her tongue. Her face is scribbled over with smoke. "Driver's license in my purse."

He uncuffs her so she can dig it out. "You gonna be a good girl or do I have to cuff you again?"

"Eat me."

"I'll take a rain check on that." He leaves, locking the door behind him.

She grinds the cigarette out with her shoe. All it did was make her sick. She lays her head on the table. *Get rid of it.* She has already tried. She'd talked with a woman on the phone who agreed to do it only because Sheila knew her niece. Two days later the woman had been arrested. Sheila didn't know where else to go. Besides, she had cried with relief after hanging up.

When Tavera returns, Sheila sits up straight and wipes it all out of her mind so she won't cry in front of a cop, for God's sake. He tosses the driver's license on the table. "I guess no one wants you."

"You wanna get the fuck off my back now?"

He smiles, watching her stuff the license back in her purse. "I ought to search that for marijuana."

"Running low?"

She doesn't ask if she's free to go, just heads for the door. Behind her she hears, "I'll be seeing you, Sheila Alvarez."

"Don't bet on it, *lechón.*"

~

The assistant DA offers Charlie a choice: eight years for manslaughter or enlistment in the army for three years. "Like going to jail," he says, "except you get paid."

Bobby sees it coming because he's heard about this kind of thing going on. "Cannon fodder, Charlie," he says. "Ever hear of it?"

Charlie scowls. "I ain't going to prison."

"This war, it's a dream come true for the Man. Wake up."

"Your ass isn't the one sitting in a jail cell."

"They tell you you're gonna be driving supply trucks in the rear? Typing up telegrams in Saigon to some dead kid's family?" Bobby shakes his head. "You'll be getting your ass shot off, and that's exactly where they want you."

Charlie skips the trial, the judge, and sentencing for basic training. Katherine comes home one night to find a month's rent on the table and a note from Sheila saying she's starting over somewhere else. Despite Bobby's offer of his place, Katie moves into the spare bedroom above the bar. Gino puts Charlie's things in storage and takes P.T. to live with him. In May of 1967, Charlie leaves for Vietnam.

5

May 1967

Hey Bro. Im sending you my address where you can rite to me. Its already summer here and everythings green. Im sweating like a pig. Dont lose this address. I want you to rite to me evry week and tell me how your doing and if your okay. They shaved my head bald. Love, me. P.S. Rite me a letter.

May 1967

Dear Charlie, Gino does not like corn flakes we went to the store and got four boxes he says I eat too much but you know what he eats more than me just not cornflakes how do I know you will get my letter rite and tell me you got this. Alrity then from your big brother.

June 1967

Hey Charlie, how you doing? You need anything let me know okay? Gil went and married that little blonde hooker. She doesn't come down to the bar except to talk to Gil, and doesn't come down to work any more at all. Damn shame, too. I got a toss out of her for introducing her to this guy whose brother can get her painkillers cheap for cramps when she's on the rag. So she gets her pills and I get a blow job. That was before she retired. Katie, she's around, but she ain't got the same spark without Sheila. I still got the word out to everyone I know, but she did a fade on us, Charlie. She's gone. Listen, I know a guy over there, Clark Joplin, supposed to be in the Ninth Cav. He's a good guy. Once you're over there, if you run into him, give him my name and he'll do what he can for you. He's got the shit figured out, you need anything. Okay? I think he's a Captain or something by now. He was a buddy of my dad's in Korea. Keep your nuts covered. Bobby.

August 1967

Dear Bro, today I got a big fat leech up my nose. We had to cross this stream but it rained evry goddamn day for a week so the waters up to our armpits and freezing and what do I do but step into a hole and go under. By the time were out the other side we got these things hanging all over us. We strip down and check our legs and each others backs. I got this monster worked his way half way up my nose. I freak out and I dont have my bug juice because it was strapped to my helmut and came loose when I went under. So I yell for some one to get this thing out of my goddamn nose. There all too busy checking their balls and peckers. I aint had one on my pecker yet. I would keel over and die right there. Colt comes over and I yell at him to spray the fucker. He says to hold on and he digs threw his rucksack and I yank on this sucker but it aint budging. Colt yells hey Snake turn around. Then the cocksucker takes a picture of me. He takes a goddamn picture while Im getting my eyeballs sucked dry from the inside. He finally hits the thing with his bug juice and it comes out deader than shit and my blood all over. These bastards are huge Bro. Big as your dick I swear to God. Im gonna get that picture off Colt and send it to you. You will flip. You write and let me know every things okay. Tell Gino I said hi. Stay out of trouble okay. Love, me.

September 1967

Gino. You gotta make sure the draft folks leave Bro alone. I seen guys here near as bad as he is. Carrying rifles, too. Do whatever you gotta do to keep him safe and Ill owe you anything you want. It's a bad trip. I got people yelling in my face all day sometimes all night. The worst is when there yelling at me while the gooks are shooting at me. Those fuckers want to kill me. My sargent says no problem just kill them first, but you cant see for shit. Its bad. Guys are dying already. I didnt think evrything would happen so quick. I didnt think they sent the new guys out in the middle of the worst shit. People back home dont got no idea whats going on over here. Its a miracal any of us make it back. I gave Bro my address but here it is in case he loses it. This place scares the shit out of me. I guess my guts dont travel outside of Ypsi.

October 1967

I got my notice. Two weeks. There's no way out of it. I got P.T. in a halfway house outside of Ann Arbor. I talked to the woman for a long time, and me and P.T. went out to look at it. She says no way is the draft board going to want anyone who lives there. He gets his own room, and he doesn't have to take any drugs, and it's part owned by the state so the money Old Jerry set aside should cover it until you get back.

I don't know what else to do. I hope this is okay, because I'm going to be gone before you even get this letter. I guess the odds of both of us coming home in one piece are pretty small. So I'll see you when I see you, one way or the other. Gino. P.S. Here's P.T.'s address as of October 20. P.P.S. You can keep writing to me if you want. I'll read them when I get back.

October 1967

Dear Bro. You gotta promise me youll tell me if you dont like it at that place. You gotta write and tell me what its like and who the people are and what you eat and what you do all day. You dont gotta be nowhere you dont wanna be. And if anyone fucks with you, call Gil at the bar. If you need anything just call him. Ill send him money every month in case you get any emergencys. Even if you just wanna buy a new shirt or something you call over there and him or Katie can take you shopping. Thanks for all the letters so far. Tell me what evrything looks like. Make it so I can see evrything in my mind. Love, me.

November 1967

Dear Charlie, The house where I live has two floors I am sitting in the front room where their is an old desk and I am riting to you from that desk. Yes I like it here no one has picked a fight with me yet their is someone here sitting on the couch reading *Hot Rod* magazine his name is Barry. I have filled out two forms that might get me a job I want to go back and work for Gil but no one will let me will you please tell them to let me work for Gil please there is a bug cralling up the arm of the couch it moves up a inch then it stops then it moves up some more it is closed to Barry's arm I will let you know if it jumps on him. Now it is gone it went back down I am sitting by a window and the sun is shinning on my head it is hot I will rite to you in two days. How is Veetnom love your big brother.

November 1967

Dear Pfc. Simpkins, I am a volunteer at the VA Medical Center in Ann Arbor. Your name was on a list of soldiers from Washtenaw

County for this Pen Pal program they have here. I chose your name because I went to school with a Charles Simpkins from Willis. The Charlie I knew dropped out after his freshman year at Lincoln High. I am curious if you are the same person.

I graduated two years ago. I still live at home on Hitchingham Road. Since graduation, I've worked as a teller for Citizens Bank. I recently applied for a position in the mortgage department, and I have an interview on Monday. That means I have all weekend to sweat it out. I will let you know if I get the job, if you still want to write back and forth. If I do get the job, I will move to Jackson. I would like to get out of here and have a place of my own.

My hobbies are reading mystery novels and whittling. If you would like to be Pen Pals, then someday when I'm good enough, I'll send you something that I have whittled if I haven't chopped a thumb off first.

I have been given your location in the Army, as far as division, platoon, company, etc. However, I have no idea where you are in Vietnam, or what your job is. I would like to know these things if you're allowed to tell us. I didn't check—maybe I'm not supposed to ask. Does the Army censor letters for security reasons? As you see, there is a lot I don't know, even after volunteering here for six months. I know how to change a dressing. I've gotten good at it. But I don't understand how the military works. We got guys here from the Navy, the Marines, some guys who get very mysterious when you ask them what division they were with. I don't know if I should say this, but it's the Marines who seem to be wounded the worst, or the most often. Do you know any Marines? Are they all crazy or just unlucky?

It seems like my biggest job here as a volunteer is to listen to stories. The nurses and doctors don't have time, and the guys are bored to death when they aren't doing physical therapy. Sometimes I write letters for guys who can't write for themselves, for guys whose families can't come to visit, or won't. But mostly I listen to them talk.

I'm getting more of an education than in all my years at Lincoln high school. I am even learning a few Vietnamese phrases, such as "dinky dow" and "choo hoy." All of this makes me curious to hear from someone who is over there. It is hard to imagine.

I have written a lot and it is late. I have to be up tomorrow at 6:30 for work, which is tomorrow evening for you, isn't it? I hope to hear from you. It would really be something if we went to school together, wouldn't it? Sincerely, Diane Porter, Volunteer, VA Medical Hospital, 2215 Fuller Road, Ann Arbor, MI 48105, USA!

November 1967

Bro, I had some freaky shit happen the last couple days. Got a letter from some chick I went to school with. She wants to be my Pen Pal or some goddamn thing. I am sending you the letter so you can see what a head case she is.

Then last night I had a lizard tell me to fuck off. I shit you not Bro. This little voice comes out of the dark and says fuck you. I look behind me like a dumb ass like who are they talking to? There aint no one behind me and aint no one in front of me. Over here you dont want some stranger saying fuck you in the dark. I about wet my pants thats how scared I was. So I wake up Junior and I wisper in his ear how some ones out there. Were listening and you know of course their aint nothing. Then this thing jumps up close and I about jump on Juniors head I swear to God. Its a lizard and hes looking at us and were looking at him. He aint that big. Juniors looking at me like Im a goddamn cherry. Then the lizard bends his front legs like hes gonna jump and he says fuck you. Junior wants to laugh but he cant because its night so you gotta be quiet. He puts his hand over his mouth but the goddamn thing does it again. He gives this little jerk and says fuck you. Junior wispers fuck you too. We both put our heads down trying not to laugh but you cant help it. We dug way back in our bunker hoping it would go away. But it keeps saying fuck you and every time it does its funnier. Goddamn thing kept cussing us out for damn near an hour thanks to Junior answering him back. I thought he was gonna jump in the bunker with us. I swear to God Bro it was like when dad used to say he was gonna kick our ass if we didnt shut up and we couldnt quit laughing even though we were gonna get our asses kicked. It was like that. No you cant work for Gil no more. I miss you. Love, me.

December 1967

Dear Diane Porter, you want to know what its like here. Well, lets see we just came back from a patrol yesterday. Ran into some light fire around noon and had to call in a dust-off to pick up Oblonsky who got hit in the shoulder and Smoke who got smoked (ha ha). He took a round in the face that pushed his eyeball out the back of his skull. Thats some sharp shooting. We called him Smoke because he could fade like smoke when the shit went down. He was firing back, aint like he wasnt fighting. He killed more gooks than the rest of us, and no one ever saw him do it. After we chase them off we start counting up bodies (Priority One: Body Count!) and Smoke would say "over there and over here and there should be two back there." Half the time the shit is flying so fast from every where you dont know whos killing who or if your emptying all your ammo into a damn mangrove tree. But Smoke knew. Whoever got him, I hope he dont come back. But he will. They always come back. Smoke had two girlfriends in Arkansas. He said which ever one wrote him the most letters, thats the one he marries when he gets home. Only had ten weeks to go. We didnt get a chance to go through his rucksack to see which girl was winning. Lieutenant Dickhead stripped it of anything we could use and tossed it on the chopper with the body.

After we wrapped up Smoke and the back of his head and tossed him in the Huey and Oblonsky crawled up in there, off goes the chopper without us and there we are and maybe the gooks are still out there and maybe they aint. Maybe they run off like they do if its a hit and run or maybe the gunners mowed their asses down when the chopper circled the LZ or maybe their a couple hundred meters away having lunch. We pick up our packs and keep on humping until we get to camp. Barely enough daylight to get dug in. I mean dig a hole and fill the sandbags and stack the bags around the hole and say a little prayer and eat your rotten C ration. Hotel Vietnam. Checking in is easy and checking out is easier.

To answer your question the Marines are all crazy assholes. Ask anyone in the Army. Your other question, where am I? Fuck I dont know. Near Chu Lai, which means dick squat to me. I am on the other side of the world I can tell you that. They got lots of rivers here. I seen some made of blood. I heard of one up north they call the Red River and they say its the red dirt every where makes it run red. But I think the dirts red because its soaked up that river of blood for so long. I am waiting for the trees to go red starting with the roots up the trunk and then spreading red all over the palm leaves. Red red red. Thats all you see besides green green green and brown brown brown. Some times you see the white of some guys teeth when hes screaming after being hit. Thats it for the view.

As for my job over here, its to kill people. Dont think it matters much who. Any thing else you want to know well you just write back and Ill tell you all about it. When you write why dont you tell me what you had for dinner and where you slept last night and who you seen killed lately. PFC Charlie Simpkins. P.S. Yeah I went to Lincoln. You were a year ahead of me.

December 1967

Merry Christmas Charlie! I hope this package gets there in time. How is it over there? How's the food? Do they treat you all right? You got enough clothes? You want me to send you anything? Can you believe Dad married that girl from Mississippi? She's okay. You heard from Gino at all? He got drafted, and no one's heard a word from him. It's been three months. We don't have any idea where they sent him or what he's doing. Man, I miss you and Sheila like crazy. And Gino, and P.T. What's left isn't the brilliant ones in the batch. Same old faded out customers, and Bobby working his deals, and Olivia flapping her jaws. I saw P.T. last Sunday. Took him out for lunch at Bill Knapp's to make sure he was getting some food, he's so God-awful skinny. He ate six baked potatoes, but nothing else. You missed all the excitement this past summer. Riots over in Lynwood and Glendale. Detroit was making national news. Hey, get this. Dad wants me and The Little Woman to take GED courses. He sent away for books and stuff. Can you see me with a high school diploma? You let me know if you hear from Gino. I'm growing my hair long. Wait til you see it. You haven't done any of the whores over there, have you? I been hearing stories about the kind of stuff you can catch over there. So keep your dick in your pants or in your hands or some place safe. Please write back if you have time, ha ha. Love, Katie.

January 1968

Charlie: My boy was born January 16, eight pounds, three ounces. Named him Jeffrey Gilbert. Got his old man's temper and his mama's looks. Katie's out of her mind, bringing home crap the kid don't need, crap we don't have room for. He's smart, though. He gets this look in his eye and you know he's planning something in his head, even if it's just taking the next shit. They shit a lot, Charlie. That's something you need to know. I forgot how much babies shit.

Katie talked to Gino's brother. Turns out our boy's a gunner with the 101st Airborne. I don't know anything more than that. She writes to him, but he never answers. His brother hasn't heard from him since he went over. Katie made him promise to call her if he gets any news. His brother's the next of kin, so you know what that means. Keep your eyes peeled, maybe you'll see him fly by. The whole thing's a goddamned mess. I know you're over there busting your ass. All I'm saying is, stay awake and don't be a hero. Gil.

February 1968

Dear Charlie Happy Valentines Day can you catch one of those lizards and bring it home we could take it to McGurks so Gil would get mad when it said FUCK YOU last week Steve and Rose took everyone to the Henry Ford Museem and we were eating lunch in a restrant there and an ant was crawling around my knee but then he left. Remember when grandpa took us to Greenfield Village to the blacksmith shop and we got rings made out of bent horseshoe nails and I lost mine but you said yours was a brass nuckle now the wind blows the shade in the window and it looks like the whole letter is dansing I wish that it would do the same thing when you open it so you could see. Steve says I am better off here then I was before but I do not think so it does not feel like Valentines Day I will tell you about the rest of the trip tommorrow remember that giant uniroyal tire on the side of the highway it is still there when are you coming home love your BIG brother.

March 1968

Bro, what do you mean you are better off. I will kick Steves ass when I come home. Today I saw a poisonous snake. We call them Five-Steppers because thats how long you got after he bites you is five steps and you drop dead. I dont know if thats true but it scared the shit out of me any way. He was brown with yellow patches. Didnt look fancy as far as snakes go but he had this little pin head sticking up looking rite at me. These little bastards arent supposed to come out except at night but I guess we woke him up crashing around in the bush like we do. I think we saw each other about the same time because he looked as surprised as I did. I didnt even break stride just kept walking. Got no business with you thank you mister. He wasnt that big but big enough to bite me above the boot. I started shaking after I passed him. I should of told the guys behind me he was there but it all went so quick and any talking might have set him off. It was just a quick look but now I know what it means to look at some one snake eyed. It means to scare the shit out of them, Bro.

You would flip over the jungle out here. When it aint raining its beautiful. We got mountains so high the clouds come down and sit right on them sometimes. Theres palm trees like they got in Florida, and elefant grass, which is like nothing I ever saw. When the winds blowing across it in waves it looks like a green lake. On a hot day you swear you could dive in there and swim. But truth is you would get sliced to pieces diving into that shit.

They got mesqitoes big as your hand. Well maybe not as big as yours but big as a normal guys hand. You slap these things dead and they leave a mess like you swatted a fucking blood bag. I guess I been bitten and sucked on by just about every inseck they got here. Were human C rations to them. Junior got some kind of bug crawled in his ear a week ago while he was sleeping. Woke up near dawn screaming and every one grabbed their guns and we were all shooting out at the trees until some one figured out there aint nothing to shoot at. Just Junior with something crawling inside his ear. They had to fly him out to the hospital and it looked like he was losing his mind. They gave him a shot to knock him out. Dont know what their gonna do about it maybe take a vacuum cleaner and stick it in his ear. So now Juniors gone.

But its beautiful here Bro even when its kicking your ass. Yesterday the air turned green, just like before a tornado back home. Crack of lightning lit up everything and then the sky went purple. The rain hit us like BB shots. The wind twirled the trees around and around.

Looked like Ma's spider plant when we put it in the vacume cleaner. I think I seen about a hundred different butter flies. I'm surprised they all aint dead by now. Remember them little yellow suckers we used to chase. Them yellow butter flies. Tell me where you are Bro I need to hear from you. Love, me.

March 1968

Dear Charlie, I got a squirrel now he sits outside the window he eats his sunflower seeds while I eat my cornflakes that is our habit together his name is Skuppers he is not here rite now because it is night I cannot sleep so I will rite to you. Marigold is in her box and she is doing fine. Do you remember the checker board ice cream we got from Missus Etter if we washed her car or mowed her lawn she might give us fifty cents or some ice cream that was checkered different flavors do you remember that. Bring home all the pitures you can I want to see Colt and Junior and the rest of your friends maybe they will all come visit when you come home Colt will show me the piture of you with the leech up your nose. They put me in charge of a vegtable garden here and I have peeple who help me weed Rose says I have a green thumb remember mama always talked about a green thumb I do not understand why you want to stay over their a extra three months you say it means you can come home sooner but I do not understand how a extra three months is sooner you said one year it has almost been a year and now you say you will come home next October I do not understand why. Rite and tell me when are you coming home Steve is nice do not kick his ass love your BIG BROTHER.

March 1968

Dear Charlie, you haven't changed much. I decided I wasn't going to write back, but what the heck. Tonight for supper I had leftover meatloaf, a baked potato, and canned peas. And a Coke. Last night I slept in my own bed with two pillows and an orange bedspread that my mom bought me when she found out I was moving out. (I got that job.) Last time I saw someone killed was when the school bus hit Pauline Haan in front of the junior high. You ought to remember that. Not as dramatic as the poke in the eye your friend Smoke got, but it was bad enough at the time. Any other questions you have, just write and I'll tell you all about it.

Everett Locklin was killed somewhere on the Mekong River six months ago. Andy Vanloo and David Brooks were both killed, but I don't know where. I don't know if you remember, but they were a year ahead of me at Lincoln. Closed casket on both of them. Do you want to hear this kind of stuff or not?

I asked some of the guys at the hospital to translate parts of your letter, words like Huey, dust-off, LZ. What do you do when it rains? Do you stay in one place or do they move you around? Are the trees turning red yet?—Diane.

April 1968

Dear Diane, when it rains we get wet. We sit in water and we walk through water up to our necks and we hump through muck that comes over the top of our boots and we drink what ever we can find and hope there aint some dead gook rotting in the water upstream.

The VC got nothing but holes and tunnels all threw this place. You could walk from Saigon to Hanoi with out ever seeing day light if you knew the tunnels. I heard the gooks have whole hospitals under ground like goddamn animals.

They move us around, yeah. First your in a chopper going here. But nope now they need you a hundred klicks over there so you pack up and another slick hawls you off flying in the breeze until they drop you in a hot zone where your ass is shot off before your on the ground. Thats a trip beleive me. Your zigzagging like a motherfucker and guys are getting hit on ether side of you and you grab one and drag him by his jacket until you hit the trees where you think maybe your safe. You look out at all the guys you didnt pick up and drag away and you gotta decide if their alive or if their dead out there. Snipers set on the wounded and wait for some dumb ass to run out there and be a hero and zap, pick us off like junebugs.

Then the gunships take over and shoot the living shit out of every thing with in a hundred feet of where the enemy might be. If your lucky you get to see a Cobra hanging there like John Fucking Wayne spraying rounds that chop the trees down for a half mile. Its enough to give you a hard on watching them bastards. By now all the VC are dead or running under ground like rats. So here we are and half of us got killed just getting here. They keep us here searching villages or playing hop scotch over mines or guarding some shit. They use us like bait until the VC comes out again and hits. We are worms on the end of a hook. If the NVA bites, the artillery yanks hard and you got a big fish called Body Count. No ones too goddamned concerned if the worms get swallowed or not.

You wanna know are the trees red. Yeah. We come up on a hill had a napalm strike maybe a week before. Dont know if you'd call them trees any more but they look red to me. I dont want to hear about any guys from home getting greased. I got enough of that as it is.

Your moving to Jackson. You gonna send me your address? Or maybe you dont got no more questions for me. That's good about your job. Really I mean it. Its smart getting the hell out of Ypsi. And that was pretty good asking around figuring out what the fuck I was talking about. Heres some more things you can ask your buddies about: Du Ma, FNG, Bouncing Betty, KIA. What did you mean I havent changed much. Charlie.

April 1968

Dear Bro. Yesterday I ate a steak. Captain Conley had them for us when we got back to base camp. Dont know whos ass he had to kiss or kick, but there they were. Biggest steaks you ever saw. I think evry one of us would of marched strait into hell for that man when we saw that. Coop had some fudge his girlfriend sent him. We had us a helluva feast, Bro. I about shit my brains out last night, but so did evryone else. It was funny cause we thought for sure the gooks could smell us five miles away. I got some good friends over here, so dont you worry about me. Im glad your liking your job gardenering. Does Katie and Gil come to see you? I sent them some money for you but I didnt here back. Im sorry about Marigold, but tell Skuppers I said hi. Love, me.

May 1968

Dear Charlie, What I meant by you not changing much was that you're still an asshole. Here's a laugh. I had a crush on you in fifth grade. We all played kickball at recess. I kicked it and accidentally hit you smack in the face. I said I was sorry but you cussed me out and said you'd beat the lights out of me. You were only in fourth grade, so I told you to go ahead, but you didn't. You called me a cootie shit, I think, and walked away. I was in love the rest of the year. See? You were an asshole even then. Diane.

June 1968

Dear Charlie I got a paper cut the last time I rote to you and it hurt from Thursday til Saturday so now I have to be careful when are you coming home I have mosqitos too but I have not even seen a garter snake any where today I heard Rose talking in the kitchen and she said that it was a crime we are in Veyetnom and we got no buziness there and she sounded *mad* are you going to go to jail did you kill somebody Rose will not tell me. Do not tell her I asked you what is your favrite color I forgot and I am making you something I grew a peony but it fell over. My friend Barry has a sister who died. Now he is sad all the time because she is the only one who visited him. He misses her and that is why he will not eat guess what I have my own room over the garage love great big brother PS when are you coming home?

June 1968

Dear Diane, seems like I remember you more and more every time you write. You and Sue Garrett were a couple of smart asses. Thanks for the picture and for wrapping it good in plastic. I got a picture of my brother and its all soaked threw and coming apart.

Yesterday we saw a big monkey of all different colors dansing around in the trees and cracking us up. I think we sat their for a hour while this monkey made faces and stuck his ass out at us. He was in the trees out side the wire and Judd raises up his M-16 and shoots it. It drops out of the tree but it aint dead because we can hear it screaming. The sergeants yelling at us to shut the goddamn thing up before every NVA cocksucker in the area crawls up our ass so Judd takes fifteen minutes to crawl threw the coils and finaly gets out there and shoots it in the head. He cut off one of the front paws and tied it around his neck and now he wears it like a good luck charm. A necklace of gook ears dont bother me near as much as that monkey paw. Lieutenant Dickhead sends Judd out there to bury it. I wish Judd had stepped on one of our own mines, I swear to God. He is out there digging and we can hear him bitching the whole time. Some of the guys asked him why he had to go shoot it. He holds up the paw and says look at it man, you cant buy that shit man. We were getting a kick out of that stupid monkey. Judd's ghosted on us a couple times on patrol. Next time we hit heavy fire he better watch his back.

I didnt tell you that to bring you down. Its just something that happened. Shit goes down over here you couldnt dream up any of this shit if you tried. I seen guys blown up like a toad stuffed with a fire cracker and I heard them screaming for a medic when no one can get to them because the enemy will mow you down if you pop your head up. I had a kid die while I was putting a dressing pack on his chest. Just gave up and died before the medic could get over to him. But that monkey wasnt doing nothing but making us laugh and now I gotta look at the fucking paw every day and it aint no little thing like a spider monkey. Its big. I had a rabbits foot I made when I was a kid. I brung it over here with me and I been wearing it but buried the damn thing so no one could find it.

Tell me about your new place. You still gonna work at the VA hospital in Ann Arbor or not? Goddamn I wouldnt mind being there. I could live without a hand if it got me out of here. Write soon. Charlie.

June 1968

Charlie, the Tigers look good this year. Looks like it might even be a World Series year. I went and saw P.T. like you asked. He's good. Some social worker there said a kid died when he fell out of a window in P.T.'s room. It's only above the garage, but the kid's neck was broke. She said P.T. was pretty shook up, it was a friend of his. He seems okay now. Nothing exciting around here. Take my advice. Never, ever, ever get married. Hurry and get home. Gil.

July 1968

Charlie, Happy Fourth of July. Thanks for the picture. You're right, you do look like a cross between Keith Moon and Anthony Perkins. I loved Psycho. You don't look much different than I remember from high school, except your hair's longer now, and the tattoos on the arm. I'm glad you sent it. Now I can see who I'm writing to.

I'm all moved into my new place in Jackson. I'm sharing an apartment here with Sue Garrett. Thanks to your comment a while back, we call it the House of the Rising Smart-ass. Yes, I still work at the VA on weekends. No need to go into any detail there. You know it all already. I'm thinking of whittling you your own short-timer stick. Is that something you'd be interested in, or is it too personal? How much time do you have left until you're out of there? Are you coming straight home? Or do you have to serve someplace over here for a while? If that's the case, let me know. Maybe Sue and I will come visit you. Diane.

August 1968

Dear Bro. I dont got much time to rite these days but I wanted to let you know that Im okay so you dont worry. Im fine. I got a new address is all. So you can rite to me here. When you rite to me tell me what vegtables are growing and what your room looks like and is it hot as hell there like it is here? Do you have corn on the cob? Im tired so goodnight for now. Love, me. P.S. Tell Rose to mind her own dammed business. You and me will have a house when I come home.

August 1968

Dear Diane, just dont freak out because I am okay. I will be back with my unit in a couple of weeks. The hospital here in Saigon hasnt had a mortar attack since Tet so Im better off now than I been since I got to this fucking place. Its just shrapnel and they got 90 per cent of it out but theres smaller pieces in there that probably wont work their way out until the next war. As it is I aint gonna be winning no beauty contest back there in the world. Dont ask me how it happened. Their were nine men on our patrol and seven of them died.

I want you to write me a letter and tell me what your livingroom looks like. Tell me every peice of furniture and every lamp and what it looks like and where it come from. Tell it to me so I can see it because I want to close my eyes and imagine I am sitting their with you in your livingroom having a beer and shooting the shit. I want to check out of here and go to your livingroom in my head the next time things get bad. When Im out of here and I served out my enlistment time, Im gonna get me a house surrounded by fields and woods where their aint a neighbor no where and all you see at night is stars, just black night with no lights and no color and no tracers, just shooting stars way up their that never land on the ground. Me and my brother gonna live out in the middle of fucking nowhere.

I feel like the world your in is another planet. You know all my friends I talk about from McGurks. Katie thinks its cool to fly in a chopper. It aint cool when your strapped in on a stretcher. Bobby asks me how many people I killed and that hooker that Gil married nitted me a wool scarf. What am I gonna do with that. Oh yeah thanks for the package. It caught up with me a few days ago. What did you do take a poll at the hospital there? Socks and Kool-Aid and Winstons and homemade peanut butter cookies. I got six guys here want your address but they aint getting it. Sherman is two beds down and he watched me open up this gold mine and he said I should marry you when I get home. He lost three fingers loading a Howitzer. Dumb bastard should of known better because you keep your goddamn fingers curled in and shove with the butt of your palm. But hes going home and I aint so whos the dumb bastard. Most the guys get hurt here because some dumb shit like that. See that smudge at the top of the paper is from me eating your cookies.

I think there gonna send me to some bull shit Army base in the States but I dont know where yet. I will let you know. I bet fifty bucks you dont come visit. You whittle me that short-timers stick and get it over here quick.

Write to me here at the hospital. If I am gone, it will get to me. Their good about that. Dont forget to tell me about your livingroom every damned detail. Love, Charlie.

September 1968

Charlie, I know this is the third letter in three days and you're going to think I'm crazy but I'm afraid if I stop writing, you'll disappear. You have to come home. You can't be who you are, and be so far away, and never let me see you in person. The pictures help, but my whole body hurts from missing you. Tell me the MINUTE you know where they're sending you.

Thanks for not minding about that stuff that I wrote to you, about those couple of years when I went a little crazy, the drugs and all the guys. I think I was trying to kill myself, if you want to know the truth. That's not me anymore. But I thought you should know about it anyway. I don't know if there's something wrong with me that I need you like I do when we don't know each other. But I do know you, and I do need you, so there it is.

I'm at the kitchen table, the dishes aren't washed, so it smells like tomato sauce in here. The back door's open and bugs are banging against the screen. That's how I feel, like I'm banging against a wall that keeps you from me. There's a breeze coming in. I wonder if you have a breeze where you are. Tell me you're coming home. Tell me I'm going to see you. Diane.

September 1968

Babe, I am coming back to the states in one week. Your gonna have to meet me half way. If you are who you say you are then you will come to South Carolina as soon as you can. I hope you do because I love you. Charlie.

September 1968

Dear Bro. You are going to live with me and that is it. You are NOT going to stay living where you are. We will make you another vegetable garden. Ill be coming half way home and Ill be able to call you and we can talk about our new house well have when Im all the way home. Ill call Rose and tell her whats what too. I thought youd be happy that Im leaving here and all you want is to live in your own place but you cant.

6

IT'S BEEN OVER A YEAR SINCE CHARLIE LEFT VIETNAM and went to Ft. Jackson in South Carolina to serve out his enlistment time. Now it's late October 1969, and Charlie has been honorably discharged. Diane's there to pick him up at Detroit Metro Airport, ninety minutes early.

She plays with the gold band on her finger, spinning it slowly with her thumb. Diane Porter Simpkins. Mrs. Charlie Simpkins. They were married August seventh at the army base in South Carolina, by an army chaplain. Sue Garrett was her maid of honor. Charlie's best man was Lieutenant Larry Swallow. Charlie said he was the only officer on the base who wasn't a dick. He didn't invite P.T. to the wedding because he wasn't speaking to him. Charlie wanted him to come and live with them in Jackson and P.T. wanted to stay where he was.

"Charlie, you're acting like a jerk," Diane told him. "You'll hate yourself later if he isn't here." Did no good. Charlie got a four-day leave and they went to Myrtle Beach for their honeymoon. That was nearly three months ago.

When he first came stateside, Diane took three days of vacation and asked Sue to go with her. They took turns driving all the way down to South Carolina. It was early fall but still humid down there. Diane cried because her hair frizzed up. She put on and wiped off four shades of lipstick before Sue told her it was time to meet him no matter how awful she looked and dragged her by the wrist out the door.

The hotel lobby was empty. Her new dress with the patent-leather belt crumpled in the heat as they waited. The door opened. When she saw him a shock passed through her, right through her body like boiled blood. She wanted to hide until he went away, but Sue pushed her so hard that she had to stand up. He took off his army hat when he saw them and smiled. Seemed like she'd known that smile all her life: smart, funny, mean, and lonely. She knew she was never going to have another day of peace as long as he was alive. She had one hand on Sue's shoulder, her nails digging in to keep her upright. She hated Sue at that moment; Sue wasn't about to have her heart smashed like cheap motel furniture. She stepped back when he got close. He sat down without touching her.

"Hi, I'm Charlie." He held his hand out to Sue once it was clear that Diane wasn't going to introduce them.

"I'm Sue. I came with Diane just to . . ." The mention of her name embarrassed everyone, because she hadn't said a word. Her eyes were glued to a spot on the floor where the linoleum was dented in random tiny smiles.

"Hey, hon." He said it softly, his head leaned toward her. She looked up at him, met his eyes, then looked at the little dents on the floor.

~

Charlie took them to a barbecue place in town, the kind of place where they could get comfortable and eat with their fingers.

"You have a good drive down?" he asked her.

"What?"

"Did you two have a good drive down here?" She nodded. "Good. Pretty soon you'll have it memorized." He gave her another smile. She couldn't breathe well enough to answer.

"What's it like, being back?" Sue asked. "Do they make you work all day now that you're not fighting, or what do you do?"

"I don't know yet," he said. "I'm still on leave. I'll probably help toughen up the new boys before we ship them off to get killed."

"You weren't," Diane said.

"Weren't what?"

"Killed."

"Promised you, didn't I?" He laughed and patted her on the leg. Sue told him about the deli store that she manages. He told them about the plane ride back, how everyone got drunk before they were out of the Saigon airport.

She let her hand creep up to rest on his and they held hands like that for a while, but she kept her eyes down. He started to wonder whether she was really the woman who had written him those letters. He watched her rub at her eyebrow with her thumb.

"I do that, too," he said, "with the eyebrow."

When they were stuffed with barbecue, they dropped Sue off at the hotel. Before she got out of the car, she shook Charlie's hand and said she was glad to have met him finally after hearing all about him every day from Diane. Diane remembered talking to Sue every day about him, about the guy in the letters, the guy who sent the Polaroids. Every word he ever wrote to her, every misspelling and every story, it was all crashing around inside her.

"See you in the morning," she said to Diane. They had separate rooms.

"I need to get drunk," she told him as they pulled away from the hotel.

"Yeah." Now it was Charlie who wouldn't look at Diane. Without the protection of Sue between them, he had nothing to say.

"Really drunk."

"Take this turn here." He lifted his arm to rest across the back of the seat. His hand touched her hair. "Soft."

Six hours later she was on her back, both legs wrapped around him. They had made love twice and she'd had an orgasm both times, something she'd never thought possible.

"Diane, babe."

"Hmm?" Her fingers ran up and down his back over the random lumps of shrapnel scars.

"I gotta have a cigarette," he whispered in her ear. He pulled himself out of her slowly. She unclasped her legs and felt cold darkness in the space where his body had been. Cold air blew through her pores. Tears came, though she didn't feel sad.

"I thought you'd hate me after the way I acted at dinner."

He picked his pants up off the floor and put them on. "Diane, honey. I could never hate you."

If she lived to be the oldest woman on earth, she would never forget those words and the tenderness in them. She wouldn't forget even if she never saw him again after that night.

"I'll be out on the balcony." He grabbed his Old Golds and his Zippo. She lay there with her chest balled into a fist and breathed through her mouth so the tears wouldn't turn to real crying. He was outside on the hotel balcony, flicking ashes down into the parking lot.

She was imagining him again. She was picturing him in her head, like she had for the past eighteen months. She got up and pulled on a robe. From the front window she watched Charlie lean with his back to her. When she came and stood beside him he smiled and put his arm around her.

"I wondered when you was coming out."

She laid her head against his shoulder and smelled the salt and sex mixed with his cigarette. "You don't feel right, being here." She tried to say it in a way that made it okay. He flicked an ash, just as she had imagined.

"I was thinking about the guys in my unit." He looked up at the stars that seemed too close to be real. "For them, it's already tomorrow." He lit another cigarette and offered her one. She shook her head no. "Whoever's left, they're out on some bullshit patrol somewhere, who the hell knows where anymore." He looked down at his hands. They were scarred and callused. "A week ago I was there. Can you believe that?" He crossed his arms on the railing and laid his head on them. "One week, and I'm fucking homesick for that place."

Later that night Diane woke up to a fist slamming into her shoulder and Charlie yelling. She woke him up and stayed awake with him the rest of the night. He wouldn't tell her about the nightmare. It was a while before he'd let her touch him. They played gin rummy to pass the time until the sun came up.

~

Now, finally, he is coming home for real. The Charlie and Diane from that first night seem like funny strangers to her. Her apartment is clean, the fridge is full. She bought clothes for him, all his favorite colors, types of shirts, pants. He isn't scheduled to start at the Stewart Tool and Die for another week. She took some vacation time, a second honeymoon. There's a heavy lump in her stomach.

She's pretty sure, as sure as anyone can be, that he loves her. She's afraid she'll find out she loves him only at a distance, afraid she'll get tired of having him around all the time. Right now, she's not sure that she loves him at all. All those guys at the VA Hospital every week, why didn't she fall for one of them? She glances down the terminal toward the exit.

He is one of the last ones out of the gate. His hair has grown out a little, combed straight back from his forehead. He carries a canvas suitcase. He told her he's straight, no drugs in four months. "Un-Vietnamization," he called it. He looks old in blue slacks and a button-down shirt that has been hit with a wall of starch. Over that, a coat that's too light for late October. He looks around him like he never saw an airport before.

She's sitting some distance from the gate. She stands up, then waits while he walks toward her. When he gets close, he looks her up and down. "You look great."

"You too."

She raises her arms and he pulls back for a second, just a small second, before leaning in and giving her a kiss and hug. He tosses his canvas bag over his shoulder. "Let's go home."

He's quiet in the car as she drives home. He doesn't have a driver's license. She takes one hand off the wheel to hold his. "How's it feel?"

"Good. Feels good." He gives her a smile, but it's not his smile, then turns to look out his window again. All this time, she's been dealing with Charlie in a cage, and now he's out. He told her about how he got dragged in the service to begin with, about killing his grandpa. For the first time, he doesn't have to be back somewhere at a certain time. He hasn't mentioned any of the folks from McGurk's in a long time. Hasn't talked about his brother, either. He's still mad about him not coming to live with them. Diane rolls down the window. As she glances at his profile, the ache inside her is worse than ever.

A billboard goes by: CITIZENS BANK WORKS FOR YOU! Picture of a blue-collar guy in a swank office, boots up on the desk, cigar in his mouth.

"That's where you work?" he asks.

"Yeah." She's ashamed of the billboard, of all the crap it implies. "I got you a carton of Old Golds in the glove box."

"Thanks, babe." He pulls out the carton, opens a pack, and lights up with the car lighter. He rolls the window down a little to let the smoke out.

"I hope you like pork chops."

"Love 'em."

Her hands shake so much that she can't get the front door of her apartment open. He takes the keys out of her hand and unlocks it. She starts to say thanks, but he lifts her up in his arms, kisses her, and carries her over the threshold. All through dinner she keeps asking him if everything is all right until he says, "Don't ask again." After they're done eating, he says, "Okay if I smoke in here?"

"Of course."

He lights one and looks around for an ashtray but there isn't one because she didn't think to buy ashtrays. In the bathroom there's the Norelco shaver and shaving cream and Old Spice and his own toothbrush and matching towels that say "Charlie" and "Diane" in green silk embroidery, the fridge is stocked with

Miller, new pajamas are hanging in the bedroom, but there isn't an ashtray in the apartment.

"I'll get you a plate." She rushes to the kitchen.

"That's all right," he says, waving his hand. He picks up his bottle of Miller and steps out to the front porch to smoke. She clears the table and washes the dishes so the place will be clean and homey for him, not the pigsty he grew up in. When she's almost done wiping down the stove and the counter, she looks up to see him leaning against the door frame in the kitchen, watching her.

"What're you doing?" he asks.

"Just cleaning up." Her voice is high and bright; she sounds like her mother. The sight of him leaning against the door frame is too big to take in. She wants to tell him, "No, that's where I stand. You are on the other end of the phone line."

They stay like that, in the kitchen, for a silent stretch of time. She is as unreal to him as he is to her. She remembers the first night they spent together down in South Carolina.

"You want to play gin rummy?"

He looks like he might laugh, or maybe cry. "Sure."

7

THE NEXT DAY DIANE DROPS CHARLIE OFF AT THE Department of Motor Vehicles. When he's done filling out the forms for a driver's license, he sits on a bench at the bus stop for forty-five minutes and smokes like he wants to hurt someone. He has seventy dollars in his wallet that Diane gave him, a temporary license, and no car. The bus back to Diane's house is thirty-five cents. She asked him what he wanted for supper later; he knows she's expecting him back by six at the latest. He lets two buses go by before he walks to a nearby Shell station and asks where he can get a bus to Ypsi.

After a forty-minute ride, he gets off at the corner of Cross and Hamilton, tries to call Diane so she won't worry, but he doesn't have her work number. He hangs up, hating it, hating her, hating himself. He's never in his life had to make a call to check in. Old Jerry figured he could take care of himself. And no way in hell would he call and let his dad know where to find him.

Some goddamn reunion, he thinks. *Some goddamn welcome home.* He steps out of the phone booth, his feet on automatic now. For the first time in nearly three years, he feels like himself. He knows every stinking, trash-filled street in this city. He knows every pebbly old back road outside of it. He walks past pawn shops and liquor stores, hotdog drive-ins and discount clothing stores. He walks until his knees are numb with the cold. A block away from Michigan Avenue and Hamilton, he sees McGurk's neon sign blinking. The "p" in "Tap" has been fixed. He stands leaning against a light pole, looking around. Two and a half years gone by. Pear's Men's Store down the block is gone. That's where Gil bought him the suit for his trial. Kresge's still sits right where he left it but it has a new sign. He doesn't recognize any of the cars in McGurk's parking lot. A Cadillac pulls in. Charlie steps behind the light pole so no one will see him. A man and woman with a baby go into the bar.

The Mississippi Blonde walks into McGurk's with Cricket on her hip and Todd at her side. When she sets the boy down he spreads his arms and legs like a little Godzilla, swaying from step to step. His coat is unzipped and half slipping from his shoulders. When Katie sees him, she jumps up.

"Cricketty-Schmicketty!"

Cricket says something supposed to sound like Katie, and takes a run at her. He goes down on his face, gets up to try again, but Katie's already there to pick him up and hold him on her lap. She's all over him like he's her own. Pretty soon he jumps off Katie's lap and onto his butt. He doesn't look around for help. He rolls over, no easy trick in that fat coat, and uses the chair leg to climb back up on his feet. Meanwhile there's Gil standing over the bar with his arms straight, braced on the counter like God waiting on the other side of the parted sea. Gil's a lot meaner when he's drunk; he almost cost a man his eye once. He cracked Leroy Simpkins's skull for him; two weeks later the man took off back down to Kentucky, without a word to his boys.

"Get me a rum-and-Coke," says the Mississippi Blonde at the bar, "and double Johnny Walker for Todd." Her words are followed by a string of firecrackers popping from her mouth. The little Mississippi Blonde's skin looks like a toad's belly. Her hair's bleached into something almost orange.

"You're not drinking in here with Cricket," Gil says to his wife.

Todd shoves himself onto the bar so his face is close to Gil's. "You don't talk to her like that no more."

"Back off." Gil wipes the counter so hard that Todd's forced to move.

"Cut it out, will you," says the Mississippi Blonde. "Just give us a frigging drink." She plunks herself on the bar stool directly in front of Gil, her old spot. "I got something I gotta talk to you about, anyway."

The kid tries to trot under the pool table after Bobby's dog and smacks his forehead. Falls backward and hits the back of his head on the floor. There's one scream from the kid.

"Cricket, shut up," says his mother over her shoulder. "You shut up right now."

He tries to cry without making any noise. Katie picks him up off the floor and rubs his head, humming. From her shirt comes a string of hiccups as the boy stops crying. The hiccups are so hard they shake his whole body. That's how he got the nickname Cricket.

Gil pulls up a chair to the table, sits down and takes Cricket onto his lap. Gino's been watching all this from a booth in the back. Now he gets up to pour himself a drink. The first thing his hand lands on is Schmirnoff. He pours some in a wine glass and drinks half. In the mirror, Gil's using Cricket's coat hood to play peek-a-boo. Looks like the hiccups have stopped.

Bobby makes his way over to Gino. "I know she's gone down the shitter and there's nothing gonna bring her back, but it's hard to see her like that."

"Somebody ought to blow her fucking head to pieces," replies Gino, pouring more Schmirnoff.

The Mississippi Blonde follows Gil to the table. She stands with her arms folded across her chest. "I gotta talk to you about something."

"What." Gil keeps rubbing Cricket's head, who's laughing until he hears his ma's voice. He slides down off Gil's lap and stands between his legs, head down on one thigh, thumb in his mouth. The dog goes over and lick's Cricket's hand, but the kid's too scared to pet him. Dog sits down and leans his head into the kid's arm.

"I need more money. For him. For child support." She uncrosses her arms long enough to yank Cricket's hand away from his mouth, saying, "What'd I tell you about that?"

"Don't be rough with him."

"I need a hundred and fifty more a week, or you—"

"Or I what?"

"You wanna see the kid, you pay for the privilege."

Bobby shakes his head. "Stone cold, man. A hundred fifty a week she's shooting up, on top of the three hundred a week I know he's already giving her." He nods toward Todd, who watches his girlfriend from the bar. "How he got his hands on her is something I will never understand."

The kid slides down Gil's leg and crawls under the table, away from his mom. He and the dog crawl until they end up next to Gino. Cricket plays with a cocktail napkin on the floor. He gives half to the dog and puts half in his mouth and chews. The napkin, it's disgusting. Gino reaches down to take it out of the kid's mouth. Cricket screams. Gino drops the napkin and jumps up out of the booth like someone put a hot iron on his back. The girl ignores her baby, but Gil's on his way to get Cricket out from under the table. Todd beats him there. He yanks the kid off the floor by one arm, slaps him on the back of the head and tells him to shut up or he'll get the belt. Bobby's dog scoots off behind the pinball game. The kid gulps in big piles of air, trying to stop crying.

Gino shoves Todd away from the kid, and in the next instant the punk goes flying back onto a table with Gil on top of him. They crash to the floor. Gil punches him four times in the face before Gino and Bobby can pull him off. Katie holds her baby brother. The blonde yells for Gil to leave her boyfriend alone, talking about assault, and how he'll never see Cricket again after this.

"Forget it, forget him, Dad," Katie says. "It's all right. Come on."

Gil turns toward the bar. "Get that cunt out of here."

He says it loud enough for everyone in the bar to hear and it sounds awful. Katherine looks at Gil's wife like she doesn't know whether to help her or slap her. When Gil tells her to get out, the little Mississippi Blonde that used to sit so cute on that bar stool across from Gil's register, she yanks Cricket out of Katie's arms and sets him on the floor, holding hard to his tiny wrist.

"Y'all done it now," she says to Gil. "I'm getting you for assault."

Gil says, "Go on before I kick your goddamn teeth in."

"Don't matter." She pulls Cricket's coat back on him. "We're going back down to Miss'ippi anyway."

Gino and Bobby drag Todd outside where Bobby sends a swift knee into his nuts. Gino breathes in the cold air and turns away, looking down the street. The blonde stands over them crying, "Leave him alone."

Bobby drags the punk across the pavement. "Gonna stuff this honky dirt bag in my trunk and dump him somewhere in Ecorse, see how far his white ass gets." But Gino says no, let him go. The two of them stay outside until Todd's Cadillac is out of sight. Bobby says, "Give me a break please, a Cadillac."

Bobby goes inside. Gino remains where he is, gazing down the street. At first he thinks maybe the drugs have got him hallucinating again. He starts walking toward the light pole.

"Charlie?"

Charlie steps out from the shadows. He recognizes the voice, but the man walking toward him looks nothing like Gino. All that long black hair that used to drive Katherine out of her mind has turned gray. With the full beard and mustache he looks like an old man. Under his coat, he wears a long sleeved shirt buttoned at the wrists to hide the track marks. Gino stops a few feet away from Charlie and smiles.

"Welcome back to the world."

"Thanks."

The two do an elaborate handshake. Charlie doesn't say a word about the gray hair, the heroin skin, the dead eyes. He saw the same look often enough overseas.

"When'd you get back?" Charlie asks.

"Year ago."

Charlie nods without speaking. He clenches his molars together so he won't cry.

Gino nods toward McGurk's. "Let's get a drink."

"I can't go in there."

"Why not?"

"I don't know," sighs Charlie. "Just don't want to see anybody yet."

"You don't want *them* to see *you*," Gino replies. "They'll take one look and see through you, see everything you done." Gino holds Charlie's gaze. He smiles and gives him a rough hug with one arm. "Let's go."

They buy a couple of six packs and climb in Gino's '67 Charger. It moves like a black shark through the streets, with an occasional purple glint under the street lights. By the fourth beer, Charlie starts to relax.

"Heard you were a Cobra gunner," he says.

"Heard you were a grunt," Gino replies. "Probably fought right over you, blowing them little shits to pieces so you could hump your sorry ass out into the mud without getting shot."

Charlie laughs. "That'd be a bitch, wouldn't it? If we were both shooting at the same goddamn gooks and didn't know it?"

Gino laughs too. "You and me within spitting distance while I blow all those fucking little doll people to pieces." They both go silent. After a few minutes Gino raises his beer and says, "Here we are, a couple of stone killers." Gino waits for Charlie to drink. When he doesn't, Gino adds, "Give it a few weeks, you'll know what I mean."

He pulls a dime bag out from under the seat and tosses it to Charlie, who says, "We aren't killers."

"Ask all these nice civilians."

"It was a goddamn war."

"It still is, baby." Gino laughs again. "Still plenty of time, too."

Charlie pulls out a pack of papers. "For what?"

"If I hang around here much longer, I'll go nuts." He looks at Charlie, but it's not Charlie he's seeing. "It ever bother you?"

"No."

"Bullshit."

Charlie busies himself rolling the joint. "One bothers me."

"One."

"Guy in another unit sent out with ours. We caught all kinds of hell coming into a village. He's burned up bad. You know. Medic tells me to stay with him until the chopper can get there. The whole time, the guy's whispering to me, 'Kill me, kill me.'"

"You do it?"

"Didn't have the nerve. I wasn't no cherry, either. I'd just had enough. You saw it, guys dying with their faces in the mud, or their dick blown off. He kept asking me to shoot him, and I couldn't fucking do it." He stops and lights the joint, pulls long and hands it to Gino. "Made it to Saigon. Burn unit. I checked on his name. Died two weeks later." He rolls down the window and blows the smoke out into the night. "Maybe someone finally did what he asked. I hope to fucking hell someone did it for him, gave him a shot of something. Anything."

"Probably."

"So it ain't the killing that bothered me. Not so much as that one guy."

"The one that got away." Gino laughs. He laughs and doesn't stop. The sound of it, the sight of that burned up kid, it makes Charlie queasy. He opens another beer.

~

Charlie has described his brother to Diane about six dozen times, but every time she asks to meet him, Charlie puts her off. He won't talk to P.T. because he's still so mad about him not coming to live with them. When Diane asks him to come with her to Ann Arbor to have lunch with Sue Garrett, he grumbles but agrees. He doesn't suspect anything until they pull into a driveway and there's P.T., huddled on the outside stairs of a garage in a Carhart jacket. Charlie's out of the car before Diane has it in park.

"Damn, you crazy? Where's your coat? It's November, freeze your ass off."

"I did not want to miss you."

Charlie crosses the driveway. "You knew we were coming?"

"Rose told me that Diane called and you were coming to visit." Charlie shoots Diane a snaky look.

Her whole body feels light and churning at the sight of P.T. She had offered to come visit P.T. once, when Charlie was in South Carolina. That was one of the nights he called her collect, saying, "No, don't go visiting him, Jesus Christ." She turns off the engine and gets out of the car. P.T. looks over and yells, "Diane?"

"Hello."

He rushes at her like a spider racing across its web and stops a few feet away. Charlie is right on his heels, and Diane can feel his nervousness spiking on every breath. She looks up at P.T., the person Charlie loves more than anyone in the world. She studies the gray flannel eyes, the hair of dead weeds. He offers his hand for her to shake. He's so thin the joint of his wrist sticks out.

"I am P.T." His long fingers wrap around her hand like ropes. She tries not to stare at them, at her hand ensnared. He lets go and reaches up to smooth down a piece of hair that springs up from his forehead. "I have a cowlick," he tells her.

"I have one, too." She lifts her bangs and shows him where the hair grows backwards. "I have to use Dippity-Doo to keep it down."

"You have a pretty smile."

"Thanks."

"Our mom killed herself."

"Don't start with that shit," says Charlie. "Let's go, I'm freezing my ass off."

It's a studio apartment above the garage. He graduated to it when Steve and Rose hired him to be the groundskeeper. Now he climbs the outside stairs, which are frozen and slippery, and tells the others to be careful, be careful. Charlie's behind Diane, his hand on her back. She wants to ask him about his mother; he'd only told her that she died when he was young. "You mad?" she asks.

"Don't know yet."

It's a clear blue day, the sky brilliant with frozen sunlight. P.T. unlocks the door and leads the way in. Diane steps in first then stands aside for Charlie. The sun shooting in the windows sends color over the floor and walls. Prisms hang everywhere. A small fan in the corner blows just hard enough to make rainbows drift all over the room, as if the place were alive and breathing. She holds the door to steady herself. The walls of the room slant until they come to a point at the top. It's all empty space and color. Charlie looks as surprised as she does, and here he's been telling her he knows exactly what P.T.'s place looks like from all his letters.

"Come in." P.T. closes the door. There's no place to sit except his bed and a chair next to a table. P.T. points to the table and says to Charlie, "That is where I wrote my letters to you."

That's what Diane had said to Charlie when he walked into her kitchen for the first time. She had pointed to the kitchen table and said those exact words.

P.T. opens a small door. "Barry and me made this closet." There's a pole to hang his clothes on, and a small dresser tucked in on the side. "I got this at a yard sale for two dollars." He pats the chest of drawers. "I painted it by myself in the back yard."

"Nice job," Charlie says. "Where's your bathroom?" P.T. points to a door on the other side of the closet. Charlie goes in and closes the door behind him.

P.T. says quietly to Diane, "She poisoned herself."

"Pardon me?" Diane says.

"Our mom. She's over there by the window."

"Jesus Christ!" yells Charlie.

"Are you okay?" asks P.T. at the door. No answer. Diane sits down on the bed, not sure what to say. "I made that, too," P.T. says, nodding at the bed. "Me and Barry. It is sturdy."

"How'd you get this big old mattress up here?"

"Oh." P.T. starts to laugh. He's at the stove, making coffee. "Oh well." He keeps laughing. It's hard for him to settle down enough to tell her. He tugs at his upper lip. "We had to fold it in half. It was me and Latasha and Steve." He pauses to measure out the coffee. "It took forty-five minutes to get it up the stairs, then it would not—it got stuck in the door and we—oh." He's still laughing. "There was a lot of grunting."

One corner of the room is filled with drying flowers hanging upside down, jars with turnips or some other vegetable in them, other jars with crushed leaves, boxes of dried twigs.

"What's all this stuff?"

"That is my hobby." There are stacks of boxes and jars. "I can make Rose's lady pains go away every month. And I cured an infection in Steve's finger."

Charlie comes out of the bathroom with his forehead puckered down. "Hard to concentrate with a goddamn squirrel staring you in the eye."

"Is he there?" P.T. steps into the bathroom, looks up, and waves. "He did not get his breakfast. I was nervous this morning. I forgot." He goes to the kitchenette, pulls out a bag of sunflower seeds, and carries a big scoop to the window. He scatters half the seeds on the windowsill and tosses the rest out into the snow.

"He is the only one comes to the window, so he gets extra." Once the window is closed the squirrel appears on the sill, shoving seeds in its mouth fast as it can and watching P.T. out of the corner of its eye. "I think he would come inside if I let him."

Diane asks if he has a name.

"Skuppers," says Charlie.

"Yes," answers P.T.

Charlie pokes Diane with his elbow. "Go look at the bathroom, babe."

"Why?"

"Just go look."

The bathroom would be horribly cramped with its slanting wall, but someone had cut out a sky light, two feet by two feet. Diane gazes up at branches and sky. Prisms hang off that window, too.

"Damn near fell in the toilet, I got so dizzy in there," Charlie says. P.T. smiles, still working on the coffee. "Then this son of a bitch," Charlie nods at the squirrel, "pops his head up at me, I nearly died." P.T. laughs at the stove. "Goddamn thing ain't more than three feet from my face, looking at me like he'd just as soon eat *my* nuts as acorns." P.T. still laughs, but Charlie breaks off and frowns. "This ain't your home, Bro."

P.T. looks over his shoulder. "Would you like milk or sugar in your coffee, Diane?"

"No, black is good."

He takes the coffee to Diane and Charlie where they sit on the bed, then gestures around the room. "Do you like it?"

"I said it ain't no home."

"Yes, but do you like it?"

Charlie looks all around him and lets out a big sigh. "I'd lay a rug down," he says.

P.T. looks around. "What kind of rug?"

"One of them big braided rugs, those oval ones, you know?"

"Why?"

"It'd keep the place warmer in the winter."

"Are you cold?"

"No," Charlie says. "I mean cozier, you know. More like a home."

"You want me to put Grandpa's rug in here?"

Charlie stops in mid-sip. "Did we have a rug like that?"

"The green braided rug in the living room."

"I'll be goddamned." Charlie stares at the floor as if he sees the rug there. "Where is it?"

"Gino was storing everything." P.T. drinks his coffee. "You knew that."

"I want the rug."

"Okay."

Charlie looks around. P.T. looks around, too. For an instant they are identical.

"Six months," says Charlie. "Then me and Diane are gonna start looking for a house."

P.T. drinks his coffee and waits.

"Then you come and live with us."

"Maybe I could get a house next door to you and—"

"We'll talk about it then," snaps Charlie. "At least come over for supper this Saturday and spend the night. We can make square pancakes for breakfast."

P.T. asks Diane if she likes square pancakes and she tells him she does. "Okay then, I will come." He touches Diane's arm and smiles at her. She's surprised at his touch: protective.

On the ride home she asks about their mother poisoning herself. "He tell you that?" Charlie laughs. "That's one thing about Bro, he can tell some stories."

8

A MONTH GOES BY AND CHARLIE DOESN'T CALL ANYONE from McGurk's. He drives to Ypsi three or four times, even manages to get out of his car and walk to the door once, but his hands shake and his throat goes sour and pretty soon he's behind the wheel and on the highway back to Jackson.

Charlie and Gino had hung out a few more times after Charlie's first night back in Ypsilanti, just driving around in Gino's Charger, drinking beer. Charlie could tell when Gino was stoned on heroin. He took over the wheel but otherwise let it alone.

Sometimes they traded war stories. One night Gino drove out to Jackson and looked up the address Charlie had given him. Knocked on the door at 4:30 in the morning. Diane was used to being awakened in the middle of the night. She made some coffee for them, told Gino it was nice to meet him, and went back to bed. The two men sat in the kitchen with a dim light burning over the sink.

Gino pulled a bottle out of his coat pocket, poured whiskey into his coffee and handed the bottle to Charlie. "Remember you said there was one that bothered you?"

Charlie nodded, pouring whiskey into his own cup. Otherwise he sat and waited. It occurred to him that this was what his wife did every weekend at VA, waited to hear the stories.

"We were shot down," said Gino. "Me and three other guys bail right into the middle of a fire fight. Bullets are whizzing all over the place and I'm shitting my pants. Two of my guys are shot to pieces before they hit the trees. I'm unstrapping myself fast as I can so I don't end up hanging there for target practice. Men are screaming and I'm on the ground. I see a gun lying next to some dead kid, so I pick it up. The barrel's burning my hands but I'm firing at anything, praying I'm not already hit and bleeding to death and not knowing it because I'm so goddamn scared while the grenades shoot the dirt up like fireworks. It probably didn't last more than a minute. Couldn't have been more than that. You know how time gets all smashed up and you got three hours worth of fighting squeezed into ten seconds and your head spins right off your shoulders. Then everything stops. The enemy's gone. It's just me and a bunch of dead guys. Dead. I check, believe me. I'm out there alone. Anything in a U.S. uniform I pull into one spot and make a little line. One of them has a map. I try to radio my position but the goddamn radio's shot to pieces next to the RTO. Ain't nothing to do but take a dog tag off each one and try to find my way to the fire base.

"Then I hear someone crying, sounds like a woman or a kid crying. First thought is to run. Just get the hell out, get to base camp and call in a dust off to get the bodies. But you know what those gooks do when they get hold of a corpse; if there's a live VC left out there God knows what he'll do to these kids. I move down the trail toward the sound. There's dead gooks all over the place. I grab as many guns and grenades as I can carry while I make my way to this crying bastard. I find him behind a tangle of Banyan vines. 'Chu Hoi! Chu Hoi!' He's surrendering. I can't fucking believe it.

"I shoot near the clump of vines and he crawls away from me. He yells 'Chu Hoi! Chu Hoi!' over and over, holding his hands over his ears and rocking back and forth. He's a kid. I mean no more than fourteen or fifteen. I search him . . . no weapon, not even a bamboo blade. I'm thinking, isn't this a bitch? One guy left from each side. I raise my gun to blow his brains out of his goddamn skull and he keeps crying and rocking and holding his hands over his ears, yelling 'Chu Hoi!' I mean, he's really a kid. He's wearing the black pajamas and everything like a real VC, but the pj's are too big, and hang on his little stick arms.

"I already done enough rotten shit to get me into hell four times over. Killing one more dink, especially in a fire fight, an official kill, wouldn't mean anything. But I decide that once, just once, I'm gonna try something different. So I tie his hands good, and gag him so he'll stop the crying, which is rubbing my nerves. I grab some extra canteens from the dead unit. I dig out some C-rations, too. Actually find a joint, and stick that in my pocket. The gook watches me. I put the extra supplies in a pack and I get the gook to stand up so I can strap it on him. I don't want to load him down too much because it'll kill him and I want him alive.

"I can't find the goddamn base camp of course. We walk in that heat, you know, that wall of evil sucking the breath out of you. I hope the camp is wondering why the RTO hasn't called in. Someone'll be out to find them sooner or later, long as I don't wander too far off track, or step on a mine, or walk into a spider hole, or any of a million things that I been hearing about, before I get this gook back to camp alive.

"We walk until seventeen hundred hours when it starts to get dark. I look for a spot well off the trail, someplace where no one's going to trip over us accidentally. Dig a hole while the gook watches, and cover it over with my poncho. Spread leaves and shit and vines over the top. It won't pass a close inspection, but it's enough to make me feel better. Inside I heat up C-rations for me and for the kid. Take the gag off him and make it clear I'll waste his ass if he yells out. But he's not going to yell. He looks like he wants to go home. When we were fourteen, we were tearing all over hell, remember? Getting into shit, getting our asses kicked. Even the time I did in juvie detention . . . that was all bullshit compared to this poor fucker.

"He's probably been half starved since he was old enough to walk. He probably doesn't give a shit about the government any more than I do. He prays, though. Maybe that's something he believes in, something he thinks is worth fighting for. He eats that nasty beans and motherfuckers like it's steak and eggs. I gotta feed it to him because I'm not untying his hands. I can't hardly keep up with him. We have enough to last us a week, so I heat up another and the guy stops and prays and looks over at me and then prays some more and wolfs down another can. I give him a couple swigs from the canteen. When night comes I pull my jacket up around my face to hide the fire as I light up a joint. It takes the edge off the situation. Still a goddamn nightmare, but now I don't see my buddies blown to pieces in mid-air every time I close my eyes. I hold the joint out for the little gook. He takes a deep drag, coughs into his shoulder to muffle the sound, and finally exhales.

"I smoke and look at him. Never took the time to look at one up close before, not a live one. He's got spaces between his front teeth, and they buck out a little. Scar comes out of the corner of his mouth, looks like he's smiling with half his face. He stares back at me. I point to myself and say, 'Gino.' He scowls. Probably Vietnamese for shit.

"I stay awake all night. He sleeps like he's in his mama-san's hooch. At one point he wakes up and doesn't move, but he stares at me hard. Two minutes of silence, then I hear the movements, the soft voices way off on the trail. I hold a gun to the kid's head to keep him quiet, but they aren't looking for us. They're laying mines along the trail and camouflaging them. You've seen the guys blown to bits stepping on those mines. You know. I damn near shoot my little gook right then, except he's my ticket out of hell, my little bit of goodness in a sea of evil. I figure if I can give this one kid a good long life then it'll all have been for something. That was my purpose over there . . . to save one little gook. I could live with that. It made more sense than anything else. I see his life in my head, the way I decide it'll be. Maybe a year in a prison camp. When the war's over he'll get home to his village, if it's still around. I decide that it is. He gets married after a few years. Has kids. Works the rice fields his grandpa worked. Grows old and dies in his bed.

"In the morning we keep walking through the bush, staying off the trails. The more we walk, the happier I am. I talk to him in a hush while we're walking through those goddamn vines that grow down from the treetops. I tell him the prison camp won't be so bad, tell him about the woman he'll marry, about the farm he'll rebuild in his village. I tell him that his mama-san'll be there still alive and she'll cry and probably pray a lot when she sees him. I tell him about my house, about my '66 yellow Marlin. I tell him about the sun coming in the kitchen window in the morning, and the grasshoppers—how they were pretty small compared to the bastards he had over here—but the crickets sound the same.

"We hit base camp at thirteen-hundred hours the next day. They already sent out a patrol and found the unit. Choppers are loading up with body bags. They went and cleaned up the whole area while me and my little gook wandered around for damn near twenty-four hours. This guy, name's Captain Lake, comes out of his tent and asks me where the hell I've been. I hand him all the dog tags I've been carrying. Then my little gook catches an eyeful of all his buddies, a pile of VC corpses stacked up near the ammo dump. He falls on his knees and starts to cry again with that voice like a woman's, rocking back and forth just like he was when I found him. He closes his eyes and tries to cover his ears but his hands are still tied. I drop to my knees in front of him and cover his ears with my own hands, I don't know why. 'It's okay,' I'm yelling. 'That's not you. I got you.' He's crying, eyes open and looking at me like I'm the fucking devil. Captain Lake steps behind me. I keep hold of the little gook, telling him everything's gonna be okay, I'll take care of him. The captain reaches over my shoulder, puts his gun to the gook's forehead. He pulls the trigger and the kid's head comes apart in my hands."

Gino rubs his eyes and says to Charlie, "Can you explain that?"

~

As the weeks go by, P.T. is at Charlie and Diane's house so much he may as well live with them. Charlie keeps pestering him, but P.T. tells Charlie he's responsible for the grounds and the garden and shoveling the snow at his old place and doesn't want to let them down. Diane asks him one day, "P.T., if they could find someone else to take care of the lawn and the snow and all that, would you come and live with us?"

"Well, honestly? I do not want Charlie cramping my style."

She tells Charlie this when they are practicing with his Colt in a snowed-over cornfield. She isn't crazy about him having it, but it's his dad's gun and he's not getting rid of it. She tells him she won't have it in the house if she doesn't know how to use it. It's been over an hour, and she's hit only one of the oil cans.

"Squeeze it soft," he says. "Don't jerk. Take your time." She misses two more cans. "Cramp his style, huh?"

"I guess you better give him his space."

"Give him a swift kick in the ass, maybe."

"You ever teach P.T. how to shoot?"

"My dad tried to." He takes the gun from her and fires a few practice shots. "You can guess how that went."

"Maybe the three of us could drive over to Ypsi one night. I could meet your friends. And P.T. would like to see them, don't you think?"

"He can see them anytime."

"But I'd like to meet them."

"Why?"

"Are you ashamed of me?"

"Are you crazy?" He stops and kisses her.

"What does P.T. stand for?"

"What's with all the questions?" He coughs the irritation out of his voice. "Let's bring the cans in closer. We'll do one more round." They walk over the thin ripples of snow and he stops to give her another kiss.

"You didn't answer my question."

"What question?"

"What does P.T. stand for?"

Charlie frowns, dumping the empty cans on the ground. "Part Time."

"Part-time what?"

He stands one can up, then another, then another. "Just Part Time. Jesus, why you gotta ride my ass about it?"

"You know what?" From the sound of her voice he's glad he's holding the Colt right now. "You could say, 'I don't want to talk about it,' instead of acting like a prick."

"His name's Gabriel Joel." He stays busy with the cans. "After our mom died he said he didn't want to be named Gabriel anymore. Wouldn't answer if you said his name, wouldn't come if you called him. Finally my dad just called him Part Time."

"Why?"

"Called him his part-time punching bag." Charlie shoots at a tree fifty feet away, imagines that it's his father. *Pow.*

Diane sets the last can on end and stands up. "Oh."

Charlie nods and take another shot at the tree. "Then Gino decides Bro's a part-time Buddha. Bobby says no, he's more of a part-time Jesus. And they got in a big argument over it. Olivia said no, a part-time witch doctor. Everyone just got to calling him P.T."

"You don't."

"I don't care what anyone calls him, so long as they act right by him."

That night Charlie has nightmares, the same nightmares he's had every night since he got home. Diane shakes him hard to bring him back. "Charlie. Charlie. Wake up, come on." He opens his eyes. She waits until his breathing evens out. "You awake now?"

"Yeah." He sits up. "I'm gonna go in the other room for a while."

"Hold on." She turns on the light to find her robe.

"Babe, you don't have to sit up with me."

When she turns around to answer, she sees blood on the sheets. It's not that much blood compared to what she sees at the hospital, but it's in her bed, and it's coming out of Charlie's back. He looks down at where she's looking. He puts his hand up to feel where the blood is coming from. "What the fuck?"

"Lean forward," she tells him. "Keep your hands down." She climbs on the bed and leans over his shoulder. It's a cut, a half inch long, and it's bleeding a steady trickle down his back. There's so much scarring, it's hard to see how deep it is.

"What'd I do?"

"Hold on."

When she sees a sharp piece of metal jutting out of the opening, she wants to scream. The war's never going to go away. He's infected with it, and it'll keep coming back, keep coming back. How many more bits of it is he carrying around?

"Okay, I see the problem." Her voice is cool, almost bored. "Don't move and I'll clean it up."

"What is it?" He sits still, hunched over. "What happened?"

"Little piece of shrapnel worked its way out." She says it the way she would to some patient at the VA Hospital, with the same efficient calm that keeps her going no matter how hard, how sad, how hopeless a guy's situation is.

Charlie looks confused, as if he hadn't heard her. She goes to the bathroom, holds tweezers under hot water, brings them into the bedroom with towels and bandages. Moving slowly down his back, she dabs at the blood.

"This'll hurt." She douses the cut in alcohol.

"Son of a bitch."

He holds still. She heats the tweezers over the flame of his Zippo, dips them in the alcohol, and pulls the piece of metal the rest of the way out. Still calm, no big deal. All those scars already, this one'll hardly show.

"Got it," she tells him. "You okay?"

"Is it fucking up the tattoo?"

"No," she lies. "Nowhere near."

The tattoo, it's the fifth one he's put on himself since he's been home plus the three he had in Vietnam. This one sits right on top of the old shrapnel scars, a palm tree on fire. Looking at it makes Diane want to kill the bastard who agreed to do it to him. She tells him they might want to have someone look at it tomorrow.

"I'll have P.T. put something on it." He lights a cigarette and reaches for the ashtray. "Is this what you do?"

"What?"

"At the hospital. You do this shit?"

She puts the things away, props him up on the pillows. "You aren't jealous, are you?"

"You sit on the bed and rub their head like you do me?"

"No." She laughs. "I sit in a chair by the bed."

"Go get a chair."

She places a stool beside the bed and sits. "Like this," she says.

"What do they talk about?"

"The worst things. The stuff they can't write home about."

"There's one thing I don't understand." Charlie keeps his face turned to the window. "I seen Smoke with the back of his head blown apart. I wrote you about that. And then Colt, drops in front of me while we're on patrol. Drops straight down like a sack of meal. I never even heard the shot. I seen a guy trip a wire that sent a machete swinging straight into his chest.

"But I don't dream about none of that. That's what I don't understand. It's always me and Gino. We're on patrol and it's the middle of the day. He goes and steps in a creek bed and that's it. The mud sucks him down to his armpits. He's holding his gun high to keep it clean, and trying not to thrash around too much cause he'll sink faster. I'm reaching for him and I get hold of his hand and I'm pulling hard as I can and he's laughing. But these snakes come up out of the mud. They're all different colored stripes and they wrap all around Gino until his head and everything's covered. I'm yelling and shitting my pants and pulling as hard as I can, but he just slips away. The snakes sink down in that mud and take him along. Then I wake up. Every night."

Charlie is quiet for a long time. He lights a cigarette off the butt of his old one. He reaches for Diane's hand. "Guys I fought with over there, they were my friends. Ain't never gonna have friends like that ever again. One after another, I watched every one of them die. Gino's the only one I ever cared about that come out of that place alive. And he's the only one that comes along every night and haunts me."

9

SHEILA ALVAREZ PULLS INTO THE DRIVEWAY OF A SMALL house in Toledo. It sits along a row of a hundred houses just like it. The woman at the door takes the sleeping little girl out of Sheila's arms and grabs a couple of Pabsts out of the refrigerator. She tells her two boys to go outside and make a snowman, go upstairs and play with Tinker Toys, poke their eyes out, just get out of her hair for an hour. "How's my little Rosalita?" she says. "She's out cold."

The six-year-old boy hides, peeking around the corner. "Hi, Aunt Sheila."

"Hi."

He giggles and runs upstairs.

"The other'll be down in five minutes, you wait."

"I brought more oatmeal." Sheila pulls bottles and diapers out of a bag. "She gets bananas when she wakes up."

"What time are you getting off?"

"Ten."

"I told you to go outside." The woman jumps out of her chair and grabs around the corner, catching hold of Sammy's arm. *"Yo digo que te vayas.* Are you deaf?"

"What? What?" He holds his hand to his ear. "Can't hear you. I'm deaf. What'd you say?"

She swats him half-heartedly on the butt. He runs upstairs to join his brother. They're both insane. They should've been put in a home six years ago.

"Mother of God, Bonita," says Sheila.

"Don't start on the boys."

"I gotta go. I can't be late again." Sheila reaches out and touches her daughter's hair, smoothing it out of her eyes. "Charlie's married."

"Carajo, ustedes dos!" Bonnie is out of her chair again. There's swearing in the front hall as Bonnie throws coats, hats, scarves on the boys.

"We want to play with Lita!"

She pushes them out the door. "Leave Lita alone. Last night it took me twenty minutes to get the toothpaste out of her ears." She comes back and thumps into her seat. "Married?"

"Yeah. He got married six months ago."

"How long's he been back?"

"About a month now. P.T. called me last night."

"How's that old knucklehead?"

"He's fine."

"So someone was dumb enough to marry Charlie in the army."

"Yeah. But look who's got him now, and look who doesn't."

Bonnie takes a minute to scratch her head like an old hound chasing ticks. "What happens when you run off and leave a man alone? He bites at the first worm that comes by."

Sheila takes a pull of her Pabst. "He's not a trout."

"He's not much of a man either."

"What would you know? You married a *lechón*." Bonnie's husband wears his shirts unbuttoned so his hairy belly hangs over his pants. He still talks like a walking burrito, as if he'd just crossed the border. He calls himself Manuel, but Bonnie says his real name is Joseph; she saw it on their marriage license when she was already four months pregnant. "You married a hairy grease ball pig."

Bonnie smiles and lifts her eyebrows. "Okay. But when you're that ugly, you try harder, you know?" Sheila looks blank and Bonnie laughs. "He knows how to please a woman."

"Bonita, fuck you with that 'please a woman' bullshit. You telling me he makes you come ten times a night? That what you're telling me?"

Bonnie nods slowly, eyebrows still in the air. "I don't have to lift a finger." She pulls another Pabst out of the fridge, shuts the door, and leans on it. "You and Charlie were all fuck, fuck, fuck, like you were dogs or something." A snowball hits the kitchen window. Screams of laughter. "You ever have a man make love to you, little sister? I mean lick you all over until the fireworks shoot?" Sheila pictures Bonnie and Manny; it makes her sick. On the other hand, no . . . she's never had that. "So don't ask me what do I know about men." Bonnie knocks hard on the kitchen window and yells, *"En el patio.* Stay where I can see you."

More snowballs hit the window while Sheila thinks about what waits for her at home: a steady paycheck, a tiny apartment that looks out on a courtyard where the trash is piled. No roommate, no johns. Most of the girls at the strip club, they do business on the side. She works for the tips but that's all. She's been two and a half years straightening her shit out, and she hasn't had sex in the last two. And here's Bonnie with a house. It's small and ugly, but it's hers. And a husband who licks her all over. The image Sheila's been trying to avoid for months comes charging in: Charlie with that girl by his side, taking her to McGurk's, introducing her to everyone.

Sheila says, "I don't know what to do now."

"About what?" Bonnie is tilted back in her chair, watching the boys out the window. It was a mistake talking to her sister. It always is. Sheila puts her head down on the table and cries.

"Hey. Hey!" Bonnie bounces the baby girl in her arms and leans over to touch Sheila's shoulder. "Oh, come on, don't sit there and—come on, girl. That's not gonna help, just crying like that." Sheila holds her breath until her ears pound. She sits up and drags her arm roughly across her eyes while Bonnie rubs her arm. "Have you seen him?" Sheila shakes her head. "Have you talked to him? Have you told him?"

"He knew when he left."

"Honey, you have to call him."

"And have some girl answer?"

"Get his number at work and call him." Bonnie knocks on the window, shakes her head and draws a finger across her throat. "Tell him you just want to talk to him. You deserve that much."

~

Sheila lays awake that night thinking about it. The next day, she calls P.T. and gets the number for Stewart Tool and Die. She calls Charlie and asks him to meet her someplace. "I'm not looking for nothing except to talk," she says.

"So talk."

"I want to straighten some things out in my mind. Christ, just for an hour."

"Not at McGurk's."

He agrees to meet her at Haab's Restaurant in Ypsi so long as she pays for dinner. She takes Rosalita to stay the night at her sister's. Bonita wishes her good luck as the boys put Indian feathers in Rosalita's hair and shoot rubber arrows at her. Haab's is a big step up from McGurk's, so she wears a yellow dress that covers everything, and pulls her hair back in a barrette. She drives through heavy snow all the way to Ypsilanti, spiking the heat in her car.

She's already seated when he shows up. He stops by the front door and looks around. Under his open coat he wears a dress shirt that his wife must have ironed for him. Looking at him is harder than Sheila had expected.

"Am I late?"

She looks up, then back down at her menu. "No."

He sits and stares at his own menu. "Got a blizzard out there."

Sheila feels like a girl on her first date. Might as well spill the water, drop the silverware on the floor, get it over with. She keeps her eyes pinned at a point just over his left shoulder.

"Look, I'm sorry," she says.

He brushes a piece of hair out of his eye and shrugs. "Okay."

"That all you got to say?"

"What do you want to hear?"

Sheila lowers her voice. "Something like 'I'm sorry, too' for a start."

"Sorry for what?"

"You never told anyone the reason I left."

"I couldn't."

"So they thought I just deserted you." She waits for an answer. "Bet you got lots of sympathy."

"It's not like everyone sat around talking about what a bitch you were for disappearing."

"Really?" He doesn't answer because she's right; that's exactly what they did. And he let them. "I was supposed to sit here, the loyal girlfriend, waiting for her soldier boy?" She waits for his answer as he brings his face out from behind the menu. He has the nerve to nod. Already she's tired of his bullshit, and it's only been five minutes. "Well, guess what, I did wait for you. I didn't expect you to get *married,* asshole."

"Now you're talking out of your ass." Charlie laughs and tosses the menu down. "Don't tell me you were the faithful one and I wasn't."

"There's faithful and then there's faithful, and you know it." The longer she looks at him, the more she wants to fuck him and hit him at the same time.

"Forget it," he says.

"What?"

"I know that look."

"Goddamn married asshole." She lowers her voice. "Does she take it in the ass for you?"

"Yeah," he says loudly. "And she sucks cock better than you." But it's like telling a redwood that a tumbleweed gives more shade, so she lets it go. He says, "Why didn't you write?"

She looks indignant. "I wrote to P.T."

"What the hell good was that gonna do me?"

"You knew the deal up front." She leans back on the seat of the chair. "I kept in touch with P.T. I didn't marry anyone."

"Are you gonna harp on that all night?" Charlie says. "I may be married, but at least I'm not a liar and a talker out of my asser."

"A what?"

"I don't run out on people."

"You ran out on your daughter."

Charlie stops. Sheila pulls out a picture that Bonita took last Christmas: Rosalita in pajamas, holding a white stuffed kitty with a red ribbon in its fur. Charlie doesn't touch the picture. The little girl's smile lies there on the table beaming up at no one. "I thought you got rid of it."

"Its name is Rosalita Lynn Alvarez."

"Lynn was my mother's name."

"No shit."

Charlie watches a waiter serve a family at a nearby table. He watches a woman walk back to the restrooms. He watches his glass of water as he takes a drink. "What do you want me to do about it?"

"I don't expect you to dump the white chick and marry me, if that's what you're worried about." She's amazed at her calm. She picks up the picture and holds it against her chest. "I just thought you should know."

"I'll give you money."

"It's not the money, Charlie."

When she says his name, something starts at the base of his spine and shivers its way to his skull. He rubs the back of his neck. "What it is, then? You want me to be her dad?"

"I just thought—"

"Because it ain't gonna happen."

"I thought you should know. That's it. The end."

When the food comes they eat and ignore each other. Sheila tells the waiter no when he offers dessert. Charlie asks for the hot fudge cake just to keep them there longer because now he's mad. "It's not like I was out there having a blast while you were knocked up."

"If you're talking about that stupid war, I don't want to hear it."

"I thought about you every goddamn day."

"Between letters to your wife."

"That place, Sheila. I wish you could have seen it."

"I said I don't want to hear it."

"I'm a different person than I was."

"You're still full of shit."

"Keep your voice down." He offers her some of his dessert; she ends up eating most of it. "You know, you'd probably like Diane."

"Would you just fucking shut up?" People stare. Sheila stares back until they turn away.

"Okay, I'm sorry I joined the army. Jesus." He pulls at the corner of his napkin. "If I knew then what I know now, I wouldn't have done it."

"Done what? Joined the army or taken the rap for your brother?"

"Don't ever say that again. Goddamnit, don't let anyone hear you say that." He puts down his fork. "Think about it. If you were me—in my shoes, now—if you were me and he was your brother, what would you have done?" Sheila starts to reply, but Charlie says, "No. Think about it."

She had heard stories from Katie even though neither Charlie nor P.T. said much about it. Katie told her about the nights when the doorbell rang and her mother shooed her upstairs because it was the Simpkins boys again. Katie got up early on those mornings, knowing that Charlie and Gabe were there for the day, maybe a few days. At first Charlie would be silent and sulky, trying to hide the bruises. Gabe was never ashamed no matter what shape he was in, which was always worse than Charlie. By noon, he had Charlie laughing at some crazy story he was telling about a fish who only drank Fresca and what a pain in the ass it was to get to the store, or the possum named Larry who lived in the refrigerator and told fortunes with pickled tomatoes, all things that had happened "before you were born, baby brother."

Katie had been thrilled when the boys came to visit. But over time things became clearer. She heard quiet conversations between her parents. "So help me Gil, if you don't then I will," whispered her mother. "How can you let him do them boys like that?"

Gil did try. He talked to Leroy Simpkins, cut him off after four drinks, offered to put him up for the night at his house rather than go home drunk and mean to the boys. It wasn't until years later, when Gabe had already started to turn funny, that Gil finally took the boys to live with their grandpa. After that, Gil beat the living shit out of Leroy Simpkins whenever he came around until Leroy figured fuck it and moved back down to Kentucky, where he had come from. Until the end, Gabe protected Charlie the only way he knew how, by taking as many of the beatings as he could. By age fifteen, he had a twice-broken nose, a permanent red blot in the corner of his right eye that made him look half stoned, mismatched cheekbones, a dislocated shoulder, three cracked ribs, and damage to the liver and brain.

With Leroy gone, Old Jerry gently drunk most of the time, and Gabe growing further into his own world, Charlie took charge at age fourteen. He dropped out of school, although he did his best to keep his brother enrolled as long as he could. He made Gil teach him how to fight, and he hooked up with Bobby, who steered him toward some professionals who didn't mind a little free help in exchange for teaching him how to keep his ass out of jail.

~

Sheila sits in Haab's Restaurant, her stomach hurting for the way things used to be. "Who would have thought we'd look back and call those the good old days, huh?"

Charlie nods, torturing the fudge cake with his spoon.

"No use arguing about it anymore," Sheila says. "I need to get home."

"Let's go have a drink," he says. "Gimme a minute." She waits at the table fighting a headache while Charlie hurries to the phone in back. He drops in some change and dials Diane's number, then hangs up. He drops more change in and dials P.T.'s number. P.T.'s on the phone immediately, as if he knew it was Charlie the moment it rang.

"Hi."

"Hey, Bro. What you up to?"

"I am eating supper. What are you up to?"

"In Ypsi. You want to meet me and Sheila at McGurk's?"

"I have to ask Rose."

"Put her on the phone."

"Okay. But be nice. Rose is nice."

Charlie tells Rose what he wants, and they discuss whether P.T. knows how to get there by bus, and how long should it take him, and blah blah blah and yes, Charlie'll make sure he gets a ride home. Rose puts P.T. back on.

"I have to change my clothes." Click.

"Come on," says Charlie at the table, putting on his coat.

Sheila wants to go home. She wants to leave him here and never think his name again. But he smiles at her, and it's the smile she remembers, the smile that's kept her heart beating. She sighs. "Just one."

10

Sheila follows Charlie's taillights through the wall of furious white beyond the windshield. The heater wheezes the last of its warmth onto her feet as she works the manual shift to keep from sliding into a fire hydrant. Charlie stands in the whipping snow outside the bar thinking this was a bad idea. But Sheila pulls her car in behind him, gets out and takes his hand. When she opens the front door Charlie walks through it. The place is half full, but Charlie doesn't recognize anyone. He wants to turn around, to remember the place as it used to be, but Sheila pulls him toward the bar.

"Hey, Daddy-O."

Gil looks past the heads of several customers until he spots them. Even then, it takes a moment to register. "I'll be damned," is all he can say for the first few minutes. He hugs Sheila, shakes Charlie's hand, and retreats back behind the bar. Charlie doesn't know what to say, either. All he feels is empty. He looks around, searching for the others. Gil leans over the bar, chin in hand, and looks around as well. The place seems to shrink away from their gaze. Olivia walks in and stops at the door. She looks at Charlie with her mouth open.

"Well, look at the low-life bastard," she says.

"Close the door, will you?" says Gil.

She closes the door and comes right up to Charlie's face. "I'm talking to you, you redneck son of a bitch."

"This is Charlie," Gil tells her. "You remember Charlie."

She gets closer in his face and looks at him. "Well, Jesus Christ, I thought you was Leroy." She settles into a stool nearby. "Anyone tell you you look just like your dad?" It's the last thing he needs to hear right now. "Hi, Sheila," Olivia adds as if it were yesterday. "God, if he wasn't a worthless piece of hillbilly shit. Used to knock you boys around something awful. Did I tell you about the time Gil kicked the hell out of him for—" Gil sets a shot of Harper's in front of her and tells her Charlie just got back from Vietnam. She pats Charlie on the shoulder and tells Gil to get him another Miller. "Congratulations. Glad you're home."

"Thanks."

"Gave me a turn, seeing your dad."

He clinks his beer against her shot glass. "How you been?"

"Oh, hell, Charlie. Same as ever. How you doing, honey?"

"Good," says Sheila. "Good."

Charlie glances at Sheila as if to ask if it's as weird for her as it is for him. She nods. Gil pours himself a shot of whiskey and drinks it with no ceremony, no toast to Sheila or to Charlie's being home. It looks like a maintenance shot. "Katherine should be rolling in any time. She'll want to see you."

"How's Blondie?" asks Sheila.

"How the hell would I know?"

Olivia gives Sheila a slight shake of the head. Gil looks older than the two and a half years Charlie's been gone. He looks even older at the mention of his wife.

"Bobby hasn't changed a bit, though," he says.

"Yeah?" This is what Charlie wants to hear, nothing's changed.

"He got picked up for a public obscenity charge a while back. He write you about that?" Charlie shakes his head. "He gets his notice, you know, telling him come in for his physical. So he's got two weeks before he goes in. Starts loading up on black coffee with salt, and diet pills. That's all he eats is pills and salted coffee for two weeks. Can't take no drugs, it'll show up in his system, get his ass busted. He even runs around the block six times before he goes in. They see his blood pressure's off the charts, and tell him to go see a doctor and come back. So he goes to the doctor, who writes a notice and he's off the hook for six months, but then he's gotta report back. Pretty soon they catch on to this shit. So he gets orders to report, okay? Bobby doesn't argue, doesn't say a word. Two days later he's picked up by the fourteenth precinct. He's got himself tied to a goddamn light pole right there where Washtenaw and Cross come together, where the Big Dick is."

The Big Dick is a stone water tower in the middle of town, a historical landmark. Looks exactly like its name. Bobby told Charlie once he wasn't going to Vietnam to kill no strangers just to make a bunch of rich honkies richer. "If I kill anyone, it'll be here at home." He smiled. "No offense."

"It's morning, rush hour, and he's bare-ass naked. Traffic's backing up all the way to Ann Arbor. He's naked, tied up all half-assed and yelling, 'White man be doing this to me! The white man be after me!' I didn't see it personally. He reenacted it for us when he got out of jail."

"They locked him up?"

"This is Bobby, all right? That shit never happens to Bobby. He wasn't in there four hours." Gil reaches behind him for the whiskey and pours another shot. This one goes down a little slower.

"Anyway, they do a psycho test on him and decide he's paranoid, thinks the Klan's after him, and he'd be dangerous in the military. Had to go see a psychiatrist at some county clinic for a while, but he loved that. He bullshitted that guy clear to China and back." Gil pauses, finishes his shot. "So Bobby hasn't changed." Charlie nods and motions for another beer. Bobby hasn't changed. Instead of feeling better, Charlie feels worse. Maybe Bobby wasn't so great to begin with. Sheila takes off for the bathroom. Charlie and Gil are quiet for a few minutes, listening to the same old pinball game talking the same old nonsense. "Hell, how about you?" Gil asks. "How's it feel to be home?"

"Feels good." It does, now, with a third pint in his hand and the same old pictures hanging behind the bar. There's a couple of pictures of Gil and that Mississippi Blonde of his, their wedding and honeymoon. In all the pictures, Gil's smiling so it's hard to recognize him, so awake and happy like that. "Feels fucking great," he adds, looking at the picture Gil took of the four boys at Old Jerry's party.

"You gonna bring your girl in so we can see what you got yourself into?"

The good feeling dies. He looks down at his beer before taking a drink. "I don't know about that."

Gil lets it go. He can't believe Charlie's married any more than he can believe his own wife isn't upstairs cooking him dinner. "Well, it's good to see you two."

He switches on the TV above the bar and Walter Cronkite's face fades in: "—supports President Nixon's campaign to withdraw U.S. troops from South Vietnam."

"Gino made it back last November, you know."

Charlie nods, noncommittal. Gil screws up his forehead and looks at the TV. "He's different. Even Katie can see it. He never had much to say before, but now he's a ghost."

Cronkite continues, "—airport in Los Angeles was filled again today with antiwar demonstrators gathered to greet—" Charlie looks up to see long-haired kids holding pictures of burned babies and screaming at the guys leaving the terminals. He wonders if they know how ugly they look with their mouths wide open and their eyes all squinty with hate. He thinks of Gino walking through a crowd like that. He wants to grab his M-16 and mow every one of them down. For a moment he panics, feeling for his weapon. He sees Gil watching him. "What?"

Gil shrugs. "Nothing."

The TV grinds on. "According to the latest polls, fifty-eight percent of Americans believe we should put an end to U.S. involvement. Forces in Vietnam now total four hundred and seventy-five thousand."

"You want me to turn this off?" Gil asks.

"No. It's all right."

He turns the station, flips past another news program, and settles on some show Charlie's never seen before. Gil doesn't have a whole lot to say. He doesn't ask about the places Charlie's been, the guys Charlie knew, none of the things Charlie's seen.

He doesn't even ask about the shrapnel scars that creep out of Charlie's collar. They watch TV and drink.

Bobby walks in carrying a cardboard box, the dog following behind. He sets the box on the bar and comes up behind Charlie, shaking his shoulders. "It's really you, you sorry son of a turkey turd."

Charlie jumps off the barstool like someone lit a firecracker under him. He backs a few steps away. "Hey, Bobby."

"That all you got to say? Hey Bobby? What's up, my man? How you been?"

"Alright." Charlie smiles, but he watches Bobby like he's afraid he'll get bitten. "Good to see you. Still got that dog, huh?"

"Say hi to Charlie, fruit loops." The dog thumps his tail while Bobby scans Charlie's face for The Look. "Dog got himself an attitude cause I took him away from an *Avengers* rerun." Sheila comes out of the bathroom. "Where you been, girl?" Bobby looks her up and down. "What are you, a movie star?"

"How you doin' Bobby?" she laughs. "What's with the hair?" Bobby's Afro has grown into a billowing brown halo.

"Well I'm great, come to think of it." Bobby looks at them both. "You two. For the love of Jesus. I thought P.T. was stoned when he called. Gil, get them a round on me."

P.T. walks into the bar wearing clean clothes and new shoes. He has a fresh haircut. Sticking out all over, but it's cut. He smiles at Gil and says, "You shrunk."

"What're you talking about?" Bobby says, looking at Gil. "Look at the gut on the man."

"No. Gil, you shrunk." P.T. tugs his upper lip. "Hi, Sheila."

"That all you got to say?" asks Charlie. "Hi, Sheila?"

"Yes."

"Hell, Bro. Tell her you missed her or something."

"I just saw her last week."

Olivia reaches over to give P.T. a hug. "Damn, you're big. Gil, get the kid a beer."

Bobby catches her as she nearly falls off her seat. "Hey, Stickweed," he says. "What are you, seven feet tall now?"

"Get him a beer, Gil," Olivia shouts over Bobby. P.T. says thanks, but he doesn't drink beer. "Okay. What do you want, then?"

"What about Vernor's?" Charlie asks. "You give that up, too?"

"I would like a Vernor's"

"Hear that?" Charlie laughs. "Some shit just doesn't change." He looks around again as if he'd just remembered he's been away.

"Swear to Jesus, it's hard not to laugh out loud at you crackers." Bobby lifts his drink. "Charlie, welcome back."

"What's in the box?" Gil asks.

"Present for Katie," says Bobby.

"Get it off the bar, will you?"

Katherine bounces into the bar in platform boots and a purple fur coat. Underneath are bell-bottom hip-huggers that ride low, and a purple halter top. Her hair's grown long in the last few years and she wears it parted in the middle and straight down her back. Silver peace signs dangle from her ears.

"Oh my God! Sheila!" She hurls herself at Sheila, nearly knocking her off her bar stool. She cries and talks and laughs and yells all at once. "Where were you? What are you doing here? Oh, my God, I don't believe it." She pulls back and looks at Sheila, who smiles and holds onto Katherine's shoulder, trying not to fall over or cry or both. Katherine catches sight of Charlie sitting nearby. "Oh, Charlie, God almighty!" She grabs him up in a bear hug and tips him back and forth a few times.

"Katherine." He's stiff, like he's wrapped in barbed wire. "Gil, where'd she get her looks from? Wasn't you."

Gil looks his daughter over. "To be any cuter she'd need fucking feathers sticking out of her ears."

"Twenty-two years old, I gotta compete with the babies now." She waggles her hip-huggers for them. "What's with 'Katherine?'" She punches him in the chest, a little hard for a peace-loving hippie. "It's Katie. What's the matter with you?" Again, to Sheila, "Where you been?"

P.T. says, "Hi, Katie."

"My old pumpkin head. I thought you were telling me one of your stories." She's tall enough to wrap her arms around his shoulders. "Angel, angel, you get longer and skinnier every time I see you. You got someone pulling on you like taffy? Hi, Bobby."

Bobby nods and smiles, knowing better than to try to get a word in. Katie knocks half her gin down. Charlie drinks slower; he's out of practice. He leans against P.T.'s shoulder. "You call the whole fucking phone book?"

"Charlie, this is too much. How's it feel?" She rubs his shoulders and pounds his back while he tries hard not to pull away. "How's it feel to be home?"

"I don't know yet."

"When'd you get out?"

"Last month."

"A month!" She shoves him again, then kisses him. "Why didn't you let us know? Where's the missus?" She stops and covers her mouth.

Sheila says, "Yeah, Charlie, where's the missus?"

Charlie looks blank for a minute, then he gets one of his devil looks. "Home."

"Forget I asked." Katherine kisses Sheila's cheek. "Who cares, anyway?"

"I only dropped in for a minute to say hello." He stands up like he's gonna leave, but Gil comes over with another Miller.

"Courtesy of the poker table."

Charlie nods to the guys from the Ford plant, still at the same table, still playing the same game. Gil reaches for a bottle of tequila, pours a shot for himself, bolts it down. P.T. stares at Gil's empty glass and says, "What did you just do?" Gil moves off with no answer. "Charlie, what did he just do?"

"Tell me about this girl you married," says Bobby. "What's she like?"

"Go ahead," adds Sheila. "What's she like?"

"She's nice."

Katie says, "What's she look like?"

"I don't know. Brown hair. Fluffy."

"She's fluffy?" asks Gil from down the bar.

"Her hair."

"Does she kick your ass when you need it?" Katie asks.

"Look, she's nice. She's nice to me, all right?" The more he talks, the more Diane sounds like a bowl of oatmeal.

"You gotta give me your number," Katie says to Sheila. "You aren't disappearing again, are you?"

"Charlie," says P.T. "Gil's drinking."

Charlie brushes aside the comment. He pulls up the sleeve of his army jacket. "Check this out, Bobby." The tattoo starts at his wrist and stops just short of the elbow. Charlie flexes a muscle and it looks as if the dragon is crawling up his arm.

"I could've got you that for free," Bobby tells him.

Charlie laughs so hard it looks like he's crying. "Not where I got it. Not even you."

"Damn it, Sheila. Where were you?" asks Katie.

"Toledo."

"Yeah, but what were you doing in Toledo?"

"Ask Charlie."

Charlie's mouth goes flat, and he looks for a moment exactly like his father. The place starts to fill up. Everyone wants to buy Charlie a drink. He relaxes, flexing his dragon for everyone. He shows off a skull on his other arm, along with the army division insignia on his chest.

Gino comes in. He's been home since last November, but he doesn't come around the bar much anymore. When he first got back, Bobby gave him the bike he'd found: a '57 Harley, beautiful condition. Gino had been looking for one as long as anyone could remember. Bobby kept it covered and protected until Gino got back, a welcome home present. Gino had looked at it, looked right through Bobby like he was talking to the air, and said, "No thanks."

Tonight he comes slowly through the crowd, meandering around the bodies like a ghost.

He stops when he sees Sheila. "Hi ya, Shell." Shelly is what Gino used to call Sheila when he wanted to piss her off. Recognition comes slowly to her face.

"Gino?"

He turns to P.T. "String bean, look at you. What are they doing to you? Medical experiments?" He reaches up and messes with the back of P.T.'s hair. "Who'd think I'd miss *you,* huh? Charlie, it was like having a horse in the house, the way he eats." Katherine sits a few stools away. He looks for a minute like his heart has broken, like she did something to hurt him, but he gives her a hug, one hand holding the back of her head. "Katydid's looking better than ever."

"Good enough to take home?"

He lets go and steps away. "Sorry, girl."

"Close your eyes and pretend I'm Richard Nixon."

"He already gave it to me up the ass."

Charlie laughs loudly and drums on the edge of the bar with his fists. "Straight up the ass from Dick Nixon!"

Gino pours Charlie a shot from the tequila Gil left on the counter. Charlie throws it back and says something about calling his wife. Katherine laughs.

"Charlie married some fluffy church girl," she tells Gino.

Bobby hustles Charlie over to a table alone. The dog jumps on Bobby's lap. "Gino's got a line on a little fleet of trucks, small deliveries, you know." He pulls the dog's head away from his beer. "Knock it off." He hits Charlie's arm to get his attention. "We're putting together some low-scale jobs," he says. "If you want, just for some start up, I can get you in on this thing we're working out now with a fur storage—"

"I don't think so," Charlie says, looking at the floor.

"What do you mean, you don't think so?"

From the bar Gil yells over the music, "Next round, on the house." Everyone stampedes at the bar.

"Thanks, papa!" Bobby yells. "That's a first." He gets a sharp knee in the ribs from Katherine standing beside him. "You trying to kill me, Miss Peace and Love?"

"Shut up, then." Katherine pulls out a picture and hands it to Charlie. "This is Cricket. My baby brother." The kid's standing with his feet apart, wearing overalls and no shirt, both hands in the air. Damn near the same age as Sheila's kid. Christ, his kid.

"Jeffrey Gilbert McGurk. Everyone calls him Cricket."

If P.T.'s paying attention to the conversation, he doesn't show any sign. He watches the room's reflection in the mirror.

"And I been calling him papa all night." Bobby smacks his own head and checks his watch. "I gotta make a call."

As Bobby stands up, Charlie takes a couple of quarters out of his pocket and sets them on the table. He asks Katie, "He ain't still hanging around Teddy?"

From the pay phone, Bobby calls the dog over. "C'mon, corn flakes, that a boy." The dog winds through the crowd, shaking himself awake. He waddles under tables and chairs until he's next to Bobby, who scratches his ears and gives him a piece of beef jerky. Over the noise Katherine tells Charlie, "Bobby's still got his dog. Gino's still a homo. Nothing's changed."

Charlie looks at Gil and wonders why everyone stood around and let him go all to pieces under their noses. He plays with his quarters on the table. Bobby comes back from the phone, checks his watch. "Dumb, fat, lazy, useless brother-in-law of mine." He slides into a chair as Charlie picks up his quarters and heads for the phone.

~

"Babe?"

"Charlie? You okay?"

"I'm okay. I'm not hurt or in trouble or nothing."

"Where are you?"

"In Ypsi."

"Ypsi?"

"At McGurk's, yeah. Brother's here too. He says to say hi."

"Tell him hi, too." There's a pause. Charlie wishes he was there in Jackson with her. "How'd you get there?"

"Bus."

"You want me to come pick you up?"

It's a forty-minute drive, and she's offering to drive all the way there to pick him up. Not even mad. "No," he says. "I'm leaving here in about ten minutes."

"You don't have to come right away."

"I know that." He wants to come right away. He's finally at home with his friends, and he wants to be there with her. Minute he gets there he'll be climbing the walls. "I ought to be home by nine-thirty. How's that?"

"Sure."

From the other side of the pool table someone says, "I'll have to show you my Little Richard painting," but the rest of the conversation disappears. Charlie tries to picture someone's painting of Little Richard.

"Charlie?"

"If I'm not home by nine-thirty, then you can worry."

"All right."

"Diane?"

"I'm here." It's quiet in the bar. The jukebox ran out of songs. Charlie's ears pop. He tells her he loves her. "Love you, too," she says. "See you in a while."

Charlie hangs up and joins Gino, who sits alone in a booth in the back.

"Fucking women."

Gino tilts his head back. "Like to take them out back, line them up, and *pow.*"

"I married one," Charlie says, sounding surprised.

"You're crazy, too." He nods toward the door. "Don't Sheila look different to you?"

"No."

"Like a doll, a little doll person," Gino says. "I forgot how short she was. So little, damn near looks like a slope-head."

Sheila slides into the booth next to Gino. Charlie gets up and joins P.T. as Katie squeals from the other end of the bar, "Holy shit, would you look at this?" She and Bobby pull six princess phones out of the big cardboard box.

Charlie leans into P.T. and asks, "What do you mean you saw her last week?"

"Who?"

"Sheila."

"She took me to see *Jungle Book*."

Charlie rubs at his eyebrow. "How long you known where she was?"

"All the time."

Five minutes later: "Why didn't you tell me?"

"Because you never asked me."

"Bullshit." All the letters to everyone: to her sister in Toledo, to the brother Charlie tracked down somewhere outside of Santa Fe. He had asked Gil in every goddamn letter if he'd heard from Sheila. Asked Katie and Bobby, too.

"You're right," Charlie says. "I never asked you." His head falls back and he looks up at the ceiling. Cobwebs blow like streamers over the fluorescent lights, like the blue streamers at Old Jerry's party. "But you knew I was looking for her."

"Yeah."

Charlie talks slowly, like navigating a booby-trapped trail. "Why didn't you help me out?"

"You didn't ask me."

"Couldn't even tell me I had a kid?"

"She asked me not to."

Charlie leans forward and drinks his Miller in disgust. He glances over at Sheila. She gives him the same old smile, like they just climbed out of bed an hour ago. He smiles back because it's easy, like breathing. Gino listens with his eyes closed as she tells him about this set up she has down in Toledo.

"The money's great," she says. "The thing is, they can look all they want, but they can't touch." Gino nods. "Unless you want the tips. I mean, they don't roll up a hundred dollar bill and just toss it to you, you know. But that's nothing. There's places down there you can make a ton of money. How big's your dick?" That's classic Sheila. Charlie smiles down at his hands.

"Eleven and a quarter."

"Lying son of a bitch," calls Bobby from across the room. "He gets away with that shit because none of you girls ever seen it."

"You gotta come down to Toledo, Gino." She taps her cigarette and misses the ashtray, brushes the ash off the table with her hand. "You'll have them lining up to get in, men and women, whichever you want."

"No thanks," Gino tells her. "I got something else I'm working on."

"What?"

"Job overseas."

Charlie looks back down at his beer. Diane comes to mind, like a leash yanking at his neck. His wife. He hates her for the supper that's waiting on the table, for the matching towels in the bathroom, for the pajamas he has to wear around the house so the neighbors won't get an eyeful.

Bobby joins them at the bar. "Gino been telling you all about the little doll people?" When Charlie nods, he goes on. "All he talks about, when he talks at all. Gil tells him to leave it alone, but he won't." Bobby glances at Gino, who's still talking to Sheila. "Maybe you could talk to him."

"Why me?"

"He looked happy to see you," Bobby says. "Don't start with the attitude already. Listen, I gotta know if you're interested in this job I got coming up next week."

"I got a job."

"Who lined you up?"

"Straight job. Stewart Tool and Die over in Jackson."

"You're so full of horse shit, Charlie." Bobby laughs. "Nice to see *you* ain't changed."

"I'm serious. I ain't interested," says Charlie. "Leave it alone."

"Charlie, you better remember who your friends are."

Bobby digs out four quarters for the jukebox, punches in some Marvin Gaye, and asks Katie to dance. Charlie tunes out and imagines himself floating up through the ceiling, over the rooftops, and safely to his living room. He pictures Diane in his mind, but she's a ghost right now. He looks at the clock, knowing she's waiting. A crack opens in his heart and something ugly squeezes out. He pulls Sheila away from Gino's booth and dances with her.

"Just like old times, huh babe?" Charlie says, looking at Gino. She hears the bitterness in his tone and holds him tight.

11

Two hours go by while Gino watches from his booth in the back corner, not moving. It's January. Christmas has come and gone for him like a bad dream. He bought himself some happiness and stayed stoned for three days. Then New Year's—1970. New decade, same old lying bullshit. The army won't let him reenlist. Nixon's Un-Vietnamization Program. Pulling troops out, they don't need guys going back for a second tour. Besides, the letter said, Gino was psychologically unfit for active duty. So he wrote a letter to Captain Valos, his senior officer who was still in country. Valos was career army but no asshole; Gino knew he'd cut through the bullshit, get him back to his unit. It's not that he loves the place for God's sake; he just can't stand to be anywhere else.

Tonight, he and Bobby have a job to do in Ann Arbor but the blizzard looks like it's never going to end so they're stuck. Katherine has the radio tuned to WAAM so they can hear how bad it is. State police have the local high schools opened up, bringing people in for shelter and food. Men are bouncing around up there on the moon, but tonight a lot of people are going to die in the snow. Everyone talks about peace and love and brotherhood but Mother Nature is still going to wipe her ass with mankind tonight. No one can get home so everyone's drinking. It's a big party, big time out. Tell the wife and kiddies you're stranded, drink, and get laid until the sun comes out. Then everyone goes back to their little doll lives in their little doll houses.

And there's Charlie right across the room. Charlie and Sheila, acting like none of it ever happened. The guys from Hydra-Matics are louder than usual tonight. Gino slides his back to the wall and stretches his legs across his seat. He watches them with their mouths open, ha ha ha. He can't imagine laughing after spending most the day making M-16s, accessory to murder, drinking beer and shooting pool and laughing like it doesn't matter. "What world you living in?" he asks, but none of them hear. Bobby's dog jumps onto the seat and noses Gino's boot. Message from Bobby: *Come and join us.* Quit brooding in a back booth like those crazy vets you hear about.

"Fade," he tells the dog, with a nudge of his foot. It totters off the seat and disappears into the legs that crowd the room.

It's busy tonight, so Gil has P.T. behind the bar helping out. P.T.'s right back at home in an instant. Looks like America all of a sudden won the war, the way people are drinking and dancing and laughing like fools while the city freezes. Now Charlie's glued to the same stool Old Jerry was glued to before he came unstuck for good, arguing with Sheila just like no time has passed. Bobby's in his glory, shooting the shit with everyone who walks by. This is Bobby's world. Happy and carefree and to hell with whatever's going on outside. The dog shows up again, jumps onto the seat. This time he's got a cocktail napkin tucked in his collar. Gino pulls it out. Bobby's handwriting, can't hardly read it: "How do you get a nun pregnant?"

He flips it over, nothing on the back. He wants to tear it up, but now Bobby's got him. He pulls out a pen. "How?" Tucks it in the dog's collar, gives him another nudge with his boot. Gino gets a few seconds of peace before Bobby's dog comes back and sits, tired of jumping up and down. Gino pulls the cocktail napkin from his collar.

Bobby's scrawl: "You fuck her."

Gino laughs out loud. That Bobby, Jesus. He has to stop laughing because tears are running out of his eyes. He has to stop laughing. Goddamn Bobby. Stop.

A blast of cold air means someone else has joined the party. Snow blows sideways and people yell to shut the door. Then who sits down in Gino's booth, where he's nice and quiet and not hurting a hair on a head, but the Mississippi Blonde.

"What d'you want?"

She leans toward him. The cold coming off her is unreal, colder than the storm outside. "Just a little bit, you know."

"No, I don't know."

"You been scoring off Todd."

"Get out of here."

"I ain't blind, honey. I seen you." She reaches for his hand. "I got money."

He grabs her wrist, skinny as a cat's leg, and squeezes hard. "Anyone here finds out I do horse, I'm gonna fuck you up worse than your boyfriend ever dreamed."

She whines, twisting her arm in his hand. "Sell me one hit, Gino."

"I don't want to hear my name coming out of your mouth." He glances up at the bar to see if Gil has spotted her yet, then lets go of the skinny arm and leans back as Katherine slides into the booth.

"What are you doing out in this snow?" she says to the stick doll next to her.

"I just came—"

"Where's Cricket?" Katherine asks. The blond mutters something. "I said, where's Cricket?"

"He's home with Joy."

"Who's Joy?"

"Todd's sister. She's okay." Her face is gray, and she won't look at Katherine. "She's good people."

"Gino, get us some coffee."

He's out of the booth like a tracer. P.T. gets the coffee for him. He leans close to Charlie and asks him, "How do you get a nun pregnant?"

"I don't know."

"You fuck her."

Sheila laughs beside him. Charlie looks at her. "That ain't funny."

"Yeah it is, man," says Gino. "It's funny."

P.T. mixes drinks, shaking and stirring like he's done it in another life. He's having such a great time he forgets to charge people and Gil has to come behind him and collect the money.

"*That's* funny," Charlie says, watching them.

Gino glances back at the Mississippi Blonde. "It's a damn shame we can't kill people who need killing, just because we're back. We ought to ask Jimmy Hoffa for a job."

"We ain't no hit men, just good red-blooded crooks."

"I would say we've been retrained." Gino blinks and the blue eyes are alive for a moment, replacing the blank stare. "That's a joke." The Animals' "Sky Pilot" fills the air. Gino looks at the jukebox as if it were Old Scratch himself.

Charlie follows his gaze. "What?"

"That song."

Charlie listens and nods. "All Along the Watchtower," he says.

"Yeah?"

"Yeah." Charlie rubs his arms. "Makes the hair on my neck stand up."

Gil brings Gino his two cups of coffee, refusing to look in the Mississippi Blonde's direction. "How you doing, Gino?" Gino nods, takes the coffee, and beats it back to the booth. Gil watches him go. "No matter where he is, he can't wait to get away."

"He's okay," Charlie lies. "Gino's okay."

Katherine and the Mississippi Blonde both have their backs to Gino, but he hears this much: "You could clear out of here, start over. And Cricket would stay. That's all."

He sets the coffee down. "Go on, talk." He stands with his back against the wall and closes his eyes. "I'm not here."

The sound of slurping coffee, then, "Ain't no way Gil's gonna sell this place."

"You take three quarters of the money and go wherever you want. I take one quarter and Cricket."

"You asking me to sell my own kid?"

"I'm his sister. This isn't about—" There's a thump on the table. "Jesus, would you think about him for once?"

The Mississippi Blonde starts to cry. Katherine wants to rip her head off, but her voice is calm. "We're all family," she says. "He'll always know who his mama is. You can visit whenever you want." The other one keeps on crying. Katherine tries to get her to drink some coffee, but the blonde needs a fix. She can't get one as long as Katherine's hanging all over her. "Just think about it," Katherine says. "Tell me you'll think about it."

Then the blonde says, "Is that P.T.'s brother over there?"

"Charlie?" Katherine says. "Yeah, he's home."

"Ain't he the one killed his grandpa?"

Gino's eyes open. Why's she asking about Charlie? The Mississippi Blonde nudges her way out of the booth. Katie follows. Gino is alone. He's in a little cage with the dolls looking in at him, looking at the freak, the rapist, the murderer. He feels the sign over his head: War Criminal. He slips down the wall until he's crouched on his heels, elbows propped on his knees, arms resting uselessly in front of him. The smoke rising from his cigarette writhes into a ghost around his head. He stares through it without blinking.

The room stands stricken under his gaze. The walls themselves shrink away from him. McGurk's Tap Room knows how to provide comfort, whether through liquor, laughter, or fighting. Now it holds its breath, mortified at its failure. No solace can reach Gino. Even the heroin fails him. The ceiling of McGurk's fades and disappears. From high in the heavens a small spotlight, like a laser, shines on the crouched figure. The bar, Bobby's dog, even Charlie, all turn to blackness. There is nothing in existence except Gino, alone, with the eye of God pressing down on him. He can't even ask for forgiveness. What good is forgiveness from a god who allowed hell to seep into the waking world? But the beam of light cuts open his chest and he sees the blame lying there, under his ribs. He stares at his sins, sickened by God and himself.

Sheila watches him from across the room. His army jacket hangs loose, his hair tangles at his shoulders. She's reminded of the guys she always sees in Toledo. Despite the difference of a wheelchair, a pair of crutches, or a sleeve pinned up at the shoulder, they all look the same . . . staring right at her and seeing something else. She doesn't want to know what they see. She doesn't want to know what Gino is seeing now. She remembers him as he was: Charlie's best friend, with wavy black hair, a perfect build, and those quiet eyes with long dark lashes that made Katie cry. For the first time she wonders who all those other guys were before they put on their army jackets.

~

Bobby comes back to Gino's booth with two Black and Tans, the dog jumping up after him.

Gino scowls. "You know I hate Black and Tans."

"This is beautiful, you know? Crazy weather." He stretches back and laughs. Stevie Wonder comes on the jukebox. "My man." The dog sniffs at the beer, but Bobby says, "Hey!" and the dog lays down beside him. "Red hot's always trying to get in my damn beer."

It never used to bother Gino that Bobby got out of the draft. Now he thinks maybe it bothers him a lot. Bobby, he thinks he's got his shit together, thinks he's got it all figured out and going his way. They watch the Mississippi Blonde at the bar, her head on Charlie's shoulder. Gino stands up so he'll have a better view when Sheila throws her against the wall. Gil throws his dish rag on the bar and unties his apron, but P.T. hurries from behind the bar and puts his hands on the Blonde's shoulders. She lets go of Charlie, who never even looks at her. P.T.'s like a stork with a baby bird, leading her through the crowd and up the stairs. Watching P.T. is almost as good as heroin. When P.T.'s been up there for a while with her, Bobby says, "You don't think he's banging her?"

"That all you think about, is your dick?"

"Yeah. Don't you?"

"I'm thinking about your dick all the time."

After a dirty look Bobby lowers his head and leans across the booth. "Wouldn't that be something, though? If he did?"

"Did what?"

"Banged her. Sweet Jesus, I'd pay honest money to see that." He laughs and rubs his dog behind the ears. "Wouldn't you, gum drop?"

12

P.T. SITS CROSS-LEGGED ON THE FLOOR AND LOOKS through Gil's 45 collection. Leslie Gore's "It's My Party" finishes on the record player. He says, "Sometimes Katie sings and I sing with her."

The Mississippi Blonde picks up a wooden-handled hairbrush from the dresser. "I left this brush here." She carries it to the bed. "Bet you got a beautiful voice."

"My mama had such a beautiful voice that two different people from the records came and asked her to come sing for them and she said, 'No, I am staying right here with my family.' Even when one of the men said he would give her five thousand dollars and five new dresses that she could pick out herself, and a new bike for me and a new bike for Charlie, even then she said, 'No, I am staying right here with my boys,' and so the second man went home and killed himself because she had such a beautiful voice."

"That's a sad story."

"I made it up."

"Sing me something." The Mississippi Blonde shrugs off her dress and sits on the edge of the bed in her slip. "Sing me something your mama used to sing to you."

P.T. sings "In the Gloaming," still rifling through 45s, while the Mississippi Blonde brushes her hair and listens. When he's done she says, "That's a sad song. I don't suppose you made that up."

"No, that song is real."

"You're a nice boy, you know?"

"Thank you." P.T. replaces Leslie Gore with Steve Lawrence.

"I'm sorry I called you a retard that night I met you."

"That's okay."

"You want me to brush your hair?"

"Okay."

She kneels behind him on the floor and runs the brush gently over his snarly hair as she talks. "I see your brother's home from the army."

"Yeah."

"He ever say why he done your grandpa that way?"

P.T. is quiet. He doesn't know what Charlie wants him to say. "Grandpa asked him to."

The Mississippi Blonde nods. "That's what I done heard."

Silence while the she strokes P.T.'s hair. Finally she says, "You think Charlie would ever do something like that for anyone else?"

"I don't know." He puts down a record and looks at his hands.

"Do you miss your grandpa?"

"Yeah."

"Come on up here next to me." She pats the bed beside her. "You think Charlie'd do the same by me?"

"I don't know." P.T.'s fingers tap on the folds of her slip. The fabric is cold and crinkly.

"It's not like I ain't been thinking about it for a long time," she says. Sirens rise up off Michigan Avenue. The neon outside makes her profile first yellow, then pink. She turns to look at P.T. beside her. He never saw anyone smile and cry at the same time before. "You could ask him for me." He holds the hem of her slip, twisting the lace in his fingers. She kisses his cheek and rests her head against his shoulder for a while. Her bleached hair bristles and tickles against his nose; he tries to scratch without disturbing her. Shouts drift up from the bar below, followed by a wake of laughter. He wishes Charlie were here right now. Her voice interrupts his thoughts. "You like my slip?"

"Yes I do."

"You want to try it on?" He thinks for a moment, then nods. "Okay," she says as she stands. "But you can't tell Charlie."

"Why?"

"Because boys don't wear slips, and people can get funny about it." The Mississippi Blonde lifts the slip over her head while P.T. unbuttons his flannel shirt. He holds his long arms in the air while she eases the slip over his head and pulls it down across his chest. "Stand up." The slip hugs tightly all the way to the waist where it bunches up over the pockets of his corduroys. "How's it feel?"

"Scratchy."

"That's the tag in back. You have to smooth it down." She tucks the tag inside the slip for him. "You're near as skinny as I am."

She stands in her light blue bra and panties as if she and P.T. were sisters. "You want to see yourself?"

"No, I'll just stay here."

"Well, you look good."

"Thank you." He sits again and smiles at her, one hand rubbing a satin shoulder strap up and down.

"You can have it if you want."

"Charlie would get mad, huh?"

"Oh, I can promise you that." She laughs and straightens a seam for him. "But you can wear it for a nightgown."

"Skuppers would be surprised."

"Go ahead." She locks the bedroom door. "No one's gonna barge in. They'll think we're fucking or something." P.T. carefully pulls one leg, then the other, out of his corduroys. The fabric barely covers his hips. "It ain't gonna keep you warm at night, but it looks nice."

"Thank you."

"You want to try the stockings?"

"No, just the slip."

"Just as well. They'd only come up to your knees anyway." She opens her purse. "Nail polish?"

P.T.'s fingernails are bitten down to little indentations in the skin. He looks at each one before saying, "Just on this one, and then these two." The Mississippi Blonde sits on the bed and holds his left hand in hers. She dabs bits of Taffy Pink as she talks.

"I don't know what happened. Coming up north, I guess that's what done it. I froze. I come up here looking for something new. I thought maybe I could do some waitressing, maybe save enough money to buy a house. Lord God I know how dumb that sounds now. I got a job but it wasn't like waitressing in a diner. I'm not making ends meet. So I do a little extra dating, if you know what I mean, and Todd takes half because he's throwing the work my way. I'm doing dope but I'm still thinking I'm gonna have myself a house someday. With a lawn too, if y'all can believe that."

The little blonde holds P.T.'s hand on her knee to steady it as she paints his thumbnail. He closes his eyes because it tickles.

"I come into McGurk's the first time and there's Gil. Next time I come, you bet Todd wasn't with me. I dropped the waitressing and I dropped Todd, and I started dating out of McGurk's. Gil, he looks the other way, you know. I'm careful not to get him in trouble."

The little brush stroking his nails puts P.T. half to sleep. The Mississippi Blonde holds his hand gently, as if it were broken.

"Pretty soon I was upstairs with Gil every night. Katie, she was a good friend to me. Kept me company when the blues hit and I thought about maybe just a little bit of dope, just until I felt better. But she never let me do it, and she never said nothing to Gil about it, either. Maybe it would be better if she had.

"I was stupid and happy. I thought Gil was the last one, the real thing. When he popped that ring on me, I couldn't get enough breath to say yes. I couldn't believe I was alive, to feel that happy, didn't seem possible. We was thinking of someday Gil expanding the bar and getting some music in there, like live music. Make it like a club or something. We was thinking about doing that.

"He was the only man ever made me feel like more than a walking cunt. I didn't date anymore, after we got engaged. I helped him close up the bar every night. After you quit, he needed someone helping out. The best part of the day was when everyone else was gone. Gil had an ear for screwy conversation and he was a wonderful copycat, though he made me swear to never, ever tell anyone. Because of course they'd all say, 'Yeah, do me! Do me!' And if he didn't, they'd get mad. But I promise you, Lord God, if he did do them, they'd get a lot more mad. One night, Gil goes off on this thing where he says, like Bobby, 'There you go, pheasant-under-glass,' with that jumpy Bobby thing in his shoulders and his neck. And he'd have the dog thinking, 'Suck my dick,' and Bobby saying, 'That's right, that's my caviar-and-tuna-fish-on-rye.' And the dog's thinking 'Fuck you, my name is Milton.' Which about made me pee my pants, because nobody knows that dog's name except Bobby and God.

"He could've been on TV he was that funny, but no one knew it. He just didn't show that part of himself downstairs. Just like I never told anyone why I come up north from Miss'ippi, except I told Gil. See, I showed him that side of me. I cried and cried while he held my hand and said it didn't matter, none of it mattered."

She sets P.T.'s hand down and reaches for the other one.

"Keep your fingers spread while it dries. Anyway, I don't know what started the first fight, but we were two hornets stinging each other to death. I sat up all night thinking how this was what I deserved, this was the real deal the Lord God meant for me, Gil just stopping his love for me over nothing. Next day Gil, he says he's sorry and I'm sorry and it's heaven again and that dumb fight, it's like it never even happened. And it'll sure enough never happen again, but it does. How could he say all these nice things he said to me all the time—how happy he is, how happy I make him, and then we get started over nothing and he's calling me a cheap little cunt? Well, how many times does a person go through that kind of talk before something has to change? I called Todd and he came around with a little dope, just a little hit, and I pay him out of the cash register because no one's around, Gil's up there asleep, or still calling me a cunt to the walls or the curtains, I don't know. I shoot up just to get through it, just to get through the night until tomorrow when we both are so sorry and we're closer than ever."

The Mississippi Blonde stops and shakes the little brush at P.T. like a chastising finger.

"Gil did not hit me, not once, and I hit him plenty. I guess it was just regular old married people fights but I loved him so much, I couldn't stand a hard word from him. So I'm in the cash register more and more and Gil, he don't even see no needle marks at first. Katie's the one hollering at me every day, threatening to tell him.

"One night, just another old fight, just the same old words, but it hits me: This is too hard, loving someone. I called Todd and told him to come over and pick me up and I packed up all my stuff in grocery bags and some cardboard boxes. Gil don't even look real to me anymore, just a cartoon person with a mouth that says, 'Come back upstairs. I love you,' he says. 'You're killing yourself with that shit.' He had big cartoon tears on his face, but I gotta get going, I gotta get fixed. 'Come back upstairs,' he says. 'We'll get you some help.' But out I go with Todd and get into his car."

She blows on P.T.'s fingers for a few minutes.

"All along I'm thinking, 'I can undo this. I can go back as soon as I calm myself down.' Cause I would never leave Gil, not really. Now Gil thinks I don't love him. But Lord, how do you stop loving in your heart, even if you can't take it in real life? You can't. The one thing I don't remember, the thing I can't hardly believe even now, is carrying that baby out with me. I didn't never mean to hurt my little boy."

After that she's quiet, holding the bottle of polish. P.T. thinks maybe she fell asleep when she says, "You tell Charlie I don't have the guts to do it myself."

P.T. admires his pink fingernails until he gets dizzy. It's not dizzy enough to fall down, and he can still hear the Mississippi Blonde talking, but he knows that this is the start of the feeling. He's not afraid of the feeling like he used to be. He closes his eyes and hears the tingle of blood in his ears. He knows that when he opens his eyes his mama will be there in the dress that she always wore when it was laundry day. And she is. She smiles. She reaches out and touches P.T.'s cheek. Inside his head he asks her if it's okay and she nods. It's so good to have his mama back that P.T. laughs.

The Mississippi Blonde turns away to put the bottle back in her purse. "What's funny?"

"It's okay," says P.T. He gently picks up a pillow and brings it down over the Mississippi Blonde's face from behind. He hugs her to his chest with his arms wrapped around the pillow, the back of her head pressed against the cool, crinkly fabric of the slip. He is amazed at how soft she is and holds her firmly without hurting her.

He rocks from side to side while his mama tells him it'll be all right, that everything's fine now, and the little gal's gonna be so glad to be home.

The Mississippi Blonde hardly struggles. She crumples and closes like a night-blooming flower. The boards of her grandma's front porch feel smooth and warm. She smells the faint, sweet rot drifting up from the river. A breeze blows white curls across Cricket's forehead. The Mississippi Blonde's fingers dig briefly into P.T.'s arms before loosening and sliding to the bed.

He doesn't let go of her even after he sets the pillow aside. He lays her carefully on the bed and stretches out beside her. Her hair smells like strawberries. He pulls an old afghan from the end of the bed and covers the two of them. He doesn't stroke her hair or pat her arm or talk to her, but he makes sure she's warm. He wonders if she feels better yet. He wonders what the chances are of her finding his mama and his grandpa and telling them how he's doing. Thinking about the three of them together, feeling fine and talking about him, makes him happy and he drifts toward sleep. He's not sure how long it is before a knock on the door makes him jump.

"Hey, P.T."

He throws the afghan off and jumps into his corduroys, tucking the slip in. "Hi Charlie." He replaces the afghan around the Mississippi Blonde because now she looks awful just lying there in her underpants and her bra.

"Open up."

"Okay." He puts on his shirt and buttons it before unlocking the door. "Be quiet and you can come in."

"I don't want to come in, I want you to come on downstairs."

"Oh. Okay." P.T. turns the bedroom light off and follows Charlie down the hallway.

"What's the matter with you?"

"What?"

"What were you doing in there?"

"I fell asleep." P.T. adjusts the strap of the slip under his shirt.

"I mean what were you doing in there with her?"

P.T. wants to tell him that he put on her slip. He wants to tell how he got Pink Taffy nail polish. "Well Charlie, I killed her."

Charlie's hand closes around P.T.'s elbow as they turn around and head back up the hall. Once inside the bedroom, Charlie locks the door. "What did you do?"

"I killed her."

"I mean, how?"

"Oh." P.T. sits on the edge of the bed and plays with a tassel on the afghan. "I smothered her."

"Why?"

"She was going to ask you to do it, and I did not want you to have to go away again." At this, Charlie pushes the butt of his palm hard against his eyes. P.T. watches him. "Do not make it a bad thing. It is not a bad thing." Charlie sits on the floor and buries his face in the bedspread. His shoulders hunch and shake.

"She was really wanting to go somewhere else," P.T. continues. "She thought it would be better." Charlie doesn't seem to hear him. He won't lift his head from the covers.

"Mama said it was okay," says P.T.

"Shut up, Bro."

P.T. smoothes out the tassel in his hand. Charlie rolls the Mississippi Blonde roughly off the bed and onto the floor. P.T. cries out and grabs Charlie's arm. "Don't do that."

"She don't feel it, Bro. Give me the brush on the bed there."

P.T. hands him the brush. "You gonna brush her hair?"

Charlie sits on his haunches over the dead body. "Go on downstairs."

"I will brush it. I will do it."

"Go down there and make sure no one comes up."

P.T. frowns. "I think maybe I should take care of this."

"How?" Charlie explodes. "How you gonna take care of it? Look at her! Look what you did!"

P.T. grabs a handful of his own hair and pulls until the veins stand out on his arm. "I helped her because she asked me to and there is nothing wrong with that." Charlie puts out a hand as if to silence him. "There is nothing wrong with that, Charlie."

"Okay, it's okay," Charlie whispers until P.T. drops his hand. "Listen, listen to me. Remember the first time she came in here? Popping that gum like the Fourth of July?" P.T. starts to breathe normally again. He smoothes down his cowlick over and over. "And you said once, you said, 'She looks like a little yellow parakeet perched there.' Remember you saying that?"

P.T. smiles. "A little yellow bird."

"You helped her, now I'm helping you. That's all. Okay?" Charlie looks away from P.T., who watches him with a grave look. "Just please—you know what? Go downstairs until I come down."

After P.T. leaves, Charlie locks the door and looks around the room. The empty turntable still spins. He turns it off. The blue lampshade on the dresser has a big burn spot from a too-hot light bulb. He rummages through Gil's drawers looking for a knife, any type of blade, but finds nothing. He sits on the windowsill and picks at the loose threads in the knee of his jeans. His ribcage contracts until his heart grows swollen and sweaty.

He lifts the Mississippi Blonde so she sits leaning against the bed. He holds her chin steady with his left hand and punches her in the face. He hits her until his knuckles bleed, then lets her go. She remains sitting upright. He stands up and kicks her in the neck. Her head snaps back and this time she falls over on her side.

He stops to catch his breath, gulping huge sobs of air. Everything tingles like he's being scalped from head to foot. He rolls her onto her back, tears the bra and panties off, and throws them on the bed. He positions her hands in front of her face and beats her with the hairbrush so it'll look like she tried to fight off her attacker. He thinks about his dad, what would his dad do? He grabs a handful of hair and uses it to slam her head into the dresser.

"Is that what you want? Huh, bitch?"

He grabs her upper arm and lifts her off the floor, jerking to dislocate her shoulder. He shakes her and throws her against the wall. Blonde hair falls across her face. He kicks at her ribs, her thighs, her head. He drops to his haunches, then onto the floor. His legs are numb with cold. Heat builds up behind his eyes and his chests turns to cement, but tears won't come. He looks at her for a long time while his heart slows down. Finally he shoves her under the bed and positions her arms and legs so it looks like she crawled under there by herself. He stands rubbing his legs. He's sick to his stomach. He's homesick for his dad.

13

NO ONE NOTICES P.T. AS HE COMES DOWNSTAIRS. HE glides into Gino's booth without a word.

"Where'd you come from?"

"Upstairs."

"You finally got her settled down?"

"Yes." P.T. taps the table with a straw, blinking his eyes to the rhythm.

"You okay?"

"Yes." He taps and blinks faster. Gino pulls the straw out of his hand and sets it on the table. P.T. puts his hands under the table so Gino won't see the nail polish. Bobby returns to the booth with another Black and Tan. "Where'd Charlie go?"

"I don't know," P.T. and Gino say together. P.T. pats Gino on the arm. "Jinx. No jinx back."

"Wasn't he upstairs with you?"

"I don't know." P.T. picks up the straw and starts the blinking and tapping again.

Bobby smiles. "You don't know if Charlie was upstairs with you?"

"Nope." The straw moves fast and light like a hummingbird. P.T. makes himself woozy blinking, trying to keep up. Gino reaches out to take the straw away, but P.T. flips it high in the air and catches it with his other hand, out of Gino's reach. He holds it suspended over the tabletop, one corner of his mouth curved in a smile.

"You better not," says Gino. The tapping starts again. "Little prick." But Gino doesn't mind. It's nice to see P.T. acting like an everyday pain in the ass.

"I can stick out my tongue and touch my nose," says P.T., never ceasing the ratta-tat-tat on the table. "Bet you can't," he adds.

"The tip or just a nostril?"

"The tip."

Gino makes a swipe for the straw and misses. He wishes he could've carried a miniature P.T. in his pocket while he was overseas. Bobby sticks his tongue out and turns the tip of it upwards. A fountain of laughter spills on the other side of the pool table. Bobby whips his tongue in and looks over, but they're laughing about something else. He tries again, but barely brushes the corner of a nostril. "Damn. That hurts."

"I thought you could do that for hours," murmurs Gino.

Bobby wipes at his nose with the side of his hand. "Listen to the next Jerry Lewis."

"Bet you a dollar I can," says P.T.

"Can what?" asks Bobby.

"Can stick out my tongue and touch my nose." Without waiting for encouragement, he sticks his tongue out and uses his knuckle to tap his nose. All the while the straw beats a small furrow into the Formica, and his eyelashes blink like butterfly wings.

Bobby shakes his head. "I been had like a sucker." He slaps a dollar on the table.

"Hey." Gino raises a hand to his forehead to indicate a headache. P.T. stops the tapping. "Thanks."

P.T. asks Bobby, "Did Katie like her record player?"

"Loved it," says Bobby. "Said now she won't have to borrow Gil's." But P.T. walks away before Bobby can finish the sentence. The two men watch from the booth as he makes his way slowly to the bar, where Charlie has reappeared. Bobby nods toward P.T. "What's up his ass?"

Gino smiles. "If I could read that boy's mind I'd be a millionaire." P.T. hovers over Charlie at the bar. Charlie puts an arm up around his brother's shoulder and rubs his head with his knuckles. Gino wonders how Charlie does it, how he lives back here in the world like nothing's wrong.

Charlie calls to Gil to pour a couple of shots of Jack Daniels. When the drinks come, Charlie holds one up for P.T. "Here's one for Old Jerry."

"I don't want that," P.T. says.

"That's right. I forgot. Get yourself a Vernor's, then."

P.T. starts to climb over the bar like he used to, but Gil grabs his wrist. "Walk around."

P.T. makes his way behind the bar and pauses at the entrance to the back room. "Guess what." He has to repeat it twice because no one's listening. When Gil pauses long enough to make eye contact, P.T. says, "Guess how many steps it took to get from there to here."

"Twenty-seven," says Gil.

"Fourteen." P.T. disappears through the door. Gil shouts for him to bring ice, too. Charlie pushes the extra shot across the bar to Gil and says, "Here's to women." Gil snorts, but swallows his drink. Charlie brings his glass down hard. "Another round."

"I got other customers, you know."

"How many of them are buying you drinks, old man?"

Gil agrees to one more shot, then goes back to pouring beer by the pitcher. P.T. returns with several cases of beer and a bag of ice over his shoulder. Charlie keeps a close eye on P.T. while he continues to buy shots for Gil. Late in the evening, they run out of small bills. Gil tells Katherine to run upstairs and grab his wallet so he can change a twenty. "It should be right there next to the bed."

"I'll go," says Charlie.

"Katherine can get it."

"No, you guys are busy." Charlie puts his hand on P.T.'s shoulder. "You stay here. I'll just be a second." He disappears into the crowd.

"What's got into him?" says Katherine. "Buying drinks, running errands."

P.T. tugs on his upper lip and folds it over his lower lip, pinning it there with one finger. "I told him that he should be nice."

"Why should he be nice?" Katherine asks.

"Because if he isn't nice, the red butterflies will eat him."

"Red butterflies."

"Oh yes. It used to happen when I was a baby. They would cover a person head to foot, all these red butterflies, and pretty soon there would be nothing left. Like flying piranhas."

"That sounds pretty awful, P.T."

"It was. It was pretty awful."

"You hear that, Dad? Charlie's being nice so the red butterflies won't eat him."

Gil nods. "Butterflies are back, huh?"

"It's pretty awful."

Charlie returns and slaps Gil's wallet on the bar. "What's awful?"

"Nothing."

"Break out some decent whiskey, why don't you?"

"Swear to God," says Gil, opening a bottle of Black Label. "Your dad beat the brains out of *both* of you."

"Hey." Charlie's tone creates a circle of silence around them. "You want me to kick your fucking teeth in?"

"Don't start up with that," calls Katherine from the cash register, brushing her hair off her shoulder.

"No offense intended." Gil pours two shots and shoves one at Charlie. "On me this time."

Charlie swallows his and calls for doubles for them both. "You been drinking, old man. You start drinking, you start running your mouth."

"Start running my mouth and the next thing I'm sending you out the door with my boot in your ass."

"Here's to old times." P.T. raises his root beer.

"No, I mean it." Charlie leans over and sticks his finger in Gil's face. "You're an old man now. Can't hold your liquor anymore." He splashes whiskey on Gil's chest. "Look at that. You spilled booze all over yourself. Old wino. Old drunk." Charlie says all of this softly so only Gil and P.T. can hear him.

"Cut it out now, I'm telling you."

"What. What are you telling me, wino?"

"Let's go dance," says P.T., but Charlie silences him with a look. Katherine is out of earshot.

Charlie picks up the bottle of Black Label and holds it under Gil's nose. "Have another one. Drunk." Gil lays his bar rag on the counter and unties his apron. "Can't even keep a little whore for a wife."

Gil knocks the bottle away with one hand and pounds Charlie in the nose with the other. There aren't many people left in the place, just a few witnesses to see Gil lay Charlie out.

"Jesus, Gil," Charlie says from the floor. "Watch the temper." He pulls himself onto his stool and continues, "What are you gonna do when she goes back to Mississippi?"

"Fuck her. Good riddance."

"Yeah, but what about your boy?"

At the mention of Cricket, the veins appears on Gil's forehead. "She's not taking him anywhere."

"How you gonna stop her?"

"Kill her if I have to."

Charlie looks around to see if anyone's listening. Under his breath he says, "Shit. You ain't got the guts to kill a woodpecker."

Gil brings his fist down hard on the bar. "I could kill that cunt without breaking a sweat."

Plenty of people hear this. Katherine looks up from counting money. P.T. watches all this with confusion bordering on alarm. The last thing he thought his brother would do was to talk about killing anyone, especially Gil's poor little wife.

"Face it," says Charlie. "She ate your balls for breakfast."

Gil comes around the counter, grabs Charlie, and carries him by the back of his belt and collar to the front door. He shoves Charlie against a wall and yanks open the front door. The freezing wave that washes into the place has everyone yelling to shut the door. Eight or nine people watch Gil dump Charlie onto the snow-drifted sidewalk.

"He'll freeze out there," says P.T.

"Then take his ass home." Gil returns to the bar with an expression that rivals Leroy Simpkins at his worst. P.T. steps back and nearly knocks over Sheila.

"Get your coat," she says. "I'll take you both home."

Gil closes the bar that night so drunk he's nearly blind. He says good night to no one, since all the customers have gone and Katherine's asleep. He makes his way up the stairs, holding onto the banister so he won't fall backwards. In his room he flops onto the bed without turning on the light. He kicks off his shoes and falls asleep in an instant. He begins to snore, his wife lying swollen and discolored underneath him.

Charlie, P.T., and Sheila drive through the winter storm to P.T.'s home. "I'll talk to you tomorrow," Charlie tells him. "I love you."

"I know." P.T. climbs out of the back seat.

They watch until he climbs the icy stairs and goes inside. As she puts the car in reverse Sheila says, "Come home with me."

He closes his eyes, but the sight of the Mississippi Blonde on the floor, hair over her face and legs bent beneath her, turns Charlie's lungs to quicksand. He looks at Sheila's profile and it looks like home, it feels like home. Diane means apologies and behaving the way she wants him to. When they reach Sheila's place in Toledo his hands move over her like a blind man's. There's her body, all of it, just as he'd left it. Time rolls back as he moves inside her. Later Charlie says to the window, "Feels like I stepped off a cliff, and just now looked down."

"We owed each other this much," she tells him.

"Yeah." He hands her his cigarette. "Didn't think it'd be like this, though."

"Relax, Charlie. Nothing's changed."

14

THE NEXT DAY, CHARLIE WAKES UP IN THE STRANGE bed. He peers at the glare of white sun outlining the window shade. It's several seconds before he realizes where he is, only a few seconds, but it feels like half an eternity to Charlie, whose first thought is that he's back in the hospital in Saigon. Reality separates from panic, and the previous night rushes through.

He looks around for a clock. The motion dislocates his brain inside his skull and makes him nauseated. He sits up. The bed tilts backward. Quarter past noon. He's supposed to be at Stewart Tool and Die. He closes his eyes and holds onto the mattress until it stops moving. In the other room a T.V. plays low, some soap opera. Sheila was always hooked on them. Sheila. Christ. He wants to fall back into the sheets, but he knows how that will feel. He sits in the middle of the bed, naked, the blankets twisting around him. He gazes again at the drawn window shade. Out there in the bright sunlight people are going on about their business, running errands, working their jobs. Out there men are earning paychecks to bring home to their wives, decent men doing the right thing, free to go wherever they want in that bright light while he's in this darkened room. He's trapped in here, always has been, and nothing he ever does will get him out. He closes his eyes and imagines himself walking down the street with everyone else, taking the bus back to Jackson, walking in the front door to a living room full of light. Diane will be there. She'll wrap her arms around his waist and squeeze as hard as she can, tell him how much she missed him, and maybe make some tuna sandwiches for lunch with thick slices of tomatoes and lots of pepper.

The phone rings in the other room. Charlie opens his eye to the dim light and all he sees is Gil's wife, the dead weight of her as he hit her, rolled her over, hit her again. In the other room the soap opera is silenced and he hears Sheila's voice: "What? Yeah, yeah, okay. Just hang on girl, sit tight. Fuck. Okay, it's okay." Charlie is half dressed when she opens the door. "Oh God, Charlie. Gil killed his wife."

By the time he's fully dressed and standing at the front door, she's on the phone again. "I know, but I got an emergency . . . goddamnit Bonnie, how often do I ask . . . fine. No, fine. I'll be there in five." Sheila and Charlie don't say much in the car. Sheila pulls in front of the little house like all the other little houses in a row. "I'll be right back." Charlie sits in her car and waits. Can't even drive home on his own. He needs to talk to Bro. He needs to call Diane.

"Hold her." Sheila shoves a little girl into his lap and tosses a diaper bag in the back seat. When she gets behind the wheel she says, "Lita, honey. This is your daddy." Lita pats his hand, which sits on the armrest. She pulls a few of the hairs on his wrist and pats his hand again. Sheila says, "Can you say hello?"

"Hi." Both Lita and Charlie say it at the same time. Lita laughs and slaps his arm. "Hi, hi, hi, hi, hi, hi, hi." Charlie's tongue turns to paste. He looks at his hand, which is nearly as big as her head. His arm goes around her waist when they come to a stop light, then quickly lets go. She bounces on his lap and hurls herself backward until her head collides with his Adam's apple.

"Aagh."

"Did she get you?" asks Sheila. "Lita, what did I tell you about that?"

Lita laughs again, two short huffs and a high scream: huh huh eeeeeh, huh huh eeeeeh. Sheila and Lita sing "Don Gato," and "The Old Woman Who Swallowed a Fly." Charlie spends the thirty-minute ride to Ypsi staring out the window while his daughter pulls out the hairs on his wrist one by one.

~

There are uniformed officers, plainclothes officers, people coming up and down the stairs, some of them looking like they haven't been outside a morgue for months. At the center of the hub sits Katherine, with Bobby beside her.

"Sheila," she says, quiet and calm. Charlie had expected hysterics. It's strange to see Katie so quiet. When she sees the little girl she smiles. "I don't believe it." Lita stands quietly beside her mother, chewing on a graham cracker. To Charlie she says, "I called your place. They took Dad in. I called his lawyer."

Bobby reaches down to pet the dog, but the dog's not there, so he scratches Lita's head. "Somebody has to go over to the station. You ought to see it up there." Bobby shakes his head. "Katie found her."

Sheila sits next to Katherine and holds her hand. Whatever she's feeling she keeps it inside. She lets Bobby take Lita, who buries her hands in his afro. "Huh huh eeeeeh!"

"What's your name, Eskimo pie?"

"Esko Pie!"

"So Mama's been holding out on us, huh?" Bobby takes Lita to the jukebox and lets her push buttons.

"What happened?" Charlie asks.

"He went nuts," Bobby says over his shoulder. "He beat her so bad you wouldn't know it was her if you didn't know it was her."

Katherine says to Charlie, "Will you go over there?"

"Where?"

"The station. See if they'll let you talk to him. See if he's okay. See if they'll set bail. I don't know."

Charlie nods. "Who else did you call?"

"Gino. He's not home either."

Charlie nods again. "Let me tell Bro myself. I'll tell him."

Katherine nods. She hasn't let go of Sheila since she walked in. Charlie doesn't stick around. He's a bad actor and he knows Sheila will see through him at any moment. He walks over to the fourteenth precinct station, no more than ten blocks away. After three hours of waiting, six attempted calls to Diane (all of them hung up before it even rang), and eight cups of coffee to settle his stomach, Charlie is finally allowed to see Gil.

Gil is dressed in his usual gray work pants and flannel shirt. Charlie didn't realize until that moment how much he'd dreaded seeing Gil in orange coveralls. But Gil looks normal: no haggard eyes, no beard stubble, none of the earmarks of a desperate man. Charlie hesitates in the doorway; maybe Gil's calm because he knows. Charlie's mind flies over the scene last night, scanning for anything he could've overlooked, while Gil beckons him to come in. It is a small room, a private lawyer-client kind of room. Charlie sits down, lights a cigarette, then slides the pack to Gil.

"Thanks," says Gil. "Didn't bring any tomato juice, did you?" Charlie shakes his head. "Aspirin?" Charlie frowns. "I'm getting too old to drink like this."

"You want me to get you something?"

"Naw. Sit down. Did you see her?"

"Who?"

"Dory. Did you see her?"

Dory. Charlie rubs his eyes. "No."

"It's bad. Katherine saw her. She saw how bad it was." Gil sits back from the table with his legs apart, one hand on each knee.

Charlie realizes he's taking a drag each time Gil does. He stabs his out. "What happened?"

"I killed her." Gil jerks the cigarette up to his mouth.

"Then it was an accident. They have to realize it was an accident."

"If you saw her—it was no accident."

Charlie rubs his eyes again. "C'mon, Gil. You wouldn't kill a woman. You don't got it in you."

"You know why Katherine's mom left me?" Gil settles back and watches Charlie, who's seated awkwardly half off the chair as if about to jump up and run. "We were arguing and I threw a pound of frozen hamburger at her."

Charlie waits. Then, "That's it?"

Gil nods, takes another jerky drag. "She said once I start, it's just a matter of time. She watched her own dad put her mom in the hospital half a dozen times. I guess I don't have to tell you how that works."

"That how come you quit drinking for so long?"

Gil nods. "So don't tell me I ain't got it in me."

"Katie called your lawyer. We'll get them to set bail."

"What the hell do I want with bail?" Gil throws his cigarette to the floor and kicks it aside. "Where am I gonna go? Back to the bar? Sleep in that room?"

"Anything you want me to do? Something you want me to bring you besides tomato juice and aspirin?"

"Did Katherine find Cricket okay?"

Shit. Cricket hadn't even entered Charlie's head. Kate had mentioned the kid but now he couldn't remember. "Yeah, she's got him. He's fine."

Gil helps himself to another cigarette before putting the pack in his shirt pocket. "I'll tell you one thing. One thing." Gil leans forward so Charlie is forced to look at him. "Whenever you see a way to start all over again, a second chance, don't you fall for it. It'll slice you up." Gil makes a small slashing motion with his hand. "Slice you to fucking pieces." He stands up. "Call Katherine for me, tell her to forget the bail. Other than that stay out of it. No reason to mix yourself up in this."

Charlie stands up with him. "Cops are gonna wanna ask me questions."

"Tell the truth. You think I care what they do to me now?"

When he steps out of the station, Charlie reaches for a cigarette only to find them gone. Irritated, he heads for the liquor store a few blocks away. It's late. He'd been in that station, feels like two days. Diane would've come home from work hours ago. He wonders what she's making for supper. He ducks inside a phone booth and sits on the frozen steel ledge. He plays with the phone, dialing random numbers just to watch the dial spin back into place. Hey, babe, got tied up, be home in a bit. Hey, babe, spent the night at Sheila's. Hey, babe, Bro killed someone, but don't worry. He bangs his head lightly on the glass wall. Worried is probably the last thing she's feeling by now. He leaves the phone booth. A dark wind picks up. His jacket is light, and he's half numb when he reaches the liquor store.

"Hey, Charlie. When'd you get back?" The guy behind the counter reaches behind him and throws two packs of Old Golds down next to the cash register. "Jesus, that's something about Gil."

Charlie pays for the cigarettes and steps back into the darkness. He could walk. He could walk until his legs freeze out from under him. He could walk south to Kentucky and find his dad: find him and put a piece of two-by-four into his skull. He stands outside the liquor store with his head scrunched into his coat collar. Under a street light he strikes a match, but the smoke makes him dizzy and sick. He tosses it down where it burns a neat hole in the snow, clean as a bullet. The blizzard from last night has left everything crystal and quiet. Ice cakes the tree branches. His nose hairs freeze.

He's been home for over a month. How many of his friends are still over there? How many are alive? It's Friday night. That means it's Saturday morning in Vietnam. The snow and the icy wind burning the back of his neck make it hard to believe such a place as Vietnam could exist. He closes his eyes and tries to put himself there, as he has a hundred times. He could never place himself home during his tour, could never come back to Ypsi in his mind. But all it takes is a moment's shift of focus and the sweat starts on his face, under his arms, trickles down his chest. The vomity odor of the jurian fruit fills his nose along with the heat of Zippos against grass, the shit-filled rice paddies. A balmy warmth brushes his face, air thick with humidity and insects. His palms sting with a thousand small cuts, his stomach begins to cramp. He opens his eyes and sucks in five or six deep waves of cold. He focuses on the neon up and down Michigan Avenue until he's safely back again. Each time he goes there it's harder to come back. Each time he tells himself he won't do it again. Even now, the snowdrift he walks through feels more like mud than snow. He continues across the street where the phone booth still stands empty and brightly lit on the corner. He drops in all the change in his pockets.

"Hello?" Her voice. Tired, worn out, but her voice. "Charlie?" He blinks melting snowflakes from his eyes. "Charlie." He leans back against the glass and lets his head fall against it. Silence on his end of the phone, silence on hers. Maybe it goes on for a long time, maybe he falls asleep.

"Please deposit forty-five cents or your call will be disconnected." He wipes more melting snowflakes from his eyes. Diane tells the operator to reverse the charges, but it's only a recording. He hangs up and heads for his car. Once in McGurk's parking lot he can't put his key in the ignition. It seems that every move he makes is countered by an opposite. Pretty soon he'll be as crazy as P.T. He puts his forehead into the palm of his hand and squeezes. Over there things were simple. There were no rights or wrongs or shades of gray. Just stay alive or get dead. He tries to let his mind go blank, but when he closes his eyes all he sees is Diane. He takes a deep breath and gets out of the car. McGurk's stands there like it always has, like an act of God.

15

KATHERINE AND BOBBY WENT TO TODD DOLPH'S house, where Joy told them the whole story. Todd and the Mississippi Blonde were fighting over Cricket. Todd dragged him out of bed and told Joy to get the kid out of his sight before he killed him. That's when she walked out. Just walked out and left her boy without looking back. She wasn't out the driveway before Todd burst in the kitchen, dragged Cricket off Joy's lap and into the bathroom. Behind the locked door, Joy heard slaps and the thud of a boot, heard Cricket crying. She called the police.

~

Now, at the hospital, Katherine storms around like Westmoreland himself until she finds someone who'll give some answers. A nurse gives her a bunch of forms. Under "Mother's Name," she hesitates, then writes Katherine McGurk. Father, unknown. She leans over the admitting nurse. "Where is he?"

"You are . . ." The nurse glances down at the forms. "The mother?" Her glance continues until it lands on Bobby, then down at the words "Father Unknown," and up again at Bobby. He gives her his patented grin and winks. "Pediatrics is on the third floor," she says in a voice as cold as a night crawler. "Take a left out of the elevator."

Bobby hustles to keep up with Katherine, who's already in the elevator. She doesn't have to tell him to keep his mouth shut; it's clear from the look on her face. A man and a woman are working at the pediatric nursing station. Katie goes for the man.

"We're here to see Jeffrey McGurk."

"Ah . . ." He searches a clipboard for the name.

"McGurk. I'm his mother. Where is he?"

Again, the sliding glance at Bobby before answering. "Mrs. McGurk. The folks from child protection will want to speak—"

"Where is he?"

He looks at Bobby again. "How are you related?"

Katie puffs up like the lizard with the big wing on its neck. "Do I gotta bust into goddamn every room on this floor?"

"I'll get someone right away."

Bobby smiles. "That's my Katie girl."

"Shut up or you'll be pissing out your ass hole."

Bobby wonders what would make a man piss out of his ass hole until the man from the nurse's station returns with another guy, who impassively holds out his hand. "Hi, I'm John Grace. Child protection."

"Katherine McGurk." She takes his hand and squeezes it hard enough to pop his fingernails. "And this is Robert Royce." Bobby shakes the man's hand with a little nod, playing it strong and silent since he's not allowed to speak.

"The police brought him in last night. We were unable to locate you."

"Where is he?"

"Just down the hall here."

Cricket is tiny in the big hospital bed. He has a cut on his nose and a bruise that spreads from one eye across the bridge of his nose. A woman sits next to the bed reading from *Raggedy Ann and Andy and the Camel with the Wrinkly Knees*. Cricket holds his stuffed bunny against his chest, chewing on its ear. Katherine leans into the room. "Cricket honey?"

"Kitty!" He's so excited that he tries to climb over the bed's guard rail. The woman holds onto him until Katherine can take him in her arms.

"Hey, buddy, look at you! Look at this big fancy bed." All the while she looks at the bruises on his arm, the dark splotches on his neck.

"I'm Ellen Knox," says the woman, oozing professional restraint.

"Katherine McGurk."

"He'll be fine. We've taken X-rays, nothing broken. There are still a few test results that we're waiting for."

Katherine plays peek-a-boo with the bunny. "What kind of tests?" she asks.

"Checks for diabetes, syphilis." At Katherine's look, she continues. "It's the standard work-up before placement."

"What placement?" Bobby asks, forgetting to shut up.

The woman glances at John Grace for help. He says, "Under the circumstances, we think short-term foster care is needed until—"

"No foster care," Bobby says. "He comes home with us."

"In these cases, Mr.—is it McGurk?"

Katherine puts up a hand to silence Bobby. "Look, we aren't his parents, okay? We're his legal guardians. His mother's gone."

"Gone?"

"Got herself beat to death last night," Bobby adds.

"I'm sorry for your loss," Ellen Knox says automatically, not faltering a hair. "We'll need to see a police report."

Katherine takes a warning breath and John Grace interrupts. "We'll take care of the paperwork later, after you've had a chance to visit." He looks at Cricket, so small in the hospital bed, and adds, "They'll want to keep him until morning. Observation."

Katherine nods, sitting next to Cricket on the bed. Bobby plays with the bunny, tossing it up and letting Cricket catch it. "Buh!" Cricket yells.

"Say 'Uncle Bobby!'"

"Bubba!"

"Say 'bunny!'"

"Bubba!"

"Great." Bobby tosses the toy up again. "Big grown up boy, talking like a Howard Cosell." Cricket laughs and throws the stuffed animal into Bobby's face. "Oh yeah, you're your dad all over, aren't you?"

Ellen Knox leads Katherine out to the hallway. "Did you bring the guardianship papers with you?"

"No," snaps Katherine.

"Does your husband have them?" Katherine looks at the woman, who has probably seen horrors that Katherine herself can't imagine, and wonders how dumb she can be to think that the man in there is her husband. "We won't release him to you without a copy of the—"

"I'll ask him." Katherine ducks back in the room. "Cricket Spigot McGickett! How are you?" He laughs hard when she calls him that. He laughs hard, like an adult, then he gets the hiccups. He tries to roll off the bed again, but Bobby swings him onto his lap. Katherine gives him water in a paper cup. "Gulp this quick as you can." Then, to Bobby, "Honey, where are the legal guardianship papers?"

He lets the "honey" slide by without comment. "Somewhere."

Gil and the Mississippi Blonde had asked Katie and Bobby to be godparents when Cricket was born. Gil wanted to make sure Cricket had spare parents in case something happened to his real ones. "They can't release him to us without the paperwork."

Cricket says, "Mama?"

"Mama wants you to stay with Kitty and Uncle Bobby," she tell him. "Won't that be fun? We do have those papers, don't we?"

"Somewhere."

"Papa?"

Katherine pushes the buttons to make the bed go up and down to distract Cricket. "Sometimes it's fun to do stuff when Mama and Daddy aren't around to scold you." She wants to bite her tongue off the minute she says it. Cricket looks down at his bunny.

"Mama."

"Do you have them or not?"

"I think so. Gil gave me a bunch of stuff when he did his will."

"Do you know where they are?"

"Yeah. Let's see if bunny wants to come visit." Bobby holds the bunny up to his ear and leans toward Cricket. "Bunny, my man, you want to visit Uncle Bobby and Kitty?" He listens to the bunny. "He says he'll come if you'll come." He turns to Katherine. "I got them at home." A young woman brings a tray with pudding on it. "Now look at this business here," says Bobby, adjusting the bed tray to Cricket's height. "Banana pudding. You are one spoiled Daddy-O."

"You should've put them someplace safe."

"I did. I put them someplace."

Katherine keeps her voice low and leans across the bed. "They're going to take him away in the morning if we don't have those papers."

"I know that. I heard you. I know it."

"And if he's taken in by CP for even one day, I'm gonna break your stupid neck."

"Bubba!" Cricket has fed a spoonful of pudding to the stuffed animal.

"That's beautiful, honey," she tells him. "Does bunny like the pudding?"

"No."

"All the more for us," says Bobby. He turns to Katherine. "Look, I have them. Just let me make a phone call." Katherine nods and settles in next to Cricket, who leans his head against her chest. The weight of him there is almost too sweet to bear.

16

CHARLIE ENTERS MCGURK'S, FROZEN AND SHIVERING. Sheila's behind the counter and the place is near empty. Guys from the Ford plant have their poker table going; guys from Hydra-Matics are shooting pool. Charlie grabs himself a Miller from the tap and sits on a stool near Sheila.

"How's Gil doing?" she asks.

Charlie shakes his head. The mention of Gil throws him off what he came here to say. He turns around on his stool and ignores her. Back by the pinball machine there's a guy leaning against the wall in a T-shirt that says *America, Love It or Leave It.* "I swear it was this big." He holds his hands a foot apart, holding both his beer and his buddy's. "Finally had to go in and cut the thing off."

"No shit?" asks his friend, who flips the flippers on the pinball machine.

"Just went in and chopped it off."

A black couple sit in a booth in the back. Looks like they're breaking up. She's crying hard and he comes to the bar for refills and napkins for her to blow her nose. They're both wearing wedding rings. Charlie stretches his neck to see if the rings match when a hand grabs his wrist. He jumps and pulls his hand away. "Don't do that!"

Sheila scowls and shrugs her black hair off her shoulders. "I said, did you hear anything from Katie?"

"How am I gonna hear from Kate at the station?"

"Okay. Don't bite my head off. Jesus."

"Last night ain't gonna happen again." He goes on before she can reply. "I'm married. I got a chance to live a good life and I ain't gonna fuck it up. You went ahead without me, now I'm gonna go ahead without you. Don't be calling me at work or hanging around thinking I'm gonna change my mind because I won't. I got a wife now." He waits but there's no reply. "I outgrew you. That's all it is." Still no reply. "Gimme your address, I'll send you money once a month for your girl." He glances over and she's pouring ashes from one ashtray to another and back again. "Say something." Sheila shakes her head no. "Where's the kid?"

"Upstairs sleeping."

A cop walks in and sits at the bar. He puts his hat on the counter and says, "Who's bartending?"

Charlie tries not to stare. It can't be the same cop. He looks again. It is. For a moment he thinks they've caught him already.

Sheila recognizes Tavera, too. She says, "Charlie, get the old guy a drink on me."

"Old Crow," Tavera tells Charlie. "And some ice."

She reads his name plate. "What kind of name is Tavera?"

"Puerto Rican."

"Right." She turns to Charlie. "Cover the bar for me." She fades to the back of the room and picks up a pool cue. The couple in the booth are still breaking up. The woman bawls her head off while Mr. Smooth tells her it's nothing she did wrong. *"Ojo de culo,"* Sheila mutters loud enough for him to hear.

Charlie looks at Tavera like he's the last thing left at a yard sale and puts his drink in front of him.

"Charlie Simpkins." Tavera pokes at the ice in his glass. "When'd you get back?"

"While ago."

"And here you are." He takes a drink. Charlie rolls his beer bottle back and forth in his hands. All those pictures of the Mississippi Blonde and Gil and Cricket are still tucked on the mirror behind the bar. No one's touched them. Tavera looks at the picture of the four boys at Old Jerry's party. He tastes his whiskey, lets his hand fall with a slap on the bar. "When's the last time you saw Dolores Sherman?"

"Who?"

"Dolores McGurk. Mrs. McGurk."

"Last night."

Tavera sticks his pinky finger in his ear and digs around. "You got a helluva nose for the wrong place and time, you know that?"

"I could say the same about you."

"Can't blame you for holding a grudge."

"Hell, that's over," sighs Charlie.

"Dead and buried, as they say," replies Tavera. "Can I get another Old Crow? Ice on the side. And another beer for yourself. To show no hard feelings." He waits until Charlie puts the drinks on the counter. "Can you tell me who she talked to last night?"

"Hell, she talked to everyone. Why d'you cops all of a sudden care about some stupid junkie whore?"

Tavera's surprised at the sound in Charlie's voice. Didn't know he felt one way or the other about her. "She wasn't born that way," Tavera says. He takes a little slurp of his whiskey and crunches his ice. It's Charlie's turn to look surprised. They drink a little, both of them watching Sheila. She chalks her pool cue, lines up a shot, and misses.

Charlie lights a cigarette. "Look, I didn't know her."

"She was in here with her boyfriend not long ago."

"There's a prince. Why don't you go talk to him?"

"He was in custody for beating the kid. Best alibi there is." Tavera leans away from the smoke. "How'd you bruise your hand?"

Charlie looks down at his swollen knuckles. The phone rings. Charlie yells to Sheila but she ignores him. He picks it up. "Yeah?"

"Charlie, listen I need a favor."

"Where are you?"

Bobby lets out a slow breath through the line. "I'm at Beyer."

"The hospital?" Charlie says this loud enough for Sheila to hear over the music and the crying woman. "The kid there?"

"The boyfriend went after him. What else is new. I need you to run over to my place and get some papers for me."

"Now?"

"Is Katie there?" Sheila asks.

"Ask him yourself." Charlie hands her the phone.

"Is Katie there?"

"Yeah. She's gonna kill me if you don't put Charlie back on. She's on her last limb, man. You wouldn't believe the shit hole that kid was living in."

"Tell him Dolph's in jail," says Charlie.

"Dolph's in jail."

"Yeah. I hope they hang his ass." Bobby sounds more pissed than Sheila's ever heard him. "Guy's an animal. Waits until his mama leaves and starts beating hell out of him. Joy called the cops."

"Who's Joy?"

"I don't know. Some chick. Put Charlie back on . . . Charlie? Listen, go over to my place and look in the bottom drawer of my dresser. Should be some big envelopes in there."

"I don't have a key."

"God, Charlie." Bobby was nearly yelling. "Use your brain. Break in. Bring me the one with the—screw it, bring all of them. Bring everything."

"Why can't you do it?"

"Can't leave Katie by herself. Excuse me, Miss, can you tell me what floor we're on? Three? Third floor. Hurry up."

Charlie finishes his Miller in two long swallows and thanks Tavera for the drink. "Close up, will you Sheila?" And he's gone.

17

WHILE BOBBY CALLS THE BAR, KATHERINE WONDERS where she's going to take Cricket. Can't raise him in a bar. Katherine's mom's house has a neat green lawn, no newspapers blowing wet in the gutters, no police sirens all night. In Katherine's mom's house you don't curse or drink and they probably still go to church. It's been ten years since Katherine has been there. When Bobby returns, telling her that everything's taken care of with the papers, she asks him to stay with Cricket. "Don't leave him alone," she says. "I'll be right back."

She can hardly see to slide the bolt on the bathroom stall before she has an attack of diarrhea that scares her to death. The tears start. She cleans herself and sits there on the toilet seat, picking lint off her shirt and letting herself cry. She knew her father; he was a bully and a loudmouth. He had a rotten temper. But he would never do this. He would never, ever do this. After ten minutes, it isn't about her dad anymore, or how she was the one in the delivery room all through that long labor when

Cricket was born, before his mother went on the junk. It isn't seeing Cricket all beat up like that, the way P.T. used to look. It's her mom, Charlie and P.T.'s mom, Cricket's mom, all those mothers in the world who let their kids in for all kinds of hell. Mothers are supposed to have some instinct, some maternal built-in instructions about how to protect their children. Where are all the mothers?

She unrolls toilet paper to blow her nose. Another wave comes, so it doesn't do any good. She's afraid she'll get hysterical and someone'll have to come in and slap her to calm her down. She leans her forehead against the cold tile wall. It's the only thing that doesn't ache, her cool forehead. She'll have to sell the bar to pay for a lawyer. Then where will she go? No McGurk's Tap Room to come home to, no dad to come home to. Without McGurk's she may never see any of her friends again. Everything's gone. Everyone's gone. She wraps her arms around herself. She's freezing from the neck down and burning inside her head. The diarrhea has gone. By now she's crying because the door of the toilet stall hangs crooked. She looks at the sad crooked door and wonders how she's going to get out of there, how she's ever going to get Cricket home, and what she'll do with him when she gets there.

Bobby keeps up a steady stream of nonsense until Cricket's eyes droop and finally close. He closes the door quietly and asks the nurse at the desk if she saw which way Katherine went.

"Mrs. McGurk?" she asks. Bobby nods. "She asked where the bathroom was about twenty minutes ago?"

"Where's that?"

"Down the hall to your right?"

Bobby knocks on the ladies' room door. He puts his mouth close to the doorjamb and calls, "Katie girl?"

"Bobby?" Her voice comes from a tin can sunk under water.

"You all right?" He opens the door. "Come on out, girl." Two nurses come up behind him in the hallway. He steps away from the door. "Ladies."

They ignore him. The shorter one calls into the bathroom, "Do you need some help?"

"No," Bobby tells her. "We just need a little privacy is all."

The second one turns to him. She's so pale her hair is white. She takes him in—black man trying to break into the ladies bathroom—and pushes her way in the door. "Miss, are you all right?" The blonde checks over her shoulder to make sure Bobby doesn't pull a knife. "Do you want us to call security?"

The door opens wider and Katherine steps out, mascara all runny, a raccoon with the flu. She says, "My stepmother just died. I wanted some privacy." Both women back up, speaking over each other with their "sorry's" and "didn't mean to bother you's." Katherine takes Bobby's hand and they walk down the hall. "I told you not to leave Cricket."

"He's asleep."

"What if he wakes up?"

"I saw the pill they gave him. He ain't waking up 'til morning." They sit on chairs outside Cricket's door. "You want something? Coffee or something?"

"Don't leave." She wipes her thumbs across the dark smudges under her eyes. "Don't leave me."

Bobby puts his arm around her. "Bobby's staying right here."

18

As soon as Charlie leaves for the hospital, Sheila tells the couple in the back booth to get the hell out. The man looks at her with his mouth open, too surprised to do anything but get up and walk out, leaving his wallet on the table. Sheila slips it in her pocket as she clears out the poker game, too. When everyone else has gone she says, "We're closing, Mr. Police Man."

Tavera carries his whiskey and ice from the bar to the jukebox. He punches in a couple of numbers, then parks himself in a chair. Aretha Franklin's "Do Right Woman" comes on.

"I need a refill," he says. Sheila isn't built like Katherine; she can't physically throw him out. She has to climb on the second rung of P.T.'s stool to grab the Old Crow. She sees him laughing in the mirror. "Get yourself something while you're back there," he says. "My treat."

"Yes, Officer." She climbs on top of the stool to reach the good Scotch. He doesn't think this is so funny. She pours a double. "How you doing on that ice?"

"I could use some more."

She plunks his ice on the table as she walks to the pool table. Tavera turns around in his chair to watch her shoot the balls around. She has nothing else to say to him.

"¿Cuanto por una buena chingada?"

If he was trying to catch her off guard, he did it. "What did you say?"

"You heard me. How much for a fuck?"

"Sesenta dólares."

"Sixty bucks for a girl your size?"

She looks at his gut. "A john your size? We come out even."

"Play you a game of pool."

"No thanks."

"You win, I pay the sixty bucks for it. I win, I get it free."

"Jesus," she mutters. "You're worse than Bobby." She takes a few more shots on the table. "I win, it's a hundred twenty," she tells him. "You win, it's a freebie."

"Hmm."

"I'm coming out of retirement. It costs."

"When'd you retire?"

"Two years ago."

He kicks his feet up on a chair. "What you been doing since you retired?"

"Dancing."

"Where?"

"Toledo, out by the airport."

"I know that area."

"I'll bet."

"Which place?"

"Am I under arrest?" She drops the eight ball and pauses for another sip of the Scotch before racking them up again.

Tavera crunches his ice. "How about that game?" he says.

"I win, it's a hundred twenty paid up front."

"You got it."

"And you can't bust me for it afterwards."

He laughs; he sets his drink down next to hers on the jukebox, and chooses a stick. "Call each shot?" She nods. Nobody ever agreed to a hundred twenty before, not for her. When they flip for the break, he wins. He makes several attempts at conversation, but Sheila isn't having any of it. Her mind is at the hospital with Katie, at the jail with Gil.

Twenty minutes later he drops the eight ball and misses scratching by a quarter inch.

"So what do you like?" Sheila is all business, like selling a car, but she'd break a bottle over his head if she could. "You want a mommy? You want it to hurt?" She narrows her eyes. "You want a little girl? I used to get a lot of those."

"Just a straight fuck would be fine."

"Lo que tu digas, Jefe."

She shuts off the lights, unplugs the jukebox, locks up the cash register and the doors. Tavera carries empty glasses to the sink. They go upstairs where police tape blocks off half the hallway. Sheila motions for him to be quiet, then goes into the living room to check on her daughter. Rosalita is curled up on the couch under a blanket, her mouth wide open, deep in dreams.

Katherine's bedroom has a window facing the street; neon blinks through the pulled curtains. Sheila strips down to nothing as if she were alone. Tavera puts his service revolver in his shoe. When he takes off the padded vest, she says, "You're not as fat as I thought."

Immediately, he's all over her legs, her hips, and the barrel stomach that leads to small, dark nipples. He tastes them, warm and sour. He pushes her flat on the bed and rolls her over on her stomach. He runs his tongue across the back of her knees, up her thighs, and along the little fold where her legs meet. He rolls her over again; she isn't going to give a freebie without seeing who she's giving it to. He has his hands in all that hair, this time gently, while his mouth sucks down her neck, her shoulder, to breasts that fit perfectly in his mouth. The nipples are like two pebbles. He rolls them around with his tongue.

She has her arms around him, holding onto his back: not doing much, but not cheating him, either. He rolls her around the bed like a dog with a chunk of bone, his nose nudging into her legs, her ass, licking everything he finds. On her back, looking up, Sheila smiles and tells him to fuck her. It's a whore's smile, and a whore's line, but it works. He spreads her legs with his knee, and feels with his fingers, then wraps his arms around her to hold her in place while he slides into her. He keeps it like that, all the way in. Then he moves, easy at first. She looks out the window. He holds her face. "Look at me."

"Fuck you."

He kisses her mouth hard enough to leave a bruise, then pulls his head away. "Look at me."

She does. Face blank, eyes blank, she lies there while his cock fills her. He doesn't break eye contact until he comes inside her, comes harder than he has in years. When he rolls off her, she gets out of bed and peels the condom off him like she's skinning a chicken. She stays in the bathroom while he dresses, then props a couple pillows under his head and waits. She comes back in, pulls on a bathrobe, and reaches for her purse. She sits on the floor by the window and opens it four or five inches. If the cold bothers her, she doesn't show it. She lights a cigarette, ignoring him. He's not sure if she thinks he's asleep or just doesn't care.

Maybe she's waiting for someone to come back, or waiting for a phone call. Maybe she's looking at the snow.

"It wasn't fair," he tells her. "I'll give you the sixty."

She flicks ash onto the ledge and the wind carries it off. "A bet's a bet." Tavera starts to say something like he's sorry but Sheila tells him, "Don't."

He changes the subject with the grace of a bull. "Why'd you retire?"

"Got tired of it."

"What got you tired of it all of a sudden?"

"Are you interrogating me?"

"Curious."

"P.T.'s like that. Curious."

"P.T."

"Charlie's brother."

"The freak?"

She shoots him a look. "The tall one."

"Why'd you retire?"

She reaches for her pack of Viceroys and lights a fresh one. "I saw a girl get killed."

Dead people, they turn your head around. They pile up like a stack of pictures in a drawer. It doesn't matter how well you knew them when they were alive; the only snapshot that stays with you is the dead one.

"How?" he asks.

"The overtime thing, you know. I did it at first. There was all kinds of sucking and fucking in that parking lot after closing time. I'm in a guy's car, kneeling over his face. He wants me to pee in his mouth."

"Did you?"

"Sure." She takes another puff and opens the window an inch higher. "I'm squatting over this guy, pissing, looking out the front windshield. At the end of the parking lot—it's a big parking lot—this girl gets out of an old Impala. She walks across the lot. Her john starts the car up, time to go home to the wife and kids. When she's near the trash dumpster, he floors it. He burns rubber across the parking lot and hits the dumpster head on, full speed, with her pinned in between. She flops over his hood. Her purse flies over the car and I think I ought to go get it before someone takes all her money. He backs up, and the top half of her folds down like she's touching her toes. He cut her almost in half. She goes down on the pavement and the guy drives away.

"The john underneath me, he throws me off when he hears the crash. I'm in mid-piss, so it goes all over the front seat. He sees that girl laying there in pieces, and he yells at me to get out of the car. I wind up on my ass, while he peels out just as fast as the guy in the Impala. All over the parking lot, girls are flying out of cars and men are driving over the curb to get out of there.

"When the pigs finally come, there's nothing left but a couple of us girls standing around. Don't want to leave her laying there all by herself. I had a good long look at her. I saw inside that girl. I saw her broke open like a dog in the road. I never believed a person's body could look so little like that person, not like any person, not like anything human. She was making sounds, up until the ambulance came.

"I quit. No more overtime. It's not like it was some ethical thing. Everyone thinks they're immortal, you know, secretly. But not after seeing that girl. From that night on, I was something that could be killed." Sheila stares at the red end of her cigarette like it holds the whole scene inside it.

"What was her name?"

"Why you want to know that?"

"I'm curious."

"You and P.T., you'd get along like couple of guppies." She flicks the cigarette butt out the window. "Nancy. We called her Nancy." She waits for another question, but he gets up off the bed. "What about you?" she asks. "You must have some great dead body stories."

"Next time."

"Ain't gonna be no next time." She pulls away as he kisses her ear. "Leave out the back door. It'll lock itself behind you." In the dark Sheila thinks about Charlie's words. *I've moved on. I outgrew you.* Fucking strangers used to drive his voice out of her head.

She puts fresh sheets on Katherine's bed. Once Tavera's car pulls out onto the avenue, she dresses and leaves the bedroom. In the hallway, the police tape glows an angry yellow, criss-crossing the door to the other room. She reaches through the tape and pushes the door lightly. It opens five or six inches. Inside is a museum piece, a police display, a life-size model of a room. It's more than the scene of a crime; it's the scene of a murder. The rest of the world will move on, day in and day out, but not this room. It will never stop holding its breath. Just like the parking lot outside that strip club in Toledo. She packs up her daughter and walks carefully down the stairs. She pulls the plug on the neon sign and closes the door behind her. "C'mon sweetheart, let's get you home."

19

When Charlie leaves Sheila and Tavera at the bar, he drives to Bobby's apartment. The dog nearly mows him down trying to get outside. Charlie stands in the cold while the dog finishes his business. It scratches and lifts its head for a minute. Its nose twitches and the ears cock forward. "What you smelling?" Charlie looks up the street. "What is it?" It's too quiet. His heart kicks every other beat. His legs begin to chill. The dog shakes itself and waddles back upstairs. Charlie stands in the doorway and sniffs the night. He lights a cigarette and watches the dead neighborhood. One or two cars go by in no hurry. Diane is probably asleep by now.

He dumps a bunch of Gravy Train into a frying pan and sets it on the floor. A couple of African shirts lay across a dining room chair. A sunburst clock hangs in the living room with Christmas ornaments hanging from several spokes. The phone rings. It's one of the princess phones. Purple.

"Yeah?"

"Bobby my brother, I got more of those Bulovas."

"This ain't Bobby."

Click. Bobby'll skin his nuts for scaring away a contact. He rummages around and finds three or four folders in the drawer, just like Bobby said. He grabs them all and heads out. The phone rings again as he shuts the door.

~

At the hospital, he forgets what floor they're on and has to ask three people for directions. Stepping out of the elevator, he flinches at the too-bright lights Floor tiles shift position and the walls grow smaller, narrower. He takes a minute to close his eyes. Damn hospitals. At room 338 he knocks, although the door's open. He beckons Bobby into the hallway, but Bobby shakes his head and motions for Charlie to come in. Keeping his eyes away from the bed where Cricket lay, he hands the folders to Bobby. "There you go."

"I didn't ask you to bring all this."

The folders are thick with notices, newspaper clippings, doctor's letters, Bobby's endless correspondence with the U.S. government concerning his draft status. He digs around until he finds the right papers and tosses everything else onto the foot of the bed. "There you go, dearest," he says, handing them to Katie.

Charlie glances in her direction; it's a mistake. He sees just enough of Cricket to send his knees cold again. It's just a regular old hospital bed, but the bottom half of it is flat. Cricket only takes up a little space, and it doesn't look right. Charlie flexes his toes to keep them from going numb. "I gotta go."

Katie stands up. "Did you see Dad? Did you talk to him?"

"Yeah, he's okay." Charlie backs up toward the door. "He's fine."

"Fine?"

"I'll talk to you tomorrow." He ducks out, but takes another glance at the bed, at the two little feet lumps under the blankets. It isn't right. Why can't they make kid-sized hospital beds? He nearly faints in the elevator on the way down. He stands outside in the falling snow, stamping warmth back into his legs. Damn hospitals.

~

It's a short drive from Beyer Hospital to P.T.'s place. Charlie takes the outside stairs two at a time, slips on an icy step, and falls backward. He lies there on his back and blinks up at the snow zooming toward him. A face appears out of the swirl.

"Hi."

"Hi, Bro," Charlie says. "I think I broke my arm."

"Does it hurt?"

"Feels fine, except I got this bone poking out."

"Really?" P.T. bends over to look.

"No."

"Then why did you say it?"

"Why'd you ask such a stupid question?" Charlie sits up. "Hey, let's go for a walk."

"Okay."

Halfway around the block Charlie wraps his arm around P.T.'s shoulder. P.T. stoops to make it easier, munching on a handful of snow. He says, "Are you cold yet?"

Charlie shakes his head so that snow flies out of his hair. "Nope."

Charlie slips on the ice and they both fall. P.T. tries to keep his hair out of his eyes and get his brother upright at the same time. Charlie lies on his back, laughing too hard to get up. Snowflakes fall on his coat and rest there like small doilies.

"I would like to go back," says P.T.

"Not yet."

"Sheila ain't changed much, huh?" Charlie stands up with a frozen stick and rattles it against a fence while they walk. "Diane's gonna kill me." He rattles the stick all up and down the fence adjoining the sidewalk, knocking the snow off the wires, and goes on and on about Diane kicking his butt for sure, and calling her the old lady, and how she will have his balls in a sling, and all the time he thinks it's funny, so P.T. laughs too.

Charlie finds a pay phone. A moment later P.T.'s on his hands and knees looking for fresh holes in the snow where Charlie dropped his change. Charlie digs down in his pockets until his pants almost fall down. P.T. finds a nickel and a penny and slips the penny on his tongue. It's so cold he lets it fall back into his hand.

"If I have to call her collect," says Charlie, "she'll really kill me for sure. Fuck." A siren blows nearby and Charlie stands still, listening, breathing hot air into his knuckles. "Hear how pretty that sounds in the snow?"

P.T. stands up and knocks the wet snow from his knees. He wonders how many other things Charlie missed while he was gone. "Yeah."

They have walked in a big circle back to the front of the house. Charlie follows his brother to the garage and up the steps. He says, "You got a long neck."

"I know." Once inside, P.T. starts coffee and turns on the space heater. "Remember Old Jerry sleeping on the fire escape when he was drunk? And we'd tie him with the belt of his bathrobe so he wouldn't fall off?"

Charlie plops on the bed. "I really think I broke my arm."

P.T. hovers over his coffee pot. "Remember when I broke my arm?"

"You never broke your arm."

"Sure I did. It was when you were a baby."

"Oh."

"Take your coat off."

"I can't," says Charlie. "My arm's broke."

"Yes, I was pretending to be Captain Hook and I swung from that old pear tree to the clothes line only it did not hold me and I broke six of my toes. And Mom put six little splints on them so I could walk. But I broke both my arms, too. So Dad called the vet and they hung me up on one of those slings like when a horse breaks a leg? I had to stay like that for eight weeks with my arms hanging down so they would heal straight."

"No kidding."

"No kidding."

Charlie takes sip of the coffee that P.T. brings him. "How come they put you in a horse harness?"

"See it was a long time ago before they had hospitals, before you were born. So everyone just had to call the vet."

"Why didn't they call a doctor to make house calls?"

"That is what they did. But he was mostly a veterinarian so he had to carry around those horse harnesses all the time in case someone broke a bone."

They go on like that all night. When they get hungry, they pop popcorn without a lid to catch the exploding pieces in their mouths. P.T. tells stories about Steve and Rose and the other people in the house. Charlie tells stories about Diane. Charlie asks for the phone, but P.T. tells him they'll have to go up to the house because he doesn't have one of his own. They play rock, paper, scissors. They try to wake up Skuppers. P.T. reads Charlie's old letters out loud to him. They spread glue on their palms, wait for it to dry, and peel it off like a layer of skin because it feels funny. P.T. sets down the bottle of glue and lies back on the throw rug that he borrowed from Rose. He looks up at the ceiling and says, "You never want to talk about Mom."

Charlie blows on his palm, drying the glue. He, too lies on his back looking up. "Nothing to talk about."

"Do you remember the day she died?"

"No."

"Do you remember that summer at all?"

"Not much," Charlie replies, "and I don't want to."

"She used to sing to herself as she hung towels on the line," says P.T., painting a picture for Charlie.

The sky was blue and empty. Gabriel played in the yard nearby. He loved the softness of her when she held him. He wanted to squish through her skin and be inside her where it was safe. He wondered if he would hear her singing from the inside. He ran into her as hard as he could and bounced off, falling to the ground. A sound came out of her, "Umph."

She squatted down next to him with one elbow resting on the clothes basket. "What'd you do that for?"

"I don't know."

"You okay?"

"I'm okay."

"All right then." She stood up with a wet towel in her hand and shook it out. "Don't run into mama like that. It hurts."

He stayed where he fell and watched two gnats circle around a sore on her ankle. "Mama, you got gnats on you."

"They ain't hurting anything."

The grass was cold because he was in the shade. He looked around the backyard and the fields beyond. He flopped his arm into the sunlight. His skin grew warm.

"We gonna go for a walk?" He watched the light on his arm.

"Depends."

"Are we?"

"If you shake out them towels for me." Gabriel shook out a washcloth and held it in the air. He held it high until she took it out of his hand. "Thank you," she said. His dad had taken Charlie into town with him. Charlie was a year younger, so he was the baby.

Once all the towels and sheets were flapping at each other on the clothesline, the woman and the boy went for their walk. The woman carried a basket that held a trowel, a pair of rubber gloves, a paper bag, and some wax paper. The boy carried a tin bucket and shovel that he used at the lake to make sand castles. When they came across some rhubarb, the woman picked the long purple stalks and the boy broke off the big leaves at the end.

"What happens if you eat those leaves, Gabriel?"

"You die."

"That's right. What about this?" She held up the stalk.

"That's okay."

She nodded, broke off a small piece, and wiped it on her dress. "Here you go."

The boy followed his mother through the field, under the early summer sun, along the trail that had always been there. If he chewed the rhubarb long enough, the sourness turned sweet.

"I'll make pie tonight," she said. At the edge of the woods, the woman pointed to a leafy thing on the ground. "Now what's this?"

The boy looked at the leaf and rubbed his ear. He got on his hands and knees and bent his head low to peek under the leaf. There was one white flower.

"Maypole!" This was his favorite flower because it was a secret, hiding flower.

"Can you eat that?" she asked. The boy shook his head. "What happens if you pick that and put it in water?"

"You could drink the water by mistake and die."

"That's good," she said. "Don't ever monkey with maypoles." They came to the stream that ran into woods. She kept one eye on the boy, who talked to each flower that he knew. Ten feet into the woods he stopped.

"What's this, Mama?"

"Them are violets."

They were small purple velvety flowers that spread along the ground like a cool puddle under the trees. He lay down on his stomach with his face flat down in the flowers. He breathed in the smell, but a bug went up his nose so he snorted it out and turned his face to rest on his cheek. The petals were as soft and cool as his mama's hands. They were a magic carpet.

"Gabriel, get up out of there." She pulled him up by his arm. "Look at that." He looked down where his body had left a flat place. "Smashing them's as bad as picking them."

He knelt and tried to fluff the petals back into shape. "I thought it was a magic carpet."

"No such thing as magic." She knelt beside him and helped fluff, then kissed him and went back to the stream, looking for something along its edges. He named the clusters of forget-me-nots, the white stars of thimbleberry, and the buttercups. He was careful not to hurt them.

His mama had said, "Never kill a flower for fun, Gabriel. I'll swat your butt if you ever come home with a handful of wildflowers." He filled his pail with dirt, then emptied the dirt on the ground and poked through it. He found two rollie-pollies, named Cindy and Sandy.

"Baby, come here," the woman said. "I want to show you."

It was as tall as he was. "Queen Anne's lace," he said.

"No. Look at it."

The white clusters were smaller than Queen Anne's lace, and not as pretty. He reached out to smell it, but she pulled away. "No," she said. "Don't you ever touch this."

He watched while she put on her gloves and took hold of the bottom of the stalks. She dug all around it until she pulled up a root. It looked like a crazy bunch of white carrots.

"This here's a water hemlock," she said. She wrapped the root in wax paper, put it in the paper bag, and started digging again. "It's poisonous."

"Who you gonna poison?"

"Medicine," she said. "It's only poison if you don't know what you're doing."

"Who's the medicine for?"

"It's just in case."

"Just in case what?"

"Go on, now. See if you can spot any of them rabbits we saw yesterday."

While he played with a fat caterpillar in the tall grass, she wrapped more white roots in wax paper and put them in the bag. He lay still and let a slug crawl up his finger. It had two black antennae that waved at him. He waved back with his free hand. His mother closed the paper bag and put it in the basket. The sun was still bright as they walked back to the house. The woman hummed and made little jokes and even broke off a second piece of rhubarb for her son.

"Gabriel, baby, this is a secret medicine, okay? It's magic. So don't tell no one we got it, or the magic will fly out the window."

"You said there was no such thing as magic."

The breeze loosened her hair and blew her housedress against her legs. "I lied."

The woman had been sick for a long time, but it was the end of summer before her husband drove her to Beyer Hospital in Ypsilanti. When she came home a few weeks later, Charlie said, "Who's that lady? Where's Mama?"

His father smacked Charlie for mouthing off, then helped his wife into the bedroom. He was in there a while with the door closed. Gabriel heard their voices but he couldn't hear their words. He and his little brother sat on the sagging couch.

"Okay, boys." The father had come out of the bedroom. He stood in front of his sons like he always did, close enough to reach out and slap either of them. "Your mama's got the cancer, so you better lay low and not make any noise. I don't want you pestering her."

"Is she gonna die?" asked Charlie.

"Damn straight she's gonna die. And she ain't doing it in no hospital with people poking at her all day."

Charlie started to cry. His father kept his hands in his pockets, and didn't yell at him to shut up. "She wanted to come home and be with you boys. So you be sweet to her." He looked at both of them. "No matter how she looks."

There were no aunts or uncles or grandmas to help out, just Grandpa Jerry, who was an old drunk. The lady down the road, Mrs. McGurk, came in every day to do for them. She had a girl the same age as the Gabriel, and the three children were in and out of one another's homes near every day. The father went to work, and the boys would wake Mrs. McGurk out of their dad's armchair when their mama needed something.

One day Katherine was sick, so Mrs. McGurk had to stay home. The father yelled about missing a day of work when he couldn't afford it. Gabriel could call Mr. McGurk at the bar in town if there was an emergency. The father showed Gabriel how to use the phone, how to match the numbers written down. Then he dropped Charlie off at the McGurk's house on his way to work.

When he left, his mother called Gabriel. Her teeth showed through her skin. "You okay, baby? Not scared?" When Gabriel shook his head no, she said, "I need you to help me today."

She told him where the sack was buried against the old barn foundation. He used his tin shovel and dug until he found an old potato bag wrapped in a burlap sack. He put it in his tin bucket and brought it to his mother.

"Open it up careful." She didn't sound like his mama anymore, but he did what she asked. He unwrapped the burlap bag, and the potato sack. He found a little jar wrapped in white cotton. The jar held syrup or honey, he didn't know, but it was brown like medicine should be. He held it out to her.

"You know there's an angel with your name," she said.

"An angel?"

"Gabriel."

It was easy to find the father's whiskey because it was never put away. He poured some in a glass, then poured in the brown medicine.

"You gonna follow the rules?"

He nodded.

"I mean it, now."

The rules were that he had to go outside and follow the trail and memorize all the flowers he saw. The flowers were different now, the wild strawberry blossoms and the thimbleberry were gone. She told him he was not to come back to the house until his daddy got home from work.

"Listen, honey. You stay out in the field. You can even go in the woods, but don't go off the trail." She closed her eyes and swallowed a few times.

"Does it hurt?" he asked her.

"Yes. This is serious now," she answered. "If you don't do it just like I say, the magic won't work."

He tried to help her sit up but he was too small. She couldn't drink it lying down. He ran in the kitchen and found the paper straws Mrs. McGurk kept in a drawer. He held the glass while his mama sipped through the straw. When she was done, she told him to put the glass under the bed and go.

"Give me a kiss, though. That's part of it. Gotta give a kiss." She turned her face so he could kiss her cheek. It felt like rotten pears but it was his mama so he didn't mind.

"You look after your brother."

Gabriel nodded.

"You promise?"

"I promise. You gonna be better now?"

"You're a good boy," she said. "Mama loves you. Go on."

He spent the afternoon making a list in his head of the flowers he found so he could tell her every single one that night. Some were still left over from summer, the red clover and the buttercups. Even the forget-me-nots had not died yet. Their secret yellow eyes peeped out at him from blue petals. Gabriel thought they were called forget-me-nots because they were so tiny, so easy to miss, all they could do was whisper, "forget me not," so he never forgot them.

There were the purple polka-dots of chicory in the field. His mom picked chicory a few times but he couldn't remember what for, so he didn't pick any. He patted the Queen Anne's lace that looked like old ladies umbrellas, but he stayed away from the water hemlock. He saw black-eyed Susans, and hawkweed that popped out of the grass like little orange spaceships. He wandered up the trail, farther into the woods. He wondered if the magic was working back at the house. He wondered if he was really an angel.

He was thirsty. Mama said not to come back to the house. The hose lay in the back yard where he left it after watering the vegetable garden. He could get a drink from the hose. That wouldn't break the rules because he wouldn't go in the house. He could tell by the sun that his father would be home pretty soon. He'd been outside all afternoon and he was too thirsty to wait. He came up through the field, brushing his hand over the goldenrod so it left yellow powder on his hands. He stood at the edge of the yard and waited. He didn't hear anything, so he walked to the spigot and turned it, just a quarter turn. He knelt down to set his mouth as close to the ground as he could. When he picked up the hose, a little yellow butterfly landed on his wrist. He blew it away and drank for a long time before turning the spigot off. He listened. Trees swished their leaves together. The field hummed with insects. No sound came from the house except for flies buzzing. His mother's bedroom window was open, and still he couldn't hear anything, no humming or singing to tell him that she was up and walking around the house. He pulled his wooden wagon up to the window. He found a wicker picnic basket and put that on the wagon.

He had done what she said. He remembered all the flowers he saw. He had stayed away all afternoon; his father and Charlie would be home pretty soon. He wasn't going inside the house. He climbed on the wagon, then tested his balance on the picnic basket. He pulled himself up to the window and looked in.

There were flies in her room. They flew and landed all around the bed. Her arms and legs were curled in, but her back was bent the wrong way. There was blood around her mouth and throw-up all down the front of her nightgown. He smelled poop.

The paint on the windowsill flaked away underneath Gabriel's fingers. His mama's hair was tossed all over the place, and some of it was lying in blood on her pillow. Her eyes were open. They looked up at the ceiling. She was looking for the angel who would come and work the magic.

"Mama?"

The flies crawled in her hair and on her bloodstained nightgown. They buzzed around the wet brown stain on the sheets. A bluebottle fly landed on her forehead and crawled across her eyebrow. She didn't blink or swat it away. More flies tapped on the window screen beside him, trying to get in.

He had broken the rules. He had come back when he wasn't supposed to. Gabriel climbed off the picnic basket, which was bent and broken now. He put it away with the wagon. He went out to the woods and stayed there, farther down the trail than he had ever gone. Shadows of the trees took away the hot sun. He walked until he found a patch of butter-n-eggs. They blinked up at him and shivered when a breeze came up the trail. Gabriel laid himself down on the yellow blanket. He curled up and pressed his cheek to the blossoms. They were as velvety as the purple violets had been, like his mother's hand before she got sick.

He didn't answer when his father and Mr. McGurk called his name. It was after dark when they found him.

"Get yourself to the house. Now."

Gabriel got up from the ground and told the small flowers he was sorry for smashing them. The father gave Gabriel a butt whipping for running off like that. Someone had already come to the house and taken their mother away. The mother's friends worried who would take care of the two boys.

"I will," said the father, and that ended it.

After the funeral, Gabriel sat on the back porch with his brother while the grown-ups stood inside and ate. Charlie asked him about the things he had overheard at the church: people saying that their mother had done suicide, that she ate poison when she couldn't stand the cancer no more.

"They don't know anything," he said. "She was trying to get better."

"No," Charlie told him. "They said she meant to."

Gabriel kicked at a piece of porch railing, knocking loose a sliver of wood that landed on the grass. "What'd she go lying for?" Two flies circled each other near his head. "All she had to do was ask me."

Charlie said, "Dad's gonna beat your ass for kicking the railing."

The father appeared at the screen door. "Get in here and say goodbye to folks."

The mother was gone for good. Mrs. McGurk helped when she could. Then one day she left with Katie and never came back. The boys were left alone with their father for years until they went to live with their grandpa.

Charlie listens to the story P.T. tells him. He remembers the day she died, he remembers the funeral. He scowls when he hears the part where his mother made P.T. promise to take care of him, but he doesn't interrupt, doesn't ask questions. When P.T. finally falls silent, Charlie still doesn't say anything. They fall asleep just as the sun is about to rise, P.T. on the rug and Charlie on the wooden floor with his head and shoulders beneath the table. He lies there, gazing up at the washers and bolts that hold the table together, thinking about his mother and slowly drifting into dreamless sleep. P.T. has already been snoring for ten minutes.

~

When they wake up a few hours later they are quiet. Charlie takes a shower while P.T. makes toast. When Charlie reaches for his coat to leave, P.T. asks, "How's your arm?"

"Not broke anymore." He stands there with his hands in his coat pockets. "Stay around home for a while. Don't go to the bar."

"Okay."

"Don't talk to anyone about anything."

"Okay."

"You gotta promise you're not gonna do this again."

"Okay."

"No, it's not just 'okay.' I'm not gonna make it without you. You can't be messing up like this."

"It won't ever happen again."

"You swear to me?"

"I swear to you."

"You're supposed to take care of me, remember?" Charlie looks out the window over the frozen yard and hunches his shoulders inside his jacket. He opens the door and turns to P.T. "She had no right."

"Be careful," says P.T., watching Charlie go down the stairs.

"You too." Charlie waves and walks to his car. "Stay away from the bar. I mean it."

~

Charlie's wide awake on the drive home to Jackson, so awake that it feels like a dream in Technicolor. He hears each ping of the pebbles beneath his tires. He sees the wind rushing up over the hood. He feels a pulse in his eyelid, his knuckle, places he never knew he had a pulse.

Diane sits at her desk at work. She has survived two nights of Johnny Carson without Charlie. She has survived two days of snowstorms and nausea. She has a dozen phone calls to make, inspections to check, an appointment with a new client at 11:00 A.M., and a closing that she is not prepared for. She has a parking ticket to pay, a hair appointment later that afternoon, and stains on the kitchen floor where she spilled a glass of grape juice that morning. She sits with hands folded on her lap. She stares at a paper clip, willing it to move with her mind. It takes an enormous amount of concentration. Once it moves, just a tiny bit, she'll be able to think about work. She's been at it since she arrived forty-five minutes ago.

"Diane?"

"Hmm?"

"You gonna get that?"

The phone on her desk is ringing. She picks it up, still staring at the paperclip. "Diane Simpkins."

"It's Maria. You got someone here to see you."

Diane panics and checks her watch. "Who is it?"

"Says he's your husband?"

"I'll come out." The whole department watches her run out the door, down the hall. "Charlie."

"Hey, babe." He hugs her. She tries to freeze the hug in her mind so she can replay it when he leaves again. She leads him to her cubicle, settles him in her chair, and seats herself on the desk close to him. "I wanted to see where you work. Never seen where you work before." He crosses his arms on her knee and lays his head down. "I'm wiped out, babe."

She rubs his head and neck. "Oh, Charlie."

He sits up and runs his hands through his hair, trying to straighten himself up. "I'm sorry."

"Come on, let's go home."

"Will you sit with me and rub my head until I fall asleep?"

Three or four heads peep up from their cubicles as she leads him out. It's the Vietnam vet, the crazy missing husband, looking just like they pictured him. "Tell me everything when we get home."

Once they're in the car, she starts crying. "Oh, Jesus, Diane. Don't cry." He bangs his head against the side window. "Don't fight with me."

She takes his hand and holds it against her cheek. "I'm happy."

When she gets him home and in bed, Charlie clings to her. "Gil's little wife died," he tells her.

"I'm sorry." She rubs his head like she promised, brushing his hair back from his forehead again and again. It's grown out, getting long again. He falls asleep. Still she rubs his head, looking down at him and thinking what life is going to be like when he leaves again: getting through the day at work, picking up some take-out on the way home, quiet evenings looking out the window as the dark comes. She won't pick up the phone when it rings. She'll have lunch with Sue once a week. She'll make herself a cup of tea and go to bed at exactly ten o'clock each night. Charlie makes a sound halfway between fatigue and pleasure, and lays his arm across her leg.

20

WITHIN THREE WEEKS, MCGURK'S LOOKS MORE LIKE *Romper Room* than a bar. Bobby brings another stuffed bear every time he walks in the door. He even let Cricket name the dog; everyone has to call him Mister Grizzlybutt. Gino hasn't been around much since the night of the blizzard, the night the Mississippi Blonde "did all of us a favor and died," as he put it.

"I heard what the bitch let her boyfriend do to Gil's kid," he told Bobby. "I seen what some of them gook women would do to save their kid's life—suck off a GI while another one holds a gun to her baby's head."

"That's beautiful, Gino."

"And then you have this lousy bitch."

"You ought to do a travel guide."

"Can't think of nothing but the next hit."

"Careful where you're throwing stones there, buddy."

Gino decided to stay away from Bobby after that remark. Tonight he's agreed to loan him an extra van, but only because he needs the money. When he walks into the bar, a blanket covers four chairs that are lined up in a row. From inside, someone makes the sound of a train. P.T. looks up from behind the bar. "Katie went to see Gil. What is wrong with you?"

"Toothache."

"Whoo-whoo," yells Cricket under the blanket.

"How much does it hurt?"

Gino curls up on the seat of a booth. "Like I'm dying."

"Did you go to a dentist?"

"Choo-choo whoo!" The front of the blanket flaps up and down.

"Who let a train in here?" Gino asks with his hands over his eyes. Cricket giggles under the blanket. "P.T., how'd a goddamn train get in here?"

Cricket giggles again. He whispers, "Whoo."

"Did you go to a dentist?"

"No."

"Do you want some aspirin?"

"No."

"Do you want something besides aspirin?"

Gino tilts his head to look out from under the table. "I just took something."

"What?"

"Choo! Whoo!"

"Never mind."

"I'll get you something else."

Gino lowers his head back down in the booth. No use arguing. P.T. lurches upstairs to get something to kill the pain. Gino lies on his back, in the seat of a booth, staring up at the ceiling fan. It's keeping almost perfect time with the pounding pulse in his jaw. Phoomph, phoomph, phoomph, like a giant fan. Phoomph, phoomph, phoomph, like a heartbeat. When he closes his eyes it sounds like chopper blades over his head.

"This will make you better," says P.T. standing over him.

"I don't want it."

"But it will make you feel better."

Gino takes the glass and drinks it. When he lies back down to watch the fan, it's just a goddamn ceiling fan. He should get up and call Charlie. P.T.'s not supposed to be at the bar. He'll get up in a few minutes.

"Would you like to go up in Katie's room?"

Gino blinks at P.T. a few times, standing so far above him. "Meeting Bobby."

"Oh." He pulls on his lip. "Would you like a pillow?"

"Nuh."

When he wakes up, half a dozen people are sitting around drinking, none of them anywhere near his booth. All the kid's toys have disappeared except a couple of couch cushions on the floor where Cricket plays with his toy barnyard. The jukebox is unplugged, so it's before six. Gino sits up in the booth. The pounding in his jaw returns. Someone's talking. The words aren't sinking in so much as the volume. He was feeling so good, sound asleep, half dead. He's all slippery from the heroin, so he sits there holding on to the table and looks around some more. P.T.'s still behind the bar. He's talking to a man in a tan overcoat. They're laughing and talking loud enough to wake a rock. Gino makes his way over to P.T. "Get me a Seven and Seven before I go under again." He balances himself on a stool next to the man in the overcoat. "Who's your friend?"

P.T. smiles. "This is George Tavera. And this is my friend Gino Firenzi."

Tavera. Gino remembers the name. He clenches his jaw; the toothache explodes across his face. He nods an acknowledgment to Tavera and carries his drink to the pay phone at the back of the bar. It picks up on the second ring. "It's Gino. . . . Yeah, I'm fine. . . . Toothache . . . Thanks, yeah. Listen, your brother's down here with that cop."

"I appreciate it," Charlie says into the phone. "No, it's no problem." He listens for a while, nodding his head. "That sounds like him, don't it? I'm on my way." He hangs up the phone, sits back down at the kitchen table.

"Who was it?" asks Diane.

"No one."

"Pass me the corn, please."

Charlie scrapes a heap onto his plate before passing the bowl to Diane. She watches the clock above the sink; seventy-two seconds go by before he speaks.

"Chicken's good."

She smiles instead of saying thank you. That's something her mother did that drove her up the wall. If she wasn't saying "Thank you," it was "I'm sorry."

"You know what Mike Sovinsky did today?" Charlie has a drumstick in one greasy hand, pointing it at his wife between bites. "What a dumb son of a bitch. He gets two plates in one socket, doesn't notice until the die comes down and *crack*. Now they gotta order a new die. I thought Delveccio was gonna blow a vein in his neck."

"Have I met Mike?"

"He's the one with the fingers. You met him."

Mike Sovinsky's missing both his index fingers. "Born without them," Charlie said once. "Just as well. He's so dumb, he'd have lost 'em sooner or later." Now Charlie grins at Diane over his drumstick. "How was your closing?"

"It went all right," she says, pouring salt all over her corn. "Everyone signed everything."

"Was that guy still a prick?"

"Yeah." The lawyer for the sellers. Expensive shirt, sincere face, gold-plated jerk. "Wasn't doing him any good, though."

Charlie likes to hear about her job, the different clients week after week, all the drama people go through when they're buying a house. "I gotta stare at the same ugly faces all day," he says. "Ain't no one said nothing new since day one. How much you make off it?" he asks.

"Five hundred and thirty."

"Jesus, girl." He laughs and takes a long pull of Miller. "Keep it up."

She looks across the table as he wipes his face with a paper towel. He gets all the grease off in one swipe, wads up the paper towel, and bounces it on his plate to signal that he's done.

"I love you," she tells him. He looks up, surprised like always. He uses his tongue to get at something stuck in his molars.

"That was Gino on the phone." He keeps working at the piece of chicken stuck in his teeth. "I gotta run over to Ypsi."

"Something illegal?" It's out of her mouth before she can stop it. He gets the piece of food and flicks it toward the sink. He's annoyed. She goes on. "What did he want?"

"Just some business."

"What kind of business?"

He doesn't look mad, but he stares out that window like it has bars on it. He says, "Don't worry about it."

"Don't worry about it." She nods her head up and down, her voice shaking. "Okay, I won't worry about it." She pushes her chair back from the table. "I won't worry about it so much, I won't even take messages for you anymore. Why don't you get your own personal operator?"

"What the—" He leans toward her. "Have I done one goddamn thing wrong? Have I?"

"Against the law? No."

"What's that mean?"

"It's not what you're doing or not doing." She backs up and stands against the counter to steady herself.

"Then what is it? What's up your ass all the time?" He's felt this coming for three weeks, ever since he disappeared for those two days. He never volunteered any information and she never asked, but she's been stewing. Now he wants to hit her. She wishes he would. Human contact. "What the hell do you want from me?"

"I want you to . . ." Her face burns red with the effort not to cry. "I want you to admit it."

"Admit what?"

"You wish you were out there right now, stealing or robbing or whatever it is you do so well that you're wasting your talent at Stewart Tool and Die."

He looks at her like she knew he would: snake-eyed and disgusted. "Hell, yeah, I wish I was out there." He gestures around the kitchen. "You think I like sitting here every night bored out of my fucking mind? This ain't how I grew up, okay?" His voice slams into her like an open palm. "Mommy and Daddy didn't sit down to supper every goddamn night with vegetables and all this shit."

"Keep going."

"We didn't have fluffy little goddamn dish towels." He throws a quilted pot holder at her. She stays where she is; the pot holder bounces off her shoulder and lands at her feet.

"Are you done?"

He doesn't answer. The kitchen vibrates with their anger. She doesn't care that she has tears all over her face, doesn't care if he sees them. She wouldn't care if he sat there and watched her bleed to death. She looks at the quilted pot holder at her feet, at the teddy bears all over it, and wonders where she got it, what something that stupid is doing in her house.

Then he says, "I gotta go out for a while."

"When are you going to treat me like a wife?"

"I bring you my paycheck," he says. "I fuck you damn near every night."

"That's not treating me like your wife."

"I take out the garbage."

"So stupid."

"Watch your mouth, I swear—"

"Don't you tell me to watch—"

"And don't *you* ever call me stupid or a dumb ass or a worthless fuck."

"I never called you anything like that."

"I'm going out." He leans against the door frame chewing on his thumbnail. "You're crazy, you know that?"

"When are you going to trust me?"

He shrugs with his thumbnail still in his teeth. "I trust you."

"Not to run off and screw the pharmacist, maybe."

"What pharmacist?"

"It was a figure of speech. I made it up." She leans her head back against the cupboard. "You never tell me what's going on. You keep half your life a secret from me. You won't talk to me about the nightmares anymore."

"That ain't nothing."

"Yeah?" She shows him the bruise on her ribs.

"What's that?"

"You did that. In your sleep."

He looks at the bruise and sighs like he's the most persecuted man in the state of Michigan, like he'd give his right arm for someone who understood him. That sigh, once she hears that, she shuts up.

"Don't give me that look," he says.

"What look?"

"Like you're not gonna waste any more breath on a goddamn idiot."

She sits down at the table and lights one of his cigarettes, pulls the ashtray towards her, and puts her feet up on the nearest chair. "I thought you had somewhere to go."

"When did you start smoking?"

"When I saw how glamorous it made you look."

"Bitch."

She looks him in the eye. "Stupid, dumb-ass, worthless fuck."

He takes two steps toward her and slaps the cigarette out of her hand. She's too surprised to pick it up. He steps on it, makes a big black smudge on the linoleum floor. A long silence. Charlie starts with his long-suffering sigh but stops himself. Instead, he sits down across from her and says, "What about you, huh?"

"What about me?"

"Admit you liked it better when I was in 'Nam."

It's like a pail of water in her face. He's got one sleeve rolled up, showing another tattoo. He keeps adding them, one after another. This one has a blue dragon head with red eyes and flames, a sword piercing through it. That's how she feels right now, on fire and pierced right through. There's a banner underneath it that says, "Brave and Bold." He doesn't look so brave and bold with his sleeve coming unrolled and falling in the chicken gravy.

"Got nothing to say?" He leans back in his chair and clasps his hands behind his head. She could punch him in the stomach before he'd have time to protect himself. "You never had to worry about where I was, who I was with, what I was doing, except getting my ass shot off."

"There was one good thing about you being over there."

"What's that?"

"I couldn't get pregnant."

He looks hard at her. "You better not be."

"Yeah, I am."

"Who's the father?"

"God, Charlie. Who do you think?"

"I don't know, Diane. You had all those orgies and shit."

"They weren't orgies."

"Going at it with two guys at once."

"I was eighteen. Stop it."

"All that shit you wrote in your letters."

"I only told you that stuff because we were friends."

"Just friends."

"I didn't think you'd marry me and go throwing it in my face."

"You been doing the guys over at the VA hospital all this time?"

"That's rotten. You know how rotten that is." He doesn't seem like Charlie anymore. His eyes are flat like P.T.'s. She hears another voice in her head, a voice that came through the soft night air of South Carolina. *Diane, honey. I could never hate you.* She looks squarely at the man in front of her until that voice goes away. "It's your baby and you know it."

"I ain't raising any goddamn kid. I don't care whose it is."

"All of a sudden I'm not good enough to have your kids?"

"Ain't gonna be no kids. Get that straight now. You decide you want to be pregnant? Just to put more shit on me? Why do you want to have a kid with me?" Images of Cricket in the big hospital bed jump up in front of him, bruises, concussions, P.T., Rosalita. He lifts the gravy bowl and bangs it down hard on the table. "You seen P.T. You heard about my dad. Old Jerry was the solidest man in the family and, babe, he told everyone it was his seventieth birthday, right? He was fifty-nine. You never saw what he looked like. You never met him or Dad or Ma. You don't know shit. Ma wouldn't protect herself, wouldn't protect us. She'd have P.T. out playing around with her goddamn garden. 'Oh look, growing things, life is beautiful.' Fucking chicken-shit bitch. You're just like her. Naïve, useless, thinking that things are all right if you think so, and you say so, and you believe so, even though you know damn well things ain't all right. Then you figure it out one day. You figure out that shit ain't right, and what do you do? Kill yourself. She fucking killed herself. Bitch did the biggest whine of them all, and did it front of her own kid. You gonna kill yourself when you figure out things ain't perfect? You don't understand shit and you know it."

She was wrong if she had thought that having him would be worth whatever pain came when he left. She thought they'd live happily ever after, right up to the day he disappeared. She thought she'd have little reminders to look at when he was gone. She didn't know he'd still be walking around, talking, close enough to touch, and a million miles off.

"I used to be like my ma. I used to think things weren't so bad, things could get better. But I went around the world and found out just how bad things can get. I got my shit set straight in a hurry and I ain't a stupid cunt no more. P.T.'s as bad as Ma, but he's my brother so I gotta stick to him no matter what. But why I married you, I don't know. Lonely and the world looks like it ain't never gonna be the same, and there's someone who swallows your bullshit and you go and marry her. Crazy shit."

"That's all it was?"

"I can't hang around here. I'll come visit some time. I mean, we can be friends if you want, but I gotta go. This is bullshit." He picks up his coat. "You can see other guys, I mean, you can fuck around all you want. Divorce me. I don't care. Look Diane, you don't want me around when I turn into anyone's dad, okay?" He puts his coat on and reaches for his keys. "I don't want to be around no kids. I don't want no family. I don't want to be here. That's it. I don't want to be here."

She breathes in the emptiness where he stood just a minute ago. She looks at the pot holder at her feet. She opens the door after him and yells, "Don't come back, you goddamn son of a bitch."

21

CHARLIE'S AT MCGURK'S BY SIX-FIFTEEN. WHEN HE gets there, Bobby's in his usual seat at the bar, watching the news, muttering to the dog who sits at his feet. P.T.'s working the bar and there's Tavera talking to him all cozy across the bar.

"Hey, Bro." He takes off his jacket and hangs it up after nodding to Tavera. "Where's Gino?"

"Hi, Charlie. In the bathroom."

"What are you doing here?"

"Katie asked me to baby-sit. She went to see Gil."

Cricket stands by the juke box, banging away at it with a Tinker Toy. Charlie grabs a stool beside Tavera and sits. "Can I get a Miller?" He watches his brother, trying to figure what they've been talking about, but P.T. won't look at him. He keeps wiping the rag in a little circle on the counter, staring at it. "Hey. A Miller?"

Tavera turns to Charlie beside him. "How you doing?"

"Doing good. How you doing?"

"I was just asking your brother here how often Dolores Sherman came here."

"Who?"

"Mrs. McGurk."

"I don't know. We don't come in that much."

"Who's we?"

"Tavera." Charlie shakes his head, disappointed. "I thought you knew everything. Me and my wife."

"Uh-hum." Tavera nods like this fits something he already knows. "They got a pretty solid case against your friend."

"So?" Charlie keeps looking at P.T. and P.T. keeps not looking back. Gil's arraignment is in a few days. Bail was too high for even Bobby to scrape up the money.

"Doesn't look like he's going to have any defense that amounts to anything," said Tavera. "What if he didn't do it?"

"Then he goes free." Charlie shrugs. "Ain't that what the American justice system is all about?"

"Would you testify in his defense? If I had evidence that he didn't do it?"

"Why you want me?" Charlie's head begins to pound. "Why not P.T.? Or Bobby over there?"

"I already asked him." Tavera motions toward P.T., who responds with a big, fake smile. "He said he'd be happy to."

"Congratulations."

"Maybe we could all work together to help Mr. McGurk," Tavera continues. "You never did tell me how you got those bruises on your hand."

"What the fuck?" Charlie shoves his beer away like he's about to get up and split. "Why is it, every time I take a shit these days, I see you climbing up my asshole?" Charlie's words echo in the quiet bar. Tavera makes a face like he's offended.

P.T. says, "Why are you mad?"

"Because if there's anything worse than a hemorrhoid, it's a hemorrhoid with a badge."

Tavera presses on. "Anything you can tell me about your friend's case?"

Charlie takes a long pull of his beer. "Other than he beat the living hell out of her? No." P.T. looks up at Charlie with puzzled eyes, about to say something. Charlie all of a sudden turns on the bar stool. "Jesus Christ, Cricket get away from there!" Cricket jumps and starts crying. Tavera and P.T. both look over and see the kid near the plug for the jukebox, sitting on the ground bawling. "Bro, get that kid away from the plug."

Cricket howls because Charlie yelled for no reason. He wasn't hurting anything, just playing with his toy barnyard set, opening and closing the barn door so it said *moo* over and over. P.T. hurries over to him to make sure he's not electrocuted. Charlie scowls at Tavera like it's his fault the kid was almost killed, asking P.T. questions and distracting him.

"Go ahead, buddy." P.T. rocks the kid on his lap with his arms wrapped around him like a human cage. "Go on and cry, buddy."

"Your brother told me a story about dressing up in the victim's slip and wearing her nail polish the night she died."

Charlie smiles. "Well, that's my brother for you."

"What about you?"

"I don't go for nail polish."

"When's the last time you saw Sheila Alvarez?"

The change of subject throws Charlie, but he shrugs like he barely remembers who she is. “I don’t know. Three weeks, maybe.”

“That long?”

His eyes shoot over to the cop. He shifts so he’s facing him with one hand still on the bottle. “Whatever shit you got on her,” he says, “that’s her problem.”

Gallant bastard, Tavera thinks. “She still a pro?”

“You been doing your homework. You tell me.”

“Don’t you know?”

“She’s straight.”

“Yeah?”

“You already know it. What’re you asking me for?”

“When’s the last time she turned a trick, exactly?”

Charlie sits looking over at his brother as if he hadn’t heard the questions. Charlie runs through the night the Mississippi Blonde died, leaving the two of them in the bar. Then, “Couple years, maybe.”

“That long?”

“Far as I know.”

“Far as you know,” Tavera repeats for emphasis. “She wasn’t friendly with Dolores Sherman?”

“Only knew her for a little while a few years back.”

“Before you killed your grandpa.”

Charlie swings around back to face the bar. “Yeah, before I killed my grandpa.” He pulls the tail of his work shirt out of his pants and leans both elbows on the bar, flashing a “fuck you” smile. “Jesus, can’t a guy live anything down?” He chuckles like he’s forgotten about Sheila already. Tavera can’t help but smile also. Far as he’s concerned Charlie Simpkins is going down a second time, but he can’t help liking the guy.

A few hours later, Katherine arrives, stamping snow off her boots. The place is doing okay business for this hour on a Saturday. Bobby's behind the bar. "Where's P.T.?"

"Upstairs getting chewed out by Charlie," he says.

"Kitty!"

"Hey Pootchie McGickett." She comes behind the bar and kisses Cricket on top of his head. He smells like baby sweat: sour and sweet. "What's Charlie's problem?" She tosses her coat in the back room and puts on a clean apron. Bobby's on the stool next to Cricket's highchair, holding up a soggy card from a poker deck.

"What's this?" Bobby asks. "What number you got there?"

"Buh," says Cricket.

"Seven. That's right. That's what you got."

"What's the matter with Charlie?" she asks again.

"Some cop came in. P.T. was talking to him." Bobby shuffles the cards. "P.T. said you were supposed to be back an hour ago."

"I went for a drive."

"A drive?"

"Yeah, do you mind? Is it illegal?"

"How's Gil?" When Katie shrugs, Bobby finishes shuffling and sets the deck on the tray of the highchair. "Cut, please," he says. Cricket cuts the deck. "Thank you."

"I went to visit my mom."

"I thought you and her weren't talking." He deals the cards.

"I was thinking she might make a better grandma than she did a mom." Bobby looks at her like she's out of her mind, but keeps still. "I thought maybe it'd be better if I moved back there with Cricket. Bring him up in a nice home, you know?"

"How'd it go?"

"How do you think?"

"I'm sorry."

"Yeah." She combs Cricket's hair with her fingers.

Bobby lays his top card face up. Cricket fumbles his top card until it turns over. "Who wins?" asks Bobby.

"Bubba," says Cricket.

"That's right." Bobby turns to Katherine. "We play aces low."

"What did the cop want?" she asks.

"I don't know." He looks at Cricket's new card. "What do you have?"

"Dog."

"Five. That there's a five." Bobby flips over a two. "Who wins?"

"Dog."

"Dog's not playing. You win." Cricket claps and reaches for the two cards. "Soon as the cop left, Charlie grabbed P.T. and hauled him upstairs."

Cricket turns over his card. "Mama."

"Eight. Say 'eight.'"

"Aye."

"Eight, right. Oh, now look here. We both got eights, so now we gotta have war."

"Wah!" Cricket shrieks. He pushes a pile of cards to the floor in excitement. Katherine helps pick them up, uses a rag to dry the drool and spilt beer off them. Bobby places three of his cards face down, then helps Cricket with his. They watch each other like thieves. Bobby lays down his fourth card face up: six of diamonds. "What is it?"

"Dog," says Cricket.

"Six," Bobby says. "Turn yours over."

Cricket gets his fourth card turned over by himself, a queen. He looks at it and screams so loud that everyone at the bar turns to look.

"Me! Me!" Cricket pulls the cards toward him. Bobby puts out his hand to stop him.

"What is it? What's your card?"

Cricket stares at his card for a long time. "Mama?"

"Close enough," says Bobby. "You robbed me blind, buddy."

"Good job, Pootchie." Katherine rubs his back. It's tiny.

Bobby says, "You shuffle now." He gathers up the cards and stacks them on the highchair tray. Cricket spreads them back and forth, bending the corners back and making shuffling noises that blow drool out of his mouth. Looks for a minute like a normal happy kid.

"Bobby."

Bobby turns his attention to her. "What's up?"

"I'm gonna ask Gino to marry me."

"You're what?"

"Gino likes kids. I don't want to raise Cricket in a bar. We could move in with him."

"Keep shuffling, buddy. You do it better than me." Bobby sits on the stool and lets Cricket stick cards into his mouth. "You know he doesn't like girls."

"He doesn't like sex with girls. But you can't say he doesn't like me as a person. Right?"

Cricket waves a card at her. "Kitty, you."

"Thanks, Pootchie." She opens her mouth and he sticks a card into it.

"No way he's gonna go for it, girl."

"He doesn't have to fuck me or pretend or anything like that." She takes the card out of her mouth. "He just has to be Cricket's dad. We'd have a good home for him. Gino could do whatever he wants with whoever he wants, I wouldn't care."

"Yes you would."

"I wouldn't complain. I wouldn't try to stop him." A guy calls for four Black Labels at the other end of the bar. Katherine jerks the tap hard. "You don't have to be such a drag," she says to Bobby. "It could work." She fills the mugs, carries them over to the guy, then pulls out a clean rag and starts on the ashtrays, looking just like her dad. "I'm selling the bar to pay for Dad's lawyer. I'll have some money left over but it won't be enough to get a decent place on my own." When he doesn't answer, she continues impatiently. "This is business. This is for Cricket's sake. I'm not asking him to support us. We'd split the rent."

Bobby's busy putting the deck of cards back together, but now he slaps them down on the tray and says, "Damnit girl, what's wrong with you?"

"What?"

"Are you playing games or are you stone blind?"

"I gotta get Cricket to bed." She pulls the tray out of the highchair as Cricket kicks and laughs. "Will you cover until I get him laid down?"

"Katie girl—"

"Please?"

"Go on then," he says. "Careful going up there. Charlie's ripping him hard."

She nods, pulls off the apron, and hurries up the stairs with Cricket, who waves halfway up. "Uncka Bubba!"

"Bobby," he says. "Uncle Bobby."

She and Cricket lie on the bed in her room. He burrows under the covers, curled against her stomach. Charlie and P.T. argue in the living room. She wants to tell Charlie to shut his damn mouth. She hasn't heard him like this since he got back from the service. Cricket plays with the locket she made for him. There's a picture of Gil on one side and his mama on the other.

"Who's this?" she asks Cricket.

"Papa."

"That's right, your papa. He's the nicest man anyone ever met."

"What else did you tell him?" Charlie yells. She can't hear much because P.T. has a quiet voice and he's talking softly. "How long was he here before me?" Mumble. "What did he say?"

Long pause where she can't hear anything at all. Cricket points to the locket. "Go see Mama."

The Mississippi Blonde's funeral couldn't even be called a funeral. They cremated her after the autopsy. There was only Katherine, Bobby, and Cricket at the little service. Couldn't find any family for her.

"No, McGickett. Can't see Mama. She can see you, though. She sees what a great kid you are. Wave to Mama." They both wave at her picture. "Now close your eyes, okay?"

P.T. talks softly for a while, then Charlie explodes. "Because you were here when I told you to stay away."

P.T. speaks louder. "She asked me. Do not yell."

"Why's he all of a sudden talking about Gil not doing it? Huh?"

"I do not know."

"Why's he all of a sudden asking me how I bruised my hand?"

"I do not know."

"This is not the time for any of your wild-ass stories, Bro. Did you tell him I was in that room?"

"No."

Katherine lies stone still, not sure she's hearing correctly.

"This time they will put me away for good," Charlie says. "Do you know that?"

"You did not do anything wrong."

There's no more yelling after that. Cricket breathes hard through his mouth, asleep at last. Katherine gets up softly so he won't wake up. At the door she hears Charlie's voice, quiet, hard, and hot. She locks the door slowly so they won't hear it click, then lies back down with her cheek against the top of Cricket's head. After Charlie leaves, P.T. moves around in the kitchen for a while. Water runs in the sink, then he goes downstairs. It's loud on Michigan Avenue, trucks and sirens all over the place. Inside Katherine's bedroom it feels quiet like a grave.

Charlie and P.T. are the closest she's ever had to brothers. Charlie used to beat the hell out of any guy that gave her trouble. Charlie, who hasn't been the same since he got back. Everyone is slipping through her fingers. She lays her cheek on Cricket's head and tries to sleep.

22

LATER THAT NIGHT, BOBBY STANDS IN A PARKING LOT near Ford Lake and watches as the wind pushes the water around. With a breeze going up and down his arm and the smell of burgers and fries in the air, Bobby feels like whistling "Dock of the Bay." It's freezing out, but the moon looks nice on the water. Gino's in the truck, sleeping. They've been waiting fifteen minutes. Five more, and Bobby's out of there.

Headlights swing down the restricted road. A woody station wagon approaches. Behind the wheel is a kid wearing a ponytail and a Rolling Stones T-shirt. Bobby wants to jump in the truck and tell Gino to head out—forget the deal. Bobby knows better than to do business with baby honkies like this, but he needs the money. Raising one little kid costs more than three apartments. Gino stays behind the wheel, in the shadows. The kid steps out of the station wagon and pushes a loose strand off his forehead. His long hair makes him look like Katherine. Bobby flips his cigarette into the water and sighs. Where are all the professionals? Where are the old guys you could trust?

"Hey," says the kid.

"You got it?"

The kid nods, rubbing his arms and shooting looks in all directions like a bad imitation of a junkie.

"Let's see it."

The kid unlocks the back of the station wagon and pulls it open slowly, like something might jump out and start humping his leg. The smell hits hard. Bobby'll have to drive back downtown with that smell in Gino's van and listen to him bitch about it all the way. Inside the station wagon are six one-hundred-pound bags of coffee beans sitting upright and held in place with seat belts. Three more are wedged in the back. One just about falls to the ground before the kid catches it with his knee.

"You said ten."

"In the front," he grunts under the falling bag. "On the floor in the front."

The bags are heavy. Gino stays put behind the wheel while the other two load them up. Bobby sits on the back fender and catches his breath when they're done. The kid's no longer nervous. He leans against the open door of the truck and pushes the same strand of hair out of his eyes.

"Okay, so I delivered, right?"

"Yeah." Bobby wants to tell him to get his punk ass out of there before he shoots a couple holes in it, but he's a professional; he pulls out his wallet and hands the kid two hundred dollars in clean tens and twenties. "Don't spend it all in one place, sonny boy."

"I won't, asshole." He stuffs the money deep in his back pocket. "You're under arrest."

Gino pounds the accelerator. Bobby falls off the fender. When he hits the ground, two bags fall out after him, split open, and bury him under a mountain of coffee beans. He sits there with the cop holding a gun to his head and watches Gino drive away. A squad car rolls out of the shadows. They take away Bobby's .32 and put him in the squad car. Bobby thanks God that Gino wasn't caught; he doesn't want to listen to the bitching.

They hold him overnight. Late the next morning, Bobby sits in the sweat room with an ashtray on a table in front of him. The cuffs are off. He ignores the cigarettes they sent in for him. Jorge Tavera takes his time, watching through the one-way mirror. The door opens and a guy with a folder and clipboard enters.

"Hello, Mr. Royce. I'm Don Fisher." Fisher says all this before he closes the door. Then he walks to the table on the balls of his feet, as if he doesn't want to get his shoes dirty. "I've been assigned to represent you." He sits down right next to Bobby, who scoots his chair away. "You want to tell me your version of events?"

"I was busted buying a half a ton of stolen Colombian," says Bobby. The guy looks blank, then turns white. "Coffee," Royce adds.

"Right." The lawyer gives a high chuckle.

"You been a public defender long?"

"Nineteen months."

"Nineteen months. How you liking it?"

"It's okay."

"Must meet all types, huh?"

Tavera enters the sweat room and slams the door for effect, then tosses Bobby's file on the table. "George Tavera." He holds out his hand. Bobby looks at it like it's holding a turd. "You want some coffee?"

"Ain't you the funny one."

"Don Fisher," says the lawyer. "Public defender."

Before the lawyer's butt hits the chair, Tavera tells them he'll cut a deal.

"What for?" Bobby asks.

"My client is not prepared to—"

"Hey, friend." Bobby looks at the lawyer. "I'll talk until I point to you, then you talk. Got it?" Fisher gets busy jotting something down on his clipboard while Bobby lights a cigarette.

Tavera tells him, "Sorry, but I'm allergic."

Bobby looks up at Tavera while he stubs out the cigarette. "How come I know your face?"

"Got any idea why I want to talk to you?" Bobby shakes his head no. Fisher looks up when Bobby is silent, waiting for a sign that doesn't come. "I want to talk about Charlie Simpkins." Bobby rubs his hands together between his knees. Tavera waits. "You've known him a long time, right?"

"Yeah."

"About what? Eleven or twelve years?"

"Maybe longer." Bobby plays with the cigarette pack, crackling the cellophane in his hand to see how annoying it'll get.

"You two were in the joint at the same time."

Bobby laughs. "Juvie. Not the joint."

"Grew up together, you could say."

"Nice guy," he says. He folds his arms and tucks his hands under his armpits.

"Served his country in 'Nam."

Bobby gives a big grin. "Doesn't mean he's not a nice guy."

Tavera makes a big show of flipping through Bobby's file. "Draft board says you got some medical problems, huh?"

The grin vanishes. Bobby leans forward and looks at Tavera like the age, the clothes, even the hair offends him. "Listen up, Pork 'n Beans," he says. "You bring us in, we're the bad guys, right? And you know we're gonna do it again as soon as they acquit us or mistrial us."

"That's not my concern."

"What if they sneak your bad guy off to the army, teach him how to be a man, fight for his country? It's gotta be a stone drag keeping America safe, scraping shit like us off the streets so they can send us overseas." He leans forward in his chair. "What kind of man you got coming home, huh? Nice squeaky clean family man?"

Tavera skips over the draft deferments and looks at the criminal record. "You deal in some exotic merchandise."

Bobby's eyelids lower. "You gonna tell me how to run my business?"

"Caught with a stolen Sphinx Hairless worth twenty-five hundred dollars."

"I thought it was a really old Chihuahua." Fisher wants to know what a Sphinx Hairless is. "Naked cat," Bobby tells him. "Ugly motherfuckers. Look like your grandmama's twat."

Fisher blushes. Tavera lets the folder fall shut. "Did you see anyone go upstairs the night Dolores McGurk was killed?"

Bobby's thrown. "I don't know."

"Did you see her go upstairs?"

"Maybe."

"Did you see Charlie Simpkins go upstairs?"

"Your point?"

"Yes or no."

"I don't remember."

"You have any reason to believe your friend would kill someone besides his grandpa?"

Bobby jumps out of his chair, knocking it back with a with a metal crash. "What?"

"Charlie Simpkins—"

"I heard what you said, you dumb piece of fried pork shit." He steps back from the table and knocks into his overturned chair. "Charlie's no killer."

"He was a few minutes ago. We agreed he's a killer but a nice guy."

Bobby's face closes up. He picks up his chair without a word and sits down. He's slouched back now, legs stretched in front of him, arms folded in the universal "fuck you" stance.

"Charlie was at the bar that night. Yes?"

Bobby jerks his finger at Fisher, who barks like a poodle. "My client is not prepared to speak at this time."

"He's been hanging around the bar with all of you since he got out, right?"

Bobby jerks his finger. Fisher says, "My client is not prepared to speak at this time."

"How many draft deferments you got, Bobby? Six? Seven?" Tavera smiles. "I got you for receiving stolen goods, carrying a concealed weapon."

He snorts. "You can't hardly call that piece of shit a weapon."

"I think I can ask the judge for ten years in Jackson State, parole after six."

"You go ahead and ask," he replies, watching the ceiling.

"We have evidence connecting Charlie to the crime scene."

"You got the usual bullshit, is what you got."

"Okay," Tavera says, "what if you're wrong? If Charlie's bumping off these folks, who would be his next shot?" No answer. "His brother?"

"Charlie'd kill anyone who touched P.T."

"Would he?"

"Look man, it's a figure of speech." Bobby rubs both cheeks as if he's trying to get rid of an itch.

Fisher decides to swing his balls around. "My client's had enough questioning. He can't give you what you're looking for." He stands up and straightens his papers.

"I'm going to let you go for now, Royce." Tavera flaps the file shut. "But I have them watching you close now. I don't know if I'll be able to help you out next time." He stands up so he can look down on the prisoner. It's a crappy trick but it works. "You can't help Charlie. But you can help yourself by helping me."

"Keep fishin' fat man." Bobby keeps a smile on his face until he's sure Tavera is out of the room.

23

"So that's it," she says. "We share a house, we share bills, we share Cricket."

Only twenty-four hours have passed since she mentioned her plan to Bobby, and now Katie sits on Gino's couch waiting for his answer. One hand rests on Cricket, who sleeps on the couch beside her. The other hand lies palm up on her thigh, ready to catch whatever part of her breaks and falls off. Unopened mail sprawls on the floor. The greasy smell of old food trickles from the kitchen. Gino wears jockey shorts and an army T-shirt in February.

He says, "I was over at Michael's house on Sunday."

"Yeah?" All he does is nod and stare off out the window until she asks, "How's Rosemary?"

"She won't come near me."

"Come on," she says, "she's your best girlfriend."

"First time I went to visit when I got home, she looked at me and ran behind her mother."

"Didn't remember her Uncle Gino?"

"That's what we figured. So I talked to her, you know. Called her Rosemaryberry and all the other names. I even sat on the floor so she could see me better."

"What happened?"

He gets up. "You want something to drink?"

"No."

He walks to the kitchen, leaning one shoulder on the wall all the way down the hall and talking over the other. "Michael pulled her out from behind her mother and told her it was okay, it's Uncle Gino."

"And?"

"Started screaming. Hid her face in Michael's pant leg. He made her look at me and she ran to her mother crying like I was killing her."

"Did she settle down?" Katherine pictures the girl tied to a highchair and set afire.

"Long as I didn't come near her. You know her mother. She looks at me like I killed every gook baby I could get my hands on." He comes back and sets a glass of whiskey on the table beside him. Doesn't take a drink. "Michael says it's better if I don't come around the house."

"Bastard."

Gino shrugs, watching Cricket as he sleeps. "No. It's his family, you know."

"*You're* his family."

"She's still a sweetheart. God, you should see her. Like a little doll." He takes a drink. His hands shake. "Look, thanks for the offer, but I can't do it."

"All right." She feels the first piece of something fall and hit her upturned palm.

"Don't cry," he says. "It's not fair if you cry and act like a girl."

"Go to hell."

Gino reaches for the afghan at the end of the couch and spreads it over Cricket. "What if you met someone else? Don't make that face, it could happen."

"Then we get a divorce."

"We can't just get a divorce."

"Why?" she asks. "Is it one of your Catholic things?"

"Catholic things?" He frowns at her. "God's a crazy old man. You better learn that now."

"Learn what?"

"God doesn't know who to punish for what anymore," he says. "He forgot the rules." Katherine lets him hold her hand so he can feel good about how well he handled her when he thinks about it later. She even smiles. He raises his glass to her and says, "Here's to Captain Valos."

"Who's Captain Valos?"

"My captain. Good guy. Died two months ago when his chopper was shot down." He shoves a torn envelope towards her. "Says so right there."

"I'm sorry."

"I'm sorry, too."

"Was he a friend of yours?"

"There's no word for what those guys meant to me." He stares at the envelope and swipes it onto the floor. "Now I'll never get back there."

"You don't want to go back."

"Well, I gotta go somewhere." He runs his fingers through his rough beard. "Maybe if I hadn't gone away, we could have done it."

"I waited for you."

"Katydid, I never came home."

"I could help you."

"You can't."

She squeezes his hands hard enough to hurt him. "Come back to me."

"Dead and gone, sweetheart."

She looks at the bottle-blue eyes, those sexy, lazy eyes that are now reptilian. "What happened to you?"

"I been home for a year and a half, and this is the first time you ask—"

"You didn't want to talk about it."

"—and now all of a sudden it's like the goddamn *Huntley-Brinkley Report.*" He rubs his finger around the rim of his glass. "It doesn't work that way."

"You said I was your friend."

"You were Gino's friend. This guy sitting here, he's the one who survived, not Gino. This guy sitting here, he's doesn't even know you."

"Yes, he does."

"He doesn't. And he never will."

And he never will. This time it sinks in. From a distance she hears, "I'm sorry."

"No, don't be sorry. You're right." She pats Cricket's head, reaches for her coat and holds it on her lap. "We wouldn't want to turn him into a faggot." The door opens and Charlie walks in.

"What's that kid doing here?"

"P.T. wouldn't baby-sit," says Katherine. "Said he's not allowed to, thanks to you. What are you doing here?"

"Charlie's staying with me," Gino says.

Katherine looks from one to the other. "Since when?"

"Since none of your business," replies Charlie, kicking off his boots.

Katherine pulls Cricket onto her lap. "What—" She coughs to clear her throat. "What about wifey?"

"Did I just say it was none of your damned business?"

"Who the hell are you, anyway? You run around playing God, ruining people's lives. Who let you decide?"

"Gee, Katherine. I didn't know you cared one way or the other." Charlie turns down the hall. His door slams.

"Goddamn him." Katie hugs Cricket to her chest. He reaches up and closes his fist around the locket.

Gino rises from the couch with his glass in his hand. He drifts into the kitchen. Katie hesitates, then stands up. Gino's voice comes from the other room. "Don't go." She sits. Her knees tremble. She sets Cricket down and puts on her coat. Gino comes back with a fresh glass and the bottle. He takes a long time setting them carefully on the coffee table. "Yell at me," he says. "Don't take it out on Charlie."

His eyes are half closed. His collarbones stick out under his T-shirt. There's hardly anything left of him to yell at. When she speaks, her voice is level and clear. "What did they do to you over there?"

"We're back on that now?"

"No. I mean both of you. All of you."

"All of us?"

Katie rests her hand on his arm. She feels the track marks under her fingertips. "You and Charlie, then. What did they make you do?"

"Charlie's all right."

"No, he's not." She pushes his arm away. "You know he's not."

Gino sits up and holds Katie's face so she'll look him in the eye. "Trust me. Charlie's gonna be fine."

"He beat Dory to death and made it look like Dad did it."

Gino lets go of her face and laughs like he hasn't laughed since he got home. It's a delightful sound, and for a moment Katie sees her Gino emerge. "Another crazed, homicidal vet, huh?" He hugs her, holding her when she tries to pull away.

Katherine breathes in the bitter accusation in his voice. She breathes it in and out several times, then says acidly into his shoulder. "Where are you getting all this self-pity? Huh?" He lets her go as she continues. "I didn't personally send you to that place; don't punish me for it. Jesus, everything doesn't revolve around the goddamn war. The world's moving on, haven't you noticed?" She grabs his hand when he starts to stand up. "I heard Charlie *say it,* all right? Him and P.T., talking about it last night." Cricket cries in his sleep. She lowers her voice. "And it's not like he hasn't done it before."

A flat pressure builds in the back of Gino's skull, like an extended electric shock. For a minute he feels light, weightless, happy. It's a physical sensation that takes him back to when he and Charlie were just dumb kids, tearing around, smoking pot, stealing cars or whatever they could get their hands on. The weight of the war hasn't found them yet. He smiles, it feels so real, like it's all happening now. He and Charlie, walking into Old Jerry's apartment and finding P.T. there on the bed with the pillow on his lap. Gino feels the bag of pot in his hand, sees the windbreaker that Charlie wore, the brown and orange afghan at the foot of the bed.

Katie's voice crashes through the lovely bubble. "He said they would put him in prison this time. P.T. was talking to a cop or something and Charlie went nuts." She hisses at him, yelling with the volume down. "You didn't *see* her, Gino. God, if you'd seen her . . ." He can picture it easily enough. It doesn't look right. It doesn't fit with P.T. holding that pillow and sitting there so quiet on the bed three years ago. Again, Katherine's voice: "I talked to Dad's lawyer this morning."

"You didn't tell him anything?"

"Didn't do any good. I'm an unreliable witness. Won't stand up in court." She shakes her head, disgusted. "So I called the police."

"Damn, Katie."

"They don't want to hear it. Far as they're concerned they got their man."

Gino is whiter than usual, and sweating. "Let it go."

"An hour later I get a call from this cop, says he believes me and would I come in and make a statement. So I did. Talked to him for nearly an hour."

Gino swallows two or three times. He picks an ice cube out of his drink and squeezes it until his palm aches. "You shouldn't have."

"Why? Because he's crazy?" Her voice rises again. "Because he's been crazy all along? They should have left him in Vietnam."

He slaps her. Twice. Without a word she bundles up Cricket and walks out the door.

"Katydid . . ." She stops, looks back over her shoulder without meeting his eyes and listens. "You're wrong," he says. "I swear to God Charlie didn't do this."

"Who else, then? Can you tell me that?" She opens the front door and waits. "I didn't think so."

In the car, Katherine lays Cricket across the front seat with his head on her lap. All she has to do is get home. Once she's home, she'll be fine. But home is going to be sold to pay for the lawyer, which means she'll have to find another job. Everything is falling apart at once. Everyone leaves. And if they don't leave, they only stay around to fuck you over. Cricket is going to have it better than that. He's her brother. She isn't leaving, and no one is going to fuck with him, ever. The night in the hospital, when they found Cricket, the crying in the bathroom, no more of that. No more crying. Charlie isn't going to get away with murder. Gino is never again going to use her heart to wipe his ass. Everything and everyone could fall down around her; she was going to raise Cricket herself with no help from anyone. She lays her right hand on his stomach and feels the rise and fall of his breath. She will be his mom.

24

After Tavera left Bobby that morning in the interrogation room, he spent the day going over the file on Jerry Moody. Cause of death, asphyxiation. In the Dolores McGurk file he reads the autopsy report again. Asphyxiation. Discrepancy between the degree of the wounds and the loss of blood. When he hears that Katherine McGurk was calling the station with some supposed new evidence, he nearly takes several heads off. "Get her on the goddamn phone. Now."

When he comes out of the office an hour later, he tells his captain he'll be gone the rest of the night. "Where are you going?"

"Toledo."

~

When Sheila's done with her set, one of the waitresses brings her a drink. "From the table by the door." The drink sits on the bar, untouched. Sheila doesn't even bother to turn around and wave a thank you. On her way to the back room, a hand closes on her arm and stops her.

"You don't like Scotch anymore?"

"What do you want, Tavera?"

"To talk."

"I'm working."

"I'll wait."

"Not here, you won't." She looks around, thinking. "A place called Sally's, two miles further up. I'll be there in an hour."

~

Ninety minutes later, Sheila pays the cover charge to a huge guy inside the door and looks to see if his eyebrows are plucked. No. Inside, she feels eyes all over her, wondering if the tits are real. He's there at the bar, talking to a woman in an Ann-Margret wig who's damn near as big as he is.

"Tavera," she says, sitting on the empty stool to his right.

"Alvarez," he says. "This is Bonnie."

Sheila pulls her jacket off and gives a butch nod to the redhead, who smiles and looks hard into her eyes, shooting sex Sheila's way like a fire hose. Sheila stares back and pulls a pack of cigarettes out of her pocket. The redhead keeps firing it past Tavera and straight at Sheila, who breaks eye contact to light a cigarette. "I got a sister named Bonnie."

"Honey," the redhead says to Tavera. "I got work to do, so I'll thank you for that drink."

"No problem," he tells her.

"I'm in the next set if you want to hear me sing." She taps his chin with a glued-on red fingernail. "I'm very good."

"I'll see what I can do." He hands her a twenty and she kisses him on the cheek. As she passes Sheila, she runs long red nails down the length of her hair.

"See ya, sugar."

"See ya," Sheila answers.

Tavera watches her walking away. It's hard not to. "She likes you," he says.

"Everybody likes me." Sheila catches the bartender's eye and orders a Cuervo. "Everybody fucking adores me."

"Hard to believe she's got a dick tucked under all that." He takes a drink and then he yawns. She picked this place to throw him off balance and he yawns.

"What are you looking for? A three-way?" She pays for her drink without looking at him. "Forget it."

"No," he says. "This is business." He leans forward with his elbows on the bar. She sees his tie all rolled up inside his jacket pocket. Just business. She'd forgotten he had such mean eyes, forgotten about the over-thirty gut, the hair doing a slow retreat, the clothes crumpled. She'd forgotten he was such an asshole. She scowls at her drink and tries not to think about fucking him. When she finally glances at him out of the corner of her eye, he says, "I want you to tell me about Charlie Simpkins."

"Never heard of him."

He smiles. That's the bitch of it. When he smiles like that, his eyes don't look mean, they look like he's got a hard-on. "His mama killed herself, right?"

"I wouldn't know."

"When he was . . . what . . . around six?"

"You're an asshole. You know that, Tavera?"

"Llamáme Jorge."

"Fuck off. George."

Music comes from the stage. Tavera sits up straight and picks up his whiskey.

"How'd you find me, anyway?"

"Went from one club to the next. Didn't take long. Come on," he says, grabbing her arm. "Let's dance." They carry their drinks to a table near the dance floor. Someone named Delilah stands under the hot lights in a long white fur, singing "I'd Rather Go Blind." Tavera grabs Sheila's arm and pulls her toward him, hard against his chest with no air to breathe. She feels a rumble from his chest but she can't hear him because he's so far above her.

"What?"

"Gilbert McGurk didn't kill his wife."

He can't force her to stay, can't arrest her, she hasn't done anything. He leans down and talks into the top of her head, burning her scalp. "You were there the night Dolores McGurk was killed."

"Yeah, well I have an alibi. I left with Charlie."

"Handy. That means you're his alibi as well." He strokes her back, her hair, all that tenderness again. "You have a great ass."

She jerks away and heads for the table, putting something solid between them. He pulls his chair out sideways, gives her a dangerous smile, and plunks himself down near her. Bonnie's act begins. On stage, she looks taller and her hair is more brilliantly red than when she was at the bar. Tavera continues like a bulldog. "The morgue tells me she received the wounds *after* she died. What kind of person would beat up a corpse?"

"You have a lovely mind, Officer Tavera."

"Your friend Charlie has a history of violence." Tavera pauses, watching her. "I have a witness says it was him killed that girl."

She plinks her glass with her thumb, sees him watching, and she stops. "You got it all figured out, why do you need me?"

"You don't want to see an innocent man go to prison."

Gil. Nothing she says is going to make any difference. It's all fucked up; the whole nightmare is starting over again. She should have known better than to go back to Ypsi. Her stomach hurts. No matter where she goes, she'll always get dragged back into Charlie's shit with no time to think, no way to stop it. Tavera slides his hand along the back of her neck and plays with her hair. "Charlie never knew what he had."

25

GINO DOESN'T MOVE FOR A LONG TIME AFTER KATHERINE leaves. Twice he starts to get up and walk down the hall to Charlie's room; twice he changes his mind. Talking to Charlie isn't going to do any good. He has the right to throw himself away if he wants. Gino sucks the last of the vodka from an ice cube. No. Charlie came back okay and he's going to stay okay, with a family of his own and a life of his own. He's going to grow old and die in his bed.

Gino dresses quietly and goes down to the basement. He rummages through an assortment of car parts and auto catalogues until he finds the white box. On his way up the stairs, the doorbell rings.

"Katydid, I'm sorry." But it's not Katherine standing on the small cement porch. "Diane. Come in."

"Thanks." She looks pale, like she's sick. She carries a can of Vernor's in her hand. "Charlie here?"

"Down the hall, second door on the right." Gino moves her gently in the right direction. "I'm on my way out."

"You don't have to leave because I'm here."

"No," he calls from the kitchen. "I really gotta go." He emerges in his army jacket, the white box under his arm. "Take care."

When he's gone, Diane walks down the hall and opens the second door on the right.

~

When he hears the knock on his door, P.T. figures it's Steve or Rose. When Gino walks in, P.T. hurries to the bed and throws the covers in place. "Hi, Gino."

"How you doing?"

"Okay." P.T. picks up three pieces of dirty laundry and tosses them in his tiny closet. Then he hurries to the kitchen to rinse a dirty glass in the sink. "I am sorry for the mess."

Gino takes in the spotless, Spartan room. "I was thinking you and me could go for a drive."

P.T. pulls on his lip. "What time is it?"

"Not that late," Gino says. "C'mon, put some clothes on."

P.T. pulls off his giraffe pajamas and a few minutes later he and Gino are cruising across the back roads of Washtenaw County. Gino lets up on the gas until they are going no more than fifteen miles per hour. The dirt road is still covered from the blizzard. "Heat too high?"

"No."

Gino pulls over and puts the car in park. "You killed that girl, didn't you?" No answer as P.T. frowns out the window. "Didn't you?"

"Look at the snow."

"Stall all you want, you're gonna talk about it, buddy." Gino puts the car in gear, turns off on an old tractor path, and kills his lights.

"You will get stuck."

"Let me worry about that."

"One time I got stuck in the snow and Charlie had to dig for seven hours to get me out," says P.T. "Then he had to put me in a bathtub of hot water to thaw me out because I was a big icicle."

Gino takes his time rolling a joint. "You killed her. Not Gil. Not Charlie."

"And then another time, I was in a boat in a little stream, and when I looked in the water there were a hundred birds swimming by, all of them flying at the bottom of the water and I almost fell in. There was a cardinal, too."

"Charlie can't take this one for you." Gino rolls down his window and lights the joint. "You might as well get used to that idea right now."

P.T. turns on the radio. "Sugar Pie Honey Bun" comes through the static. He nods his head and taps his toes to the music. Gino smokes, feeling better in his mind than he has in years. "You're not gonna talk about it, huh?"

"I like this song."

Gino reaches around in the back seat and pulls the white box onto the front seat. "Charlie ever tell you much about where he went when he went away?"

P.T. turns down the radio, relieved at the change of conversation. "He got a leech up his nose." It catches Gino off guard and he has to laugh. It's exactly the kind of thing that would happen to Charlie. P.T. relaxes more. "He said there were giant blue butterflies and trees in a blender and talking lizards.

"That so?" Gino isn't sure if these are stories or not; anything was believable in that place. "He ever show you any pictures?"

P.T. shakes his head. "His friend took a picture but I never got to see it."

The moon reflects the snow-laden field all around them. It's bright enough to see inside the car. Gino opens the box on the seat between them. "You want to see some?" P.T. sits up in his seat, curling one long leg underneath him. Gino isn't mad at him anymore. It was going to be okay. "This here is a rice paddy." Gino hands him a picture. "They have rice paddies like we have cornfields. That there's a water buffalo, like a Vietnamese cow."

P.T. touches the photo like it's something magic. "Charlie did not like rice paddies."

Gino chuckles. "Probably had to walk through them. Mud up over your ankles." He pulls out another photo. "This is a shot from the helicopter."

"All pink."

"It was taken at sun up. Everything turned pink for five minutes, then it was gone. You had to see it."

"Charlie said it turned green, too. Like here before a tornado."

"Yup. And purple, too. The rain could turn everything purple." Gino puts out the roach and rolls up the window. "You gonna tell me what happened?"

P.T. looks up, smiling. "What happened where?"

"You gonna tell me why you killed that girl?"

The roof of the car comes down around P.T.'s head all over again. He slouches over. "I cannot talk about anything like that."

"Why not?" Gino carelessly rifles through the box of photos.

"Charlie will really yell at me."

"What if I yelled at you?" Still quiet, still unhurried. "You wouldn't like that, either."

"No, but I promised Charlie."

"Okay." Gino pauses his search and smiles at P.T. "Let me tell you why Charlie can't take the blame this time."

P.T. pulls on a small lock of hair at his temple. "Okay."

"This is where Charlie really went." Gino hands P.T. a photo, nudging his hand until he takes it. "That's where he went because he covered for you."

P.T. can't make sense of what he's looking at. He holds it up to the window for better light. Before he can react, Gino hands him another one. Then he sits back and waits. P.T. holds both pictures in his shaking hands. He stares at them for a long time, even turning one sideways and back again. A droning sound builds inside him, an off-key "aaaaaeeh." It rises and falls with his breathing. Tears build and leap off his eyelashes, splashing onto his coat.

"That is not it," P.T. says. "That is not where he was." He searches through the remaining photos that Gino hands him. "There were mountains and trees and clouds and monkeys." He continues his horrible internal keening. Each picture he sees increases his terror. A few photos spill across the front seat, landing near Gino. He pushes them lightly aside and looks out the window while P.T. clutches at each picture, looking for the beautiful ones. "That is not it," P.T. cries again. "That is not where Charlie was. He never told me this. He was not there."

Gino grabs P.T. by the back of the head. His grip isn't painful, but it's unbreakable. "He didn't tell you because he didn't want to make you feel bad. But *now* it's time for you to feel bad."

P.T. covers his ears. "He told me not to tell."

"He told *me* not to tell, either. Do you think I feel any better than you do?" Gino shakes P.T. a little to make him open his eyes. "I helped him dump Jerry's body. I stood by and let him go over there."

"Does Charlie have pictures like this?"

Gino lets go of P.T.'s head. "There's something I don't understand."

"What?"

"Why did you hurt her?"

"She asked me to. Does Charlie have pictures like these?"

"She asked you to beat her up?" P.T. looks blank. Gino goes on. "Don't play stupid. Tell me."

"She asked me would Charlie help her and I helped her so Charlie would not get in trouble."

"Then what?"

"Then Charlie came in and made me leave. He said he was going to take care of it."

Gino rubs at his eyes to erase the picture that is suddenly so clear: closed fists on a body that lies limp; a small out-flung arm unmoving, unresisting. He remembers all the things that can be done with a corpse. He pulls a bottle out from under the front seat. "You want some?" P.T. shakes his head. "That's right. You don't drink." Gino takes a long slug of whiskey.

"Charlie knows how to take care of things," says P.T., trying to calm down.

Gino waits for the warmth to crawl across his belly. "If you do something bad, you go to hell for it. You know that much, right?"

P.T. thinks about that. "But he did not do anything wrong."

"If it wasn't wrong, why did they send him there?" Gino's finger jabs at the photos. "And now you went and did it again."

P.T. lets out a sigh and pulls his lip. "What should I do?"

"What do you think you should do?"

"Charlie will be really mad."

"Do you know how many guys died over there?"

"Oh, Gino. Do not yell at me, please."

Gino runs his hand through his black hair, clenching his scalp. He screws the cap onto his bottle and puts it back under the seat. "Remember the first time I met you?" P.T. shakes his head without looking up. "You had caught this garter snake. And you told us it came right out of the kitchen faucet into your hand, and that it was running away from a fox in the back—"

"A coyote."

"I thought it was a fox."

"It was a coyote."

"From this coyote in the back yard."

"I remember."

"You let Charlie name it 'Boy.' And you were going to keep him in the house."

"Except Dad found it."

"I figured that's what happened. But you told us you mailed Boy to the zoo because he wanted to be with the other snakes." P.T. smiles. "And you used to read these pretend letters from him, all about the cobras and the rattlesnakes and their feud. You did that all summer."

"I made those up."

"You were always doing shit like that. You made that secret room for Charlie under the back porch."

"He was not supposed to show anyone."

"I know, but I was there one time when your dad came home."

P.T. puts up a hand to keep Gino from saying any more. They sit in the moonlit field until P.T. starts to shiver. Gino turns the heat back on, but P.T. only shivers more. "That garter snake did not really come out of the faucet," he says.

Gino starts to laugh. Surprised, P.T. laughs, too. Gino pulls a Luger from the white box. "Charlie can't have any kind of life long as he keeps protecting you."

P.T. gets dizzy, but not dizzy enough to fall down. He hears the tingle of blood in his ears. When he opens his eyes there's his mama, standing in the field with the breeze blowing her house-dress against her legs.

"You take care of your brother."

P.T. nods.

She smiles. "You promise?"

Gino raises the gun so the muzzle rests against P.T.'s ear. "I don't see any other way to fix this," he says. "I can't let Charlie fuck up his life for you anymore."

P.T. sighs and gives Gino a long, slow smile. He reaches up and takes the gun easily from Gino's hand, then replaces it in the white box. "I will take care of it," he says.

26

While Gino and P.T. talk, Bobby pulls up to McGurk's Tap Room and bangs on the door even though the neon is off. He pounds until a light comes on upstairs. He looks up to see Katie turning away from the window.

"Open the door, girl." He backs up, but can't see anything. "Goddamn you, woman." He pulls out his driver's license and sets to work on the door. Just as he feels the latch, the door opens. Bobby pushes past her and closes the door behind him. "I been looking for you all day."

"I was out." She's in a nightshirt that comes to her knees. Her eyes are swollen. "Cricket's asleep."

"You'll freeze in that." He shrugs off his coat and puts it over her shoulders. "I got some news for you, Katie girl." He leads her to a table where they sit down. He takes one of her hands and holds it in both of his. "They're trying to pin this thing on Charlie."

"I know."

"How do you know?"

"I talked to someone this afternoon, at the station." Katherine pulls her hand away. "Stopped and saw Dad, told him Charlie did it."

"Hold it, honey." Bobby's knocked so far off his stride, the "honey" slips out. "You can't listen to that honky bullshit."

"He did it, Bobby. I heard him say it himself."

Bobby still doesn't believe it, except that Katie's dead sure, and dead calm. "You telling me he just let Gil go to jail for him?"

"That's right."

Bobby stands up, but there's nowhere to go. "How come you closed the place up?"

"Because I'm tired." More than tired, she sounds old. Her voice is almost a whisper. "Sit down."

He sits. Stares at his thumbnail, trying to make sense of things. "You're glad about Gil, I guess. Huh?" She nods, but she doesn't look glad about anything. "So where's the spark, then? Where's my Katie girl?"

"I'm not your Katie girl."

"Yes, you are. You are. You always have been, and you know it."

She dismisses him with a brush of her hand. "I don't want to hear that."

"Because of Gino?"

"No."

"Then why? Never been a time I can remember when you weren't my number one."

"I don't know. I never thought you were serious."

Bobby's mouth drops. "Never thought I was *serious*?"

"Yeah."

"Why?"

Katherine shifts in her chair. "I don't know."

"Because I'm black?

"I don't know."

"Is that it?"

"Yes." She looks surprised, puzzled, rubbing her forearms to counter the chill. "I'm sorry. I never thought about it, but yes."

Bobby sits back in his chair, stunned. After a long silence, he asks, "You want a drink?"

"No."

He goes behind the bar and busies himself with a Black and Tan.

"I'm sorry" comes from the table again. He leans against the bar for a while, drinking and tilting his head this way and that in an interior discussion. Katherine hunches beneath the coat and asks herself again why everything's falling apart at once, why she has to lose her best friend. Because she realizes now, now that Bobby's gone, that he's the best friend she'll ever have.

Bobby sits down across the table from her with his drink. He lays his palms flat. "Okay, this is what it is." She makes herself look him in the eye. He taps the table a few times. "In six months, if I can teach you not to be a racist cracker nitwit, then you have to go to dinner with me."

She reaches for his hand and holds it against her cheek, laughing. "For fuck's sake, Bobby." They lean forward until their foreheads touch.

He knows his Katie girl. This is all he needs. "Don't you know by now Bobby's never gonna leave you?"

27

TAVERA GOT BACK TO THE STATION TWENTY-FIVE MINUTES ago. It was a long drive up from Toledo, and he was thinking about Charlie Simpkins all the way. At least he'd managed to get Alvarez to tell him that Charlie was covering for someone. She even claimed he hadn't killed Jerry Moody, that it was another cover job. Most likely bullshit. She wouldn't say who he was covering for, which made the information useless even if it was true. No matter how hard he pressed her, she closed up and shook her head, as if just the thought of it pissed her off.

The closer he gets, the further Charlie Simpkins slips away from him. He can't let go of it; it's like a sliver under his fingernail. The phone rings. "Tavera."

"Got a guy out here. Simpkins."

Tavera finds the crazy brother sitting with another guy. "George," he says, putting out his hand. "How you doing?" He endures the ropy handshake. "You want to follow me?"

Gino starts to accompany P.T., who tells him to wait. "You sure?" asks Gino.

"I will take care of it."

"I'll be out here." Gino settles in as P.T. follows Tavera down the hallway.

Once in the little office, Tavera asks P.T. if he wants anything. "Water? Coffee?"

"I am hungry."

Tavera tells him to have a seat, he'll go see what he can do. P.T. sits, looks around the room. He spreads his fingers wide across his knees. He curls his toes, then uncurls them. He looks at the phone for a while, then picks it up. He pulls a tiny address book out of his sock. It has four numbers in it: Charlie's, Gino's, McGurk's, and the halfway house. He dials Gino's number and waits while it rings forever. He looks over his shoulder for Tavera.

"Yeah, what?" Charlie nearly shouts into the phone.

P.T. says, "Do you have pictures like that?"

"I'm in the middle of something."

"Do you have pictures like Gino has? Do you?"

"What?"

P.T.'s voice begins to shake, his hands and stomach as well. "Did you go to hell?"

After a silence Charlie says, "Where are you?"

"I am taking care of it."

"Is Gino there?"

"Yes."

"Let me talk to him."

"No."

"Why not?"

"He went to the bathroom."

"Bro, where are you?"

"Just tell me if you have pictures like that." He waits, swallowing air in the silence. His heart breaks when Charlie doesn't answer. "Okay, I am going to take care of it."

"Tell me where you are." Charlie hears another voice in the background before P.T. hangs up. Tavera.

"Goddamnit."

"What's wrong?" asks Diane.

"Nothing." He picks up his coat.

"I'm coming with you."

"No, you're not."

They've been arguing for the last hour, Diane methodically wearing Charlie down to the point where he doesn't know what either of them have said, or what's left to say. Despite several demands and one outright threat, she refuses to leave. Now Charlie pushes past her for the door. "Go home," he says. "I'll call you tomorrow."

Diane has her coat on by now and follows close behind him. "God damn you. I'm your wife."

"Yeah, you've said that fifty times."

He hurries down the front steps and into his car, leaving her behind. He's at the station in minutes. He doesn't bother to park, just leaves the car askew in the middle of the lot. It's begun to snow again; he half runs, half slides into the building. Gino stands up and grabs Charlie before he can get past him. Charlie pushes Gino against the wall. "What did you do to him?"

The officer at the desk looks up. "We're cool," says Gino. "Waiting for a friend." He pulls Charlie into a chair beside him. "Keep it down, man. What are you doing here?"

"He fucking called me. What do you think?"

Gino keeps a claw-like grip on Charlie's arm. "You got a family. You got a home."

"He's my family. He's my home."

"He's not gonna fuck you up again."

"You got nothing to say about it."

Gino's grip sinks in deeper. "You're the only good thing left," he says. "He's fucked, I'm fucked. All those guys we knew over there, all fucked. We don't have a choice. You do."

"Where is he?"

"You gotta live your life, Charlie. Go home to Diane, have kids, do all that shit."

"Not without him."

~

When the commotion outside starts up, Tavera goes out into the hall. He says to Charlie, "Why am I not surprised to see you?"

He brings Charlie into the office. P.T. slumps over in his chair at the sight of his brother, as if all his nerves have been severed. Charlie bends down to him. "You okay? You okay, Bro? What happened?"

"You have to go home."

"What'd you do to him?" Charlie asks, turning to Tavera. "He tells stories. He's not right."

"Do not say that, Charlie," P.T. says.

Tavera leans forward and points to a tape recorder on the desk. "You mind if I keep this going?"

"Go ahead. I'll put it in writing for you. I killed that stupid bitch. He'll tell you all kinds of bullshit to keep me out of trouble."

P.T. waves to get Tavera's attention. "I would like to talk to my brother please."

"Go ahead."

"Go away for a minute."

"Sorry, can't."

"Okay, but do not listen."

Tavera turns off the tape recorder. Charlie jumps up. "Turn it back on. I have a confession."

P.T. pulls Charlie's arm. "Now you shut up."

"Don't tell me to shut up."

"You lied to me."

Charlie takes real offense at this. "I have never lied to you."

"Gino told me. He showed me."

"Gino's crazy."

"Okay, so Gino is crazy and I am crazy."

"I never said you were."

"I know that!"

Charlie can feel this sliding into another unwinnable argument. "Bro, stop."

"I am not your brother," says P.T. "I remember when I was your real brother. I took care of you."

Charlie's legs freeze. Something slips inside him. "Bro—"

"Say my name." Sorrow sifts through the gray eyes. "Say my name, Charlie."

"Gabriel. Gabe."

"Let Gabe take care of this." P.T. slips an arm around his little brother's shoulders. Charlie can't answer. Everything is coming loose in his chest. P.T. kisses him on top of the head. "Oh, Charlie."

Tavera waits behind the desk while Charlie cries, wishing that he hadn't taken that first call for Jerry Moody, that he'd never stepped foot inside McGurk's Tap Room, that he did something else for a living.

Forty minutes later, Tavera has a full statement from P.T., and a promise of cooperation from them both. When it's over, Charlie says, "Don't handcuff him. Don't hurt him."

P.T. says, "I will see you tomorrow."

"You're gonna see me every damned day. I won't let them send you far away."

"Good, because I have to keep an eye on you." The last thing P.T. says as Charlie walks down the hall: "Do you have any pictures? Of that place?"

Charlie shakes his head. "Sorry, I don't."

"That is okay. That is fine."

Charlie walks down the hallway and out of his brother's sight. When he gets to the waiting room, he finds Diane waiting beside Gino. She takes Charlie's arm and leads him outside where the snow stings his hot face.

"Where's the Charger?" he asks Gino.

"Over at the bar. I couldn't park it at a police station."

"We'll give you a lift."

Inside the car it's quiet except for Charlie wiping his nose on his coat sleeve. When they reach the bar, Gino says, "Wanna hear something funny?"

"Sure."

He climbs out of the back seat and looks at Charlie. "Never mind," he says. "It wasn't that funny."

Charlie pulls away from McGurk's Tap Room with Diane beside him. He asks, "How'd you find me?"

"Followed you."

"You even gonna learn to listen?"

"Pull over." When the car stops, she opens the door and vomits into the slush.

"Jesus. You all right?"

She nods. He offers his sleeve, but she pulls tissues out of her purse. "Part of the package."

"Let's get you home."

~

As Gino drives away, he feels the weight falling from him like poisoned scales. He could float right out of the car if he opened his window. He arrives at a junkyard on the other side of town where he parks the Charger. He tucks the white box under one arm and slams the door shut. He rubs the gleaming hood. At the nearest trash can he uses his Zippo to burn his three drivers licenses, his VA card, every piece of identification. Then he slowly burns each photograph until the box is nearly empty. He hugs his army jacket close around his toothpick frame and looks up at the black sky.

"Charlie's going to be okay," he says up to the sky. "He'll have a long life and die in his bed." Gino pulls the Luger out of the white box. "Was that the purpose of me coming home alive?" he asks the frozen stars. "To save one little redneck?"

He laughs, lifts the Luger to his forehead and fires.

28

P.T. IS SENT TO A PSYCHIATRIC HOSPITAL. AFTER P.T.'S trial, Sheila returns to Toledo for good. Seven months later, Jorge Tavera quits the force and takes over a private investigating firm in Toledo. Lita calls him Horse Hay.

Gil is released the day after P.T. confesses. He still runs the bar, and he still holds a grudge.

Charlie and Diane have a baby daughter and name her Gabriella after her uncle Gabriel. Katie and Bobby have a baby boy and name him Leon. Cricket goes to live with them for good. Mister Grizzlybutt dies in his sleep, and even Katie cries.

The children grow up hearing stories about Cricket's mom, who was the most beautiful woman in the world, who loved Cricket and Gil more than anything in the world, and who died in a car accident. If Cricket has any memories of his mother, he keeps them to himself. The kids also hear stories about Old Jerry, who shot off fireworks in the house and broke his foot when he tried to dance on the roof of a moving car. They hear all about Ella's grandmother, who talked to flowers and knew how to make magic.

When Gabriella is thirteen, Katie shows her a picture of four young men, taken a long time ago. Katie points to each face. "That's your uncle Gabe behind the dog. Then that there is your dad, then Uncle Bobby. That's half of Uncle Gino because he fell down when the picture was snapped."

Her father tells Gabriella that Uncle Gino died in Vietnam. When Ella asks her father about the Vietnam War, why he volunteered to enlist, Charlie tells her it was a long time ago. He tells her the world was a different place.

"Who knows why any of us did what we did back then?" he tells her. "We were all just young and stupid and having a good time."

Printed in the United States
by Baker & Taylor Publisher Services